ALSO BY J. PENNER

Adenashire
A Fellowship of Bakers & Magic
A Fellowship of Librarians & Dragons
A Fellowship of Games & Fables

DEATH
Meets
CUTE

J. PENNER

Copyright © 2026 by J. Penner
Cover and internal design © 2026 by Sourcebooks
Cover design by Erin Fitzsimmons/Sourcebooks
Cover and internal art © Emma Gillette
Internal images © KaterinaKr/Getty Images, Natalia Churzina/
Getty Images, Olga Shipilova/Getty Images

Sourcebooks, Poisoned Pen Press, and the colophon
are registered trademarks of Sourcebooks.

All rights reserved. No part of this book may be reproduced in any form or by
any electronic or mechanical means including information storage and retrieval
systems—except in the case of brief quotations embodied in critical articles or
reviews—without permission in writing from its publisher, Sourcebooks.

No part of this book may be used or reproduced in any manner for the
purpose of training artificial intelligence technologies or systems.

The characters and events portrayed in this book are fictitious or
are used fictitiously. Any similarity to real persons, living or dead,
is purely coincidental and not intended by the author.

Published by Poisoned Pen Press, an imprint of Sourcebooks
1935 Brookdale RD, Naperville, IL 60563-2773
(630) 961-3900
sourcebooks.com

Cataloging-in-Publication Data is on file with the Library of Congress.

The authorized representative in the EEA is Dorling Kindersley
Verlag GmbH. Arnulfstr. 124, 80636 Munich, Germany

Manufactured in the UK and distributed by Dorling Kindersley Limited, London
001-358652-Apr/26
CPI 10 9 8 7 6 5 4 3 2 1

For everyone who's ever thought a hedgehog might be a good companion.

Prologue

Her belly churning, Iris Weyward leaned her back up against the rigid rock cave wall at Hillock and studied the rain falling outside the craggy mouth opening. The storm's wormy aroma had invaded her nose long before fat raindrops plunked indentations into the dirt just outside, promising a muddy mess.

The weather in itself wasn't a problem for Iris. She liked the rain. And its smell. She didn't even mind the impending mud.

It was something else needling inside her. A mystery she had been unable to solve.

She shook her head.

Maybe it was just the sandwich she'd eaten for lunch

even though she and her sisters had left them out a little too long.

To distract herself from the irritating sensation, Iris ground her boots into the floor dirt, drawing familiar energy from the earth. She slid her arms inside her chocolate-brown cloak and conjured magic to her hands...as if she were pulling a shimmering string from the ground and weaving it up the contours of her body. Warmth danced on Iris's palms, and, careful to keep the temperature reasonable, she rubbed them along her upper arms.

The witch should have been elated. Instead, the entire realm didn't feel right. *She* didn't feel right.

And it was more than the past-due sandwiches.

The Weyward sisters had just finished a project that went fairly well. A while back, they'd heard a few rumors about a ruthless general who wanted more power, so they'd set the right vibe in a dark cave with moody lighting, invited him over, then prophesied his "fate" to become king.

Which, of course, he wanted to hear.

Who wouldn't?

People, Iris found, particularly humans, were easy to manipulate and practice casual havoc on. All the witches needed to do was cast a few spells and fudge a prophecy or two in order to complete the simple task of getting people to turn on each other...cause a little mayhem...off their enemies...invoke a civil war. All in all, they'd found this project interesting and had taken a lot of notes. And their success should have set the stage for the next step in gaining authority over the entire Veronian Region, as well as sealed their place among other local scoundrels, malefactors, and otherwise unscrupulous folks who had high ambitions.

Toil and trouble…on the double.

Or something like that.

"Something wicked this way comes, all right." Iris's sister Poppy gushed as she held up her hand, waiting for Iris to give it a smack of solidarity. "You know…us!"

Iris shook herself out of the place she'd gone in her mind and glanced at her ridiculous redheaded younger sibling. Poppy wore a wide smile that stretched her lips, and enthusiasm sparkled in her eyes. The hand that wasn't waiting for Iris held a petite ball of fire Poppy was fiddling with.

"Thanks for leaving me with this mess," Dahlia groaned from behind her. The witch flicked one side of her blond bob behind her ear while gazing at the large black cauldron along with various scattered empty and half-empty potion bottles littering the cave floor in front of her.

Just beyond that, their three familiars—Iris's hedgehog, Dahlia's striped cat, and Poppy's raven—let out a chorus of snores as they slept on the ground, completely useless other than to dreamland. Iris did her best to ignore that nonsense and brought her attention back to Poppy, who *still* had her hand up.

Of course, Iris should have wanted to celebrate with her sisters. They'd succeeded in sowing discord, just as they'd intended. But the satisfaction she had expected wouldn't come. Only hollowness waiting to be filled by…*something* other than the life she currently led crept into her mind.

And stomach.

Instead, Iris produced her own hand from under her cloak and patted Poppy on the shoulder. "Sorry," Iris said to Dahlia and quickly averted her attention to the ground. "I'm not feeling myself." She hurried past her younger sibling to help with the cleanup.

They'd been using the cave as a hub for months to carry out their plot against their latest victim. However, it was time to move on to the next project. After all, being evil took practice.

"What's gotten into you?" Poppy complained from behind Iris, a whine playing at her tone.

Iris didn't look back.

"Let's just get this done," she insisted, retrieving several glass vials of herbage from where they'd been scattered on the ground.

"What do you mean, you're not feeling yourself?" Dahlia asked, flourishing her cape. The witch drew up her hand and conjured a misty blue tendril of magic. Seconds later she'd filled the cauldron with water to rinse it out with.

Iris shrugged and gazed around the dark cave. "Nothing feels right, okay?"

"Of course it feels right," Dahlia sneered. "Everything I prophesied came true. This only sets us up for the next success."

There she was…telling Iris how to live her life again.

Poppy scoffed. "Um…we were *all* there. They weren't only *your* prophecies, Sister."

But Dahlia was well known for trying to take credit for everything. It was a pervasive problem, likely stemming from childhood insecurities.

As she had hundreds of times before, Iris rolled her eyes at her older sister. But Dahlia wasn't one to talk out feelings even if Iris had wanted to call her out, so it wasn't a good subject to bring up at the moment. "Can we please get this over with?" Iris made her way to the cauldron of the now-watered-down potion, which had lost its potency days before anyway. Without another word she picked up the receptacle, swirled it around, then walked to the cave opening and tossed the contents out into the rain.

"I did most of the research...*as usual*," Dahlia scoffed.

Flames caught Iris's gaze as she twisted to face her sisters. Poppy stood before her with a much larger ball of fire dancing on her palm, matching the color of her curly hair. "I did *plenty* of footwork and spell casting around the realm."

"We *all* played our part." Iris shook her head and let the cauldron drop to the ground with a thud. She'd been the one to come up with all the poetry and rhymes to make the whole act sound important and official. And the Scottish king gobbled it all up. (Pride and the promise of power are funny bedfellows.)

But Iris decided not to bring up the specifics.

Immediately after Iris spoke, her familiar—Quince— let out a grunt but still didn't wake. None of the familiars did, but it wasn't a surprise, since they were used to the sisters' quarrels over the last months and could sleep through mostly anything.

But Poppy's flame only grew larger, as did the scowl pulling at the corners of her lips. In seconds, Dahlia flicked her fingers at their youngest sister and the fire went out with a hiss, as if water had doused it.

Poppy bared her teeth as her magic fizzled in her palm, failing to ignite. "You vain toad-spotted harpy!"

"Toad-spotted?" Dahlia brought her hand to her porcelain cheek in great offense.

A growl played at the back of Iris's throat. Barely able to stand her sisters anymore, she pinched the bridge of her nose. *This* was not what she'd envisioned her life to look like. "I think I'm going to bow out of the next project. I need a little break." The words came out of her mouth all too quickly, and Iris could barely believe she was saying them out loud.

Both sisters stopped arguing for a moment and spun toward her. "You can't do *that*," they demanded in unison, finally able to agree on something.

Dahlia's eyebrows squinched together in immediate judgment.

"I can," Iris stated plainly. And it was the first time in months she felt like herself again.

"What's going on?" the hedgehog asked in a groggy tone from his cuddle puddle with the other familiars.

"Nothing," Poppy said, not even turning his way. "Go back to sleep."

"Don't tell Quince what to do!" Iris's tone was short, but she didn't regret the outburst. "Everything we did here turned out this time. But barely. If we hadn't spent so much time arguing, we may have been able to wrap this up a month ago. Plus, we haven't even discussed that some things went wrong…like the guy who escaped. That could come back to bite us!"

"Fleance?" Dahlia scoffed and gestured dismissively at the air. "He should thank us. Who knows? If he becomes a king someday, maybe he'll call on our services."

"Or chop off our heads," Poppy interjected. "Since his dad got the ol'…" She ran her index finger across her neck.

Iris balled her fists at her side, trying to ignore her youngest sister, and kept her heat magic to herself. "You won't listen to me. How is this ever going to work when we aren't really a team? We haven't been a *team* for a long time… maybe when we were younger. But we haven't been young for a very long time. I need some space from the two of you. Permanent space."

Maybe this was the right choice…to forge her own path.

Her oldest sister pulled her chin back in offense.

"You're not the only one who needs space." Poppy's magic crackled, and then her hand lit with flame again as she stared at Dahlia. A blink later, however, she whipped her attention to Iris. "Wait? Space from *me* too?"

Almost on cue, Dahlia flinched as if she were about to extinguish Poppy's fire magic again.

"What's going on?" Quince echoed.

"Nothing!" Iris shouted, marched over, and plucked him from the others, who had finally woken. "We're just leaving."

She deposited him in her cloak pocket. More muffled questions came from the fabric, but Iris ignored the hedgehog.

"But the other realms," Dahlia insisted. "We have plans."

"They were never *my* plans." Iris waved at the air in the direction of her sister. "Since you always do most of the work, I'm sure you can manage an evil empire all on your own."

Like a boar, Poppy snorted a laugh, and Dahlia shot an electric gaze at her.

"And can *you* manage on your own, Sister? With that bubble brain of yours?" Dahlia snapped.

"Hey!" Poppy's mouth pursed in offense. "Maybe Iris is right. I could do evil better myself too."

"Maybe you're *both* right," Dahlia growled. "Since I do everything around here anyway." She flicked her hand at Iris. "Your magic isn't even as strong as ours." The witch snarled at their youngest sister. "And *you*? Don't get me started."

Iris winced at the dig on her magic. Heat magic. What kind of elemental magic was that? She couldn't even conjure a flame like Poppy could. But she didn't want to hear about it again, since she knew she was good at channeling her magic into potions and spells. She was capable. Gritting her teeth, Iris shook her head and took their new spat as her permission to leave. Before she could change her mind, Iris pulled her cloak's hood up over her head and walked straight from the cave's mouth.

A long breath left her lips as heavy rain soaked her cloak. Was she making the right choice?

"That's not fair and you know it!" Poppy's muffled, high-pitched voice chided from behind.

"Fair is foul, and foul is fair," Dahlia said in a flat tone.

But Iris didn't look back at them. They obviously hadn't noticed she'd left. Instead, she trudged farther into the rain, with her hedgehog in her cloak pocket still babbling questions.

Yes. It was the right choice. She wouldn't come back to Dawndale, where she'd always be overshadowed. Despite the echoes in the back of her mind, the needling in her middle had already subsided.

She didn't need a coven to wreak havoc on the realm. Iris could do it better all on her own.

And there *was* a village she'd recently heard of that was only a realm and a half away called Fraywell that needed a little…shaping.

So they had better get ready for something wicked…for she was on the way.

Chapter 1

Second Witch: Thrice, and once the hedge-pig whined.

—*MACBETH*: ACT 4, SCENE 1

No one ever said being evil was easy. Particularly not Iris Weyward.

Evil took work.

As a matter of fact, Iris knew exactly what to do to conjure the perfect mindset every morning:

1. Wake.
2. Throw her blanket off with a dramatic flourish.
3. Repeat this very intonation: *Love the life you live... and destroy those who get in your way.*

In that order. Wash, rinse, repeat.

Most days it worked. That morning would be different.

Much different. That day would begin a cascade of events that would forever change her life.

But we'll get there.

That morning Iris's eyes blinked open to the sun streaming through her cottage's bedroom window. And, as always, her first instinct was to grab the blanket and toss it freely in the air, but instead something heavy…and poky…lay across her neck and half of her cheek.

A tiny black, cold, wet nose pushed into the side of hers, and the creature snored like a dragon with a stuffed-up nose.

Iris groaned and gently drew the brown hedgehog from her face and dangled him in front of her. Using her bare feet, she pushed the blanket off her body and into a rumpled mess at the bottom of her bed and propped herself up on her elbow.

Somehow the beast still slept as if he hadn't a care in the world, while his little pink tongue lolled out of his open mouth.

She cringed at his sulfury breath and wondered if there actually was a dragon in his lineage.

"Quince," Iris said, sitting upright and running her free hand over her cheek. Unfortunately, she found a smattering of indentations pressed into her skin from the sleeping animal's prickly spines.

But Quince didn't wake. Instead he only grunted multiple times and kicked his back right foot as if fending off some unseen attacker in his dreams.

Iris sighed.

Of course she'd taught her familiar several defensive

moves in the time she'd known him...which added up to all of her twenty-seven years. When a person was the village witch, they—and their associates (hedgehog or otherwise)—needed to know how to physically defend themselves from potential attacks at any time in case magic failed.

And Iris did regard herself as a villain. Even if she hadn't quite achieved the reputation she desired.

Not *yet* anyway.

The hierarchy was steeper than one might think.

After the whole debacle with her sisters back at Hillock, Iris was still trying to figure out how to realize her journey on her own, and there had, admittedly, been a number of bumps in the road...including the fact her magic hadn't been up to par in the previous weeks.

She watched her still snoring familiar and blamed her problems on a lack of sleep.

Not to mention the letter from one of her sisters sitting unopened on her dining table.

But there were more immediate problems to deal with. Starting with Quince, who continued kicking and chopping the air with his outstretched paws in his sleep.

"Quince!" Iris shouted while swinging her legs over the edge of the bed, all while doing her best to avoid getting poked with her familiar's sharp spines.

"I'll get you!" His little chestnut-colored eyes finally popped open, and he threw his front paws out as if to attack. His voice leaned toward high-pitched, as someone might expect from a small creature such as a hedgehog.

Iris carefully plopped him down on her bed before his spiny body poked her fingers...which happened too often and made it that much more difficult to mix up potions to sell for purposes like taking revenge on cheating lovers and nosy mothers-in-law.

"You done?" Iris asked. She crumpled her brow, pursed her lips, and pointed to her indented cheek. "We've discussed this."

His pupils enlarged. "I can't help myself at night," Quince admitted while wrapping his arms around his belly and squeezing. "Your neck is so warm and cozy."

"Cozy?" Iris gritted her teeth. "The last thing I want to be known as is *cozy*." Her voice remained flat with a tinge of forced annoyance. Of course, she loved her little near-constant companion, even if he was a pest. But she never wanted to dwell on the affection for long, lest he mention it too often. "Even to you."

The little familiar closed his eyes and continued squeezing himself, apparently forgetting all about his nightmare. "No one has to know," Quince whispered dreamily.

A growl rumbled in the back of Iris's throat, but in lieu of saying anything else she rose and beelined to the mirror over the chest of drawers. Ignoring the ridiculous indentations on her lightly tanned face—perhaps if someone arrived for an early pickup they'd think it an old scar she'd earned doing *something* nefarious...one could only hope—she quickly worked to tie back her curly brown hair, but one piece in the front forever refused to stay put. The twist fell into her face, and she tucked it behind her ear, not bothering to secure it any other way. As always, it would only fall out again, so the task was useless. And Iris had given up long before.

She studied herself, considering her gray-blue eyes, the color of her father's. But instead of dwelling on something as meaningless as eye color when there were tasks to be done, she pulled a plain brown skirt and a white cotton blouse from her drawer next to the bookcase containing her father's old spell books. Quince snorted loudly again, and through the mirror's reflection Iris watched him lying flat on his back with all four legs sticking straight out, nose twitching.

Iris shook her head at her familiar, quickly exchanged her nightdress, which fit a squinch more snugly than it had the year before, for the fresh skirt and blouse, then made her way out of the bedroom and down the short hallway containing her room and one other.

Her cottage was fairly meager, as the coin she earned from her small-scale potions business was still limited. The tiny living area waited to her left, complete with a fireplace and hearth. Two worn but comfortable overstuffed green chairs sat close to it, with several books stacked beside one of them. In her spare time, Iris had been teaching herself the art of reanimation. The thick book on the top of the stack was titled *The Dead Don't Have to Stay That Way*. It had been extremely interesting. Iris hadn't tested many of the spells, but she had successfully raised a mouse from the dead after Quince had found it outside. Though she hadn't had any other test subject available, she still believed herself ready to try the magic on someone larger if she got the chance.

If Iris perfected the spell, it might eventually bring in serious coin and recognition around the Veronian Region.

As it was, the kitchen was almost completely dedicated to potion and poison making, since that paid the bills. Iris had built and installed a series of shelves to hold all measures of interesting things. There were, of course, the standard herbs that tended to round out most concoctions, but intermixed were rare ground-up bits of this and that, such as cobweb, pea blossom, moth, and mustard seeds. Unfortunately, the organization had fallen into disarray, but Iris rarely had a moment for rearranging.

Case in point, the jar of her favorite tea sat next to a container of ground scale of dragon. One day she'd find the time to get everything back in order, but in the meantime, she eyed the three bottles and a shiny red apple scheduled for pickup that day.

Two of the potions as well as the apple were lethal, but Iris rarely asked too many questions concerning orders…as she didn't want to really get involved with whatever grievance the buyer had with the victim—*person*—they intended to use the mixture on.

Not her business.

The bigger problem was that she'd stayed up half the night to make them properly. Potions that normally should have come together easily were not…and it had been happening for weeks. And the annoyance was entirely unacceptable.

Iris had come from a long line of competent witches. If she could barely manage something as basic as potions, how would she leave the legacy that was expected of her?

Nearly mindlessly she placed a black kettle on the stove and filled it with water from a pitcher waiting on the counter. Iris placed her palm on the side of the kettle and out of habit drew magic into it to heat the water. Slight warmth spread over her palm and then dissipated.

"Oh, snails," she complained. Nothing really seemed to be going right that morning. Out of frustration she grabbed the matchbox on top of the stove, dug out a match, and struck the head on the box. Gritting her teeth, she touched the match to the wood below and leaned against the counter while the water heated.

Iris sighed as the letter on the table caught her eye. Irritatingly, the perfect handwriting indicated it had come from Dahlia, who, being the older sister, always wanted to be in charge. Iris didn't want to read what she had to say. She quickly drew her attention away from it and chose a cup and saucer from her cabinet. Once the water was hot enough, she poured some into the cup and sprinkled in a generous number of tea leaves from a jar next to the one labeled *hemlock*. Iris had mixed the tea blend herself. While the brew steeped, she grabbed one of the *non*poisonous ruby-red apples from the wooden bowl on her counter.

She took the cup, saucer, and apple and sat down at her dining table. Iris wasted no time munching on the sweet fruit as she drew out her pencil and notebook, then opened it to review her orders, check the moon cycle, and map out her day's activities.

But she didn't get far, since one major point on her to-do list had not been checked off for too long.

Find a new bodyguard, the sentence read.

Iris doodled a face onto the paper, then added horns to its head and two little pointy fangs coming from the lips. For a moment she considered the doodle, since there was a time she'd enjoyed drawing, but she quickly scribbled it out.

Not that a bodyguard was truly essential for her current level of villainy, but having one gave a certain air to it. And a girl had to dream big. She hated to admit it to herself, but sometimes a witch had to fake it to make it. Plus, having muscle patrolling your house was an easy way to convince people of your importance.

The month prior, her ogre bodyguard, Jamy, who'd worked for her for the year she'd lived in Fraywell, had wanted to take a holiday with his family for a week. He'd been quite loyal and done an excellent job of helping maintain the look of an established villain. So she couldn't say no. The problem was that he hadn't returned, and she needed someone new.

She took a gulp of the slightly bitter tea and swished it around in her mouth before swallowing.

A new hire was a task easier said than done. Fraywell was a small, quaint village, beneficial for Iris in that her business competition was nonexistent, but the smallness made hiring vicious-looking employees difficult to say the least.

Her eyes dropped to her sister's letter again. Dahlia might be able to help. But then Iris would have to admit she needed assistance.

Iris sighed, leaned back in her chair, and took a bite of her apple. She worked her way through the entire fruit still not knowing what to do. Finding Jamy had been a bit of serendipity. When they met, the unemployed ogre had been lunching at the local inn, The Boar's Head.

At the inn, Iris could don her cloak, sit at a corner table, and have a drink or a meal, all while looking quite menacing. It was a good opportunity to relax and pick up orders from travelers passing through Fraywell and staying the night.

Plus, Herman and Lysander Quickly, the owners, didn't mind her presence. Lysander always said a little skulduggery added to the pub's charm. But Iris was never sure whether he was serious or just liked that Iris was a paying customer. The elf *was* a mite over the top.

In the beginning, Jamy had been down on his luck and needed a job. Iris needed a bodyguard and had a barn for him to sleep in. It had been the perfect arrangement until a couple of months later when Jamy had met an ogress from the next village called Springburn who already had a couple of kids. After that, he started smiling more and sleeping in the barn less.

Iris knew happiness seemed to ruin everything.

And since he'd disappeared entirely, business *had* declined.

She growled and bared her teeth, then quickly scrawled a circle around the words **Find a new bodyguard** on the day's list.

She hovered her hand over the paper, closed her eyes, and uttered an incantation.

"Night by night the moon doth rise,
Day b' day a cat will cry.
Focus on the goals to seek,
Only then shall you bespeak."

Calm inched over her body as the words flowed from Iris's mouth. That day would be the day. She had to get back on track with her goals. Once her pickups arrived she'd head into town for news of anyone suitable for the bodyguard job. Maybe even organize her kitchen shelves. And all of a sudden she felt better than she had all morning…lighter. Iris reached up to her cheek and found the indentations from Quince's spines gone.

She smiled and proceeded to gnaw her sweet apple all the way down to the core, then leaned out from her chair and tossed it one-handed into the garbage basket at the end of the kitchen. After that she gulped down her tea and flipped over the cup on the saucer. She didn't always read the leaves, and it wasn't as if she'd even asked it any questions. But that day she thought a read might be a good idea.

Iris flipped the cup back and guided the handle to the left. Then she glanced at the leaves lining the inside of the cup, hoping for the best. Instead, she gulped at what she saw.

There was very clearly a bouquet of flowers at the bottom of the cup.

Good luck. Good friends and…worst of all…*love*.

Her eyes widened. She'd take the luck part… She could use luck in finding her new bodyguard, and possibly some new clients. But friends and love? *That* she didn't need. Mayhem didn't want friends or love. Those things were distracting from her goals. Not only that, but she'd also chosen her path for a reason. She'd forever been odd. Her sisters had been too, and people in their past had let them know it.

Even more, the thought of having friends…other than Quince, of course? Horrifying. Unsafe.

This was undoubtedly the worst news she'd heard in a long time.

As Iris's heart picked up speed, she shoved the prediction away.

Tea is not always right reverberated in her mind. Could have been a bad batch.

But she didn't have the opportunity to fully dwell on her thoughts.

Bam, bam. The sound came from her front door.

Almost relieved at the distraction, she pushed the cup and saucer away and rose from her chair. "Be right there." Iris straightened her blouse and patted both her cheeks.

"Love the life you live," she said under her breath and eyed the cup. "And *destroy* those who get in your way." Without a second thought, Iris swiped the cup onto the floor, where it shattered.

"Good," she muttered. She'd get the mess later, but she instantly felt better about her life prospects.

Bam, bam came again.

"Coming!" Iris spun around on her bare feet and walked toward the noise, where she unlatched the lock and flung open the door. "Yes?"

But there was no one. She didn't even see her neighbor Kate, who lived across the road working in her garden.

Iris's brow frowned and she looked around. "Hello?" Those were the times she really preferred having a bodyguard around to take care of that sort of thing.

But again, there was nothing but the sign outside her door reading *Spells and Potions* (she'd kept the business message simple).

Iris almost closed the door and chalked the whole incident up to imagination when moaning came from around the corner of her cottage. She threw out her hand to ignite her heat magic, but it popped then snuffed out.

"Snails!" She seized an empty ceramic vase and clutched it by the neck, ready to break it if necessary. Iris gritted her teeth and hurried after whoever or whatever had trespassed on her property.

It turned out to be a who.

But Iris only saw the back of him as she rounded the corner with her vase ready. And from her view, he was tall, muscular, green, black-haired, and, judging by the blood on his dirty shirt and his stumbling…injured.

She froze as the orc (likely half orc by his leaner build) turned and snarled at her, showing off the white tusks at the corners of his mouth. Iris had never seen the guy in her life.

A shiver rippled down her spine, and Iris glanced down at the vase clutched in her hand. She'd need a bigger weapon *and* working magic if the orc had nefarious intentions.

"What do you want?" she growled, trying to sound tough.

But he didn't answer. Instead, his eyes rolled back, and the orc fell face-first to the hard ground.

Surprised by the turn of events, Iris gasped and for a split second wasn't sure what to do. But her mind cleared slightly, and against her own better judgment she eased up to him. Mouth dry, she stood there for a moment watching the unmoving body and then reached out her bare toe and poked him in the shoulder.

Nothing.

She bent and took his wrist. Again, nothing. He was dead.

Iris stood, pushed the familiar stray-hair tendril from her vision, and tossed the vase onto the ground. Then her lips twisted into a wry grin while her mind worked.

She'd found her new bodyguard.

Now to solve the problem of getting him inside.

Chapter 2

"What's that?" Quince's voice came from the ground behind Iris.

She flinched and caught her breath, not at all expecting the hedgehog to get up before noon.

Or a dead body in her yard, for that matter.

"My new bodyguard." Iris chewed on her thumbnail, still trying to figure out how in the realm to get the body inside the cottage.

Quince's nose twitched as he surveyed the body. "He doesn't smell good."

Looking down at the green orc she considered him. Holes had been ripped in his clothes in multiple locations, and his shirt was stained with blood on his left side, likely the location of the deadly blow. But his face still looked good... attractive even, if Iris cared much about that. He had a square jaw and bright amber eyes. His head was turned and one eye was wide open, as if staring at her. Another person might find the sight creepy, but Iris only saw opportunity.

A little death never hurt anyone.

"Well." Iris ripped off the jagged piece of nail with her teeth and spat it on the ground. "He's *dead*, so of course he doesn't smell good."

"Dead?" Quince's voice raised at least an octave, and his spines stood on end. "Why would you want a *dead* bodyguard?"

Iris scoffed at the hedgehog's lack of vision. Plus, she didn't have time to answer those sorts of questions since, first, whoever had whacked the guy might still be around and might want the body and, second, her neighbor Kate Elworth, across the road, had seemingly very little to do except stare out her window at whatever was going on at Iris's cottage. Luckily the patch of dead grass the orc had landed on was just out of her window's sight line...*unless* she'd seen him at Iris's door. But if she had, the nosy woman was likely to already be over to scope out the situation.

Iris probably should have already disposed of Kate months prior. But the situation was complicated, and for the time being she tried to keep her more heinous crimes a minimum of a day's ride away...not that she'd committed any for quite some time. And straight out *dispatching* people had never really been her cup of tea... She and her sisters had always gone about that sort of thing in a much more roundabout way. Like getting someone else to do the dirty work.

That being said, in reality, the most she would do was cast a dis-remembrance spell on the woman...but that could only be done so many times before it had...side effects. And Iris had already done that.

Multiple times.

And she had more important, immediate problems to deal with.

Without another word, Iris fisted her skirt into bunches and trudged toward the barn, past the well and the run-down henhouse with three scrawny chickens pecking the ground, barely realizing she still didn't have shoes until a thorn poked her square in the middle of her foot.

"Snails," she complained as her foot stung at the punctured spot.

Thorns in the yard were not a surprise though, since she did nothing with the outside of her home. It was all dirt and weeds except for some scraggly bushes lining the back of the cottage. Iris didn't have time to deal with them—and in what realm did a villain think about yard care? Gritting her teeth, she simply lifted her foot up, swiped away the spike, and kept going despite the trail of blood seeping from the angry skin.

"Wait up," Quince called from behind, but Iris did no such thing.

She was on a mission. The witch could conjure a little low-effort magic to help her lift the orc, since she didn't want to damage him further by completely dragging him across the dirt into the cottage. Not only that, the quicker she'd be able to complete the task the better…with a potential murderer on the loose, or worse…Kate across the way.

Neither of which Iris would allow to thwart her plan.

She made it into the barn and gazed around the dark space while her vision adjusted. Iris didn't actually keep any large animals in the barn, since she didn't have time to take care of them. It was hard enough to feed the chickens daily and listen to Quince and his whining if she forgot a meal… but she seemed able to manage both somehow.

Even someone who was depraved was aware animal neglect was *entirely* inappropriate.

"Now where did I put it?" Iris wondered out loud as she studied the stacks of wooden boxes filled with books and projects she'd forever put off to explore one new thing or another.

Finally, she spotted the handle of what she had been searching for next to the spot where her former bodyguard slept. A flat, wheeled cart she'd built a while back, because living on her own, she sometimes needed a little assistance moving large objects. Like today.

She hadn't used it in an age, and the thing was covered in old hay left over from the previous cottage owner. Iris jogged over to the cart and yanked it out from underneath the mess. Must and dirt wafted into the air and tickled her nose. Iris ignored the smell and pulled again, but one wheel dragged a bit. As she reached to correct it, Quince leaped on top of the platform and collapsed over onto his back.

"Instead of doing that, you might think about helping," Iris grumbled.

The little hedgehog flipped over and scurried to the edge of the wooden platform then flopped himself half over the side.

Iris couldn't quite see what he was doing, but the little creature grunted, pulled, and came up with a bunch of hay in his paws and a grin on his face. "Got it!"

"You're a gem," Iris said in a flat tone, but she pulled the handle, and the cart rolled freely over the hay-covered ground.

"Right?" The hedgehog puffed his chest with pride.

But Iris knew she'd need Quince's help with the next step, so she didn't say what she wanted to. She almost never did when it came to her familiar.

"Let's get this over with," she said instead and yanked the cart, with her familiar still on it, toward the barn's exit.

At the opening, she scanned outside for any unwelcome visitors or clients. It was clear, other than the giant dead body lying sprawled out in her side yard of course. Moving on, Iris bumped the cart across the ground and stopped at the side of the orc, pursing her lips.

"Head or feet first?" Quince said as he climbed down from the cart.

Iris was considering the same thing, but she didn't want to appear indecisive, so she quickly chose one. "Feet."

"Then I'm ready," Quince said.

Iris didn't *need* Quince for all her spells, but he helped

amplify them and speed them along in situations like the one she was in now. Plus, her magic had been so iffy lately, a boost was welcome. Without wasting any more time, she positioned the cart beyond the orc's feet, then lowered her hand and allowed Quince to crawl into her palm. His cream-colored underbelly was a soft contrast to the dangerous spikes on the opposite side.

The witch kneeled beside the orc and held out her free hand over the middle of his back. Quince's temperature rose noticeably, and she muttered a few words under her breath while both hands heated up.

Inhaling a deep breath, Iris settled her fingers on the orc's back. Her breath hitched. He wasn't cold yet. Of course it was silly to assume he would have been. He'd just died.

"You okay?" Quince asked.

"Why wouldn't I be?" Iris snapped, but she hadn't really meant to. She refused to admit to him or herself that this might be a bigger job than she'd originally thought.

The hedgehog eyed her. "I'm only concerned about your emotional health when you do this sort of thing."

She kind of despised the bond the two of them had. The hedgehog knew too much about her—life was easier when a person was a mystery, not an open book. "You're ridiculous." Iris refocused, finished the spell, and placed Quince on the ground.

"I'm ridiculous?" the little hedgehog muttered and waddled away from the form. "I'm not the one with a dead body in my yard."

Iris ignored him and the fact it was *his* yard as well. She had business to attend to.

Steeling herself, the witch stood and walked to the orc's feet, positioned at the end of the cart. Iris stretched out her hands and lifted his back half from the ground. Then she dragged her hands over the air and pulled. The body moved and scraped on the dirt then inched onto the cart. Iris continued to pull until the orc draped onto the cart, his top and bottom hanging off to the ground from either side.

Quince's head tipped back and forth in question. "How are you going to get him through the door?"

"Do you have to ask quite so many questions?" But he was right. She'd be in for trouble. The orc was too wide in his current position. "We'll figure it out," she said, trying to remain positive.

"If you say so." Quince sat on his haunches and crossed his tiny arms over his chest.

With a grunt, Iris grabbed the handle and pulled. The spell *had* made the orc lighter; otherwise any of what she had been doing would've been impossible considering their weight and size difference was substantial. She guessed he was at least a head and a half taller than her.

Since the wheels were worn, they creaked as she pulled the cart over the dirt. Iris glanced again at Kate's cottage, which was a stark contrast to Iris's dull one that needed several repairs.

The place was a cheery white with bright yellow painted trim, including the shutters. On top, the thatched roof was recently repaired, and her garden overflowed with flowers and all sorts of produce and herbs. In addition to the woman's habit of nosing into neighborly business, Kate was a massive flirt. Despite being well past her prime years, she was attractive, and Iris had witnessed her using that fact to her advantage with the men of Fraywell and beyond. From her revolving guests, Iris assumed she probably had no less than five suitors on the line who truly thought she might marry them at any moment.

Iris scoffed at where her mind had traveled, refocused, and kept pulling while she huffed and puffed. The spell had not lightened the orc nearly as much as it should have.

"You can do it!" Quince called out in encouragement, and Iris realized the hedgehog was square in the middle of the orc's back.

"Is that how you help?" she groaned, fully considering banning the creature from her room that night. He could sleep in the barn.

"Pshaw." Quince waved his paw in her direction. "I did what you needed from me."

"And I'll bet you're expecting breakfast as payment." She tugged the cart a little farther around the corner of the house and put all her effort into it.

"If you wouldn't mind," he said and jumped to the ground. "I haven't had mealworms in a while, if you need a suggestion."

Iris shivered at the thought and continued pulling. Even she drew the line at preparing mealworms.

Not long after, she'd managed to get the cart to the door. Taking a moment of consideration, she shoved it open and dumped the body off the cart in a heap. The orc had only been dead a few minutes, so he wasn't stiff. She pushed the cart out of the way.

"Now what?" Quince asked, still not doing anything to help other than asking annoying questions.

Iris blew out a big breath, bent down, and grabbed the orc under the arms, pulling him into her cottage's opening. The entire operation, even with magic, took more effort than she'd hoped, but she dragged the body inside, avoiding any of the broken teacup shards, and shut the door.

Mission accomplished, Iris flopped down in the overstuffed chair, panting.

"About that breakfast?" Quince asked.

Iris shot the familiar a deadly glare and he snapped his lips shut.

The little guy pointed to the kitchen. "I can likely find something to stave off the hunger."

"Good plan," Iris managed as she considered the giant dead orc in her living room. He was definitely bigger than she'd thought he was outside.

But none of that mattered. She needed to get to work. Iris eyed her necromancy book on the top of her stack while Quince ransacked the kitchen in search of some breakfast. But then she remembered the potions and apple sitting next to the door and the clients who'd likely stop by at any time. Iris wasn't too sure how kindly they might take to a dead body in the middle of her floor if they tried to come inside. Most people didn't *actually* use the deadly potions she concocted for them, but she was happy to get paid either way.

So she avoided tripping over the orc, found a basket, pencil, and paper and penned a note: *We're closed today. Take what is yours, pay your fee, then leave.* She chewed the end of the pencil, wondering if it sounded threatening enough. Then she decided to add, even though it wasn't true, *Thieves will automatically have a curse placed on them.*

Who had the time to come up with automatic curses?

Satisfied, she loaded the sealed and labeled jars along with the apple into the basket, attached the note, and placed it outside her door.

Iris needed to hurry. From reading the book, she knew that the faster she raised the dead, the better the outcome. Leave someone dead for too long, and their brain might never be as it once was.

With the door shut and locked, Iris made her way back over to the book and flipped it open to the place where she'd stuck in a slip of paper for a bookmark. It was the same recipe she'd used on the dead mouse. She ran her finger down the page to find the spell and skimmed over the passage.

As she might have expected, larger bodies took more effort than something like a mouse, and a potion was involved. She just hoped she had all the ingredients in stock.

Book in hand, Iris stood over the orc, studying him, then looked back at the spell instructions. The potion recipe was weight sensitive, and she had no idea how much the orc weighed.

"You might want to interview the guy first," Quince said, interrupting her thoughts.

"What?" she shot back.

The hedgehog had perched himself on the counter's edge with his feet dangling off the side while he munched on a piece of buttered bread. Iris was pretty sure he hadn't used a knife, and she'd likely find his paw prints in the butter. But that was a problem for later.

"Interview him. You know, before you go to all the trouble of actually bringing him back to life," the beast said with his mouth full of bread. "Who knows if he *wants* to be a bodyguard? Or if he's even *qualified* for that matter."

Iris's eyes widened, then scrunched into tight slits directed at her familiar. She already had a dead body in her cottage… She'd gone too far not to finish the job. But once again Quince was right. Iris couldn't only go off the fact the orc *looked* perfect for the position. And it would be better if he was willing to take the job.

She scoffed and guessed that consent wasn't such a bad idea. Without saying a word, she flipped back a few chapters for instructions on *Communion with the Dead*. There were no potions involved in that part, just a small incantation to recapture his soul. It couldn't have gone far.

"I'm going to need you again then," she said to Quince and presented her hand.

"Say please," he said.

Iris pursed her lips briefly. "Please."

He stuffed the remainder of the bread into his mouth, hopped off the counter, and scurried over to Iris and up her arm.

Looking down at the words on the page, Iris muttered the incantation and held out her free hand over the body.

"Swirl and tumble spirit wild
I bid you speak and fall beguiled."

Several sparks sputtered off the tips of her fingers and fell onto his back, then vanished.

"Snails," Iris complained when she listened for a voice and nothing happened. "I'm going to need a little more from you," she said to Quince.

"Gladly," he replied as he snuggled closer to Iris's neck.

She winced from the jabbing spines but spoke the words again.

Magic glimmered, and warmth from it traveled down her arms from the spot Quince pressed into her neck as she listened for what would happen next.

"Where am I?" a deep voice came into her head. The orc actually said several other choice words too, but Iris didn't pay attention to them at all. She was focused only on the rich tone of his voice and the way the sound of it made her light up inside.

"Um, um," she managed and decided not to tiptoe around the situation. "You're dead."

"Dead?" His tone was incredulous. "What did you do to me, witch? I can't be dead. There's a job I need to finish."

Iris shrugged even though he couldn't see the gesture, since his voice was only in her head. "I didn't *do* anything to you. You knocked on my door and then proceeded to meet your demise in my side yard. May I ask your name?"

He growled. "Who's asking?"

"Well," Iris said, fairly confident about her choice. He seemed aggressive. "I'm Iris Weyward. The local witch here in Fraywell—"

She was about to hype up her villainous aspirations to make the job more appealing but didn't get to it.

"Yes, Fraywell. That's where he was," the voice reverberated in her mind.

"Who?" Iris asked.

"The *yeasty, milk-livered bastard* I was supposed to take out!" The voice peppered in some more choice curses.

Iris ran her hand over her chin. Yes. He seemed like he would do. But did he want the job? She needed to ask. "You're a mercenary then, I presume?" But the second she asked, Quince let out a snore from her shoulder and she nearly shook the familiar onto the floor.

"Yes, damn it," he said. "And how am I supposed to get paid now if I'm dead?"

Iris gave Quince a poke to wake him. "I do have a solution for that if you're interested, Mr.…?"

"Talon Gefroy." The answer was low and gravelly.

She enjoyed the tone more than she wanted to admit.

"Talon," Iris said, considering the fact the orc looked as fierce as he did and had mercenary experience, even if he had failed at his last job. Excitement at the prospect stirred in her chest. He seemed the perfect fit. "Can I call you that?"

There was a pause before he answered, "Why not, witch?"

"Iris," she corrected, but he didn't respond, so she cleared her throat and continued, "You're dead, so your choices are limited. You can either stay that way or you can help me."

"How would I do that?" Talon asked with a snarl.

Iris chewed her lip. "I need a bodyguard. The pay isn't great, but you'll have a place to sleep [she left out it was the barn] and meals provided [they probably weren't going to be great if she was being honest]. You need…well, a heartbeat. I can make that happen."

"Oh…you have some skill? You're a necromancer?" he asked, sounding slightly impressed.

Iris gulped. She'd only successfully raised one mouse from the dead, but she was all about—at least feigning—confidence in her talents. "I'm talking to you, aren't I?" she said, although necromancer wasn't exactly a title she'd give herself after the mouse.

"And what's going to stop me from simply walking off after you complete the process?" Talon asked.

Iris chuckled, reveling in the newfound sense of power in her middle, albeit manufactured. "What do you take me for? Fresh born? There'll be a binding spell involved."

This would, of course, take care of the problem of him running off for a better life, as her prior help had.

Talon growled and cursed again.

"Well?" Iris asked, completely intrigued by the prospect of what would happen next.

"Deal."

Chapter 3

The hairs on Iris's arms stood on end at his confirmation. All the while, she envisioned a new and positive future for herself. Everything about the morning had gone unexpectedly but was seemingly moving in her favor despite what the tea had read.

She withdrew her hand, and Talon's voice in her mind was silenced.

At once, something deep inside her missed it, but it was likely only the sensation of power that vanished instantly from her chest. Iris gazed at his dead body, and her eyes traveled to the blood on the back of his shirt. It was already turning brown. Her eyes moved up to his short black hair and again to the square cut of his green jaw. The shade was slightly warmer than a full-blood orc's…more olive.

She liked it too.

"How'd it go?" Quince's voice in her ear broke her from her meddling thoughts.

"Oh, good, good," Iris said, excited to start the full necromancy spell and truly meet the real Talon. "He's on board."

The hedgehog's spines poked into Iris's neck as he perched on her shoulder, and she pushed him slightly off-kilter. Then she continued studying Talon.

"Not sure what you're waiting for," he said dryly.

Iris wasn't quite sure either as she brought her attention back to the spell. Hesitating a little, she flipped to the bookmarked page. So much of her simply wanted to do it right… not to mess up the spell. And a tiny voice in the back of her mind gave her doubt.

Iris's free hand balled into a fist, and she whispered, "Love the life you live…and destroy those who get in your way."

"You tell 'em," Quince said, rubbing his little paws together. "Now what do we do?"

She'd show the realm the kind of chaos they'd created. A growl rumbled in Iris's throat and her attention focused on the words in the book. The first steps were to create the potion.

Leaving Talon on the floor, she moved into her kitchen and deposited Quince onto the counter. After plunking the book next to him on the counter, she brought out a pot from the cupboard and placed it on the stove. It was already hot from her morning tea, but she opened the door and placed in another log to really get the fire going.

"Thanks," a voice called from outside the cottage just as Iris shut the door.

She flinched but quickly realized it was only Phebe from Fraywell picking up the potion she'd ordered to prepare for her annoying mother-in-law coming into town the next week. It was the only one of the three items in the basket that wasn't *completely* lethal. Phebe had considered going stronger when she placed the order but decided against taking it that far. Iris didn't care either way.

"She'll leave," Quince said as he lounged against the apple bowl.

He was right, so Iris kept her mouth shut, not wanting to alert *anyone* that she was even home. Instead she drew her attention back to the recipe.

This one wasn't that difficult, at least no more difficult than most of the other potions she created. Iris just needed to be careful with the measurements and timing. First she added the water from the pitcher on her counter into the pot and went down the list, adding the ingredients.

Wool of bat
Tongue of dog
Adder's fork
Blind-worm's sting
Lizard's leg
Owlet's wing

Plus several other ingredients she'd soon get to.

While she added each to the pot, she took another look at Talon on her floor, estimating his size for the measurements. She definitely didn't want to underdose him and have the spell not work. There was a little leeway in these things, but with necromancy spells there was only one opportunity. If she failed, then she'd simply have a useless dead body in her house and *still* no bodyguard.

Not to mention she really wanted to meet Talon in his full form.

He seemed...*interesting*.

Quince fiddled with the cork cap on a jar of dried beetles and pulled one out. He was about to deposit it whole in his mouth when Iris snatched it from his paw and tossed it into the pot.

"Hey," the hedgehog complained and wrinkled his nose.

"I need it for the recipe," Iris said as the mixture came to a bubble and she stirred. The witch muttered words over her concoction that brought everything together. As it sputtered beneath her, a terrible, acrid aroma burned her nose. And fighting the urge to pinch it shut, she grabbed a bottle and funnel then spooned exactly one tablespoon of the dark liquid inside to cool.

Iris held it up high and admired the rich color, glad she didn't have to drink it.

After a moment, she quickly flipped to the binding spell and confirmed it needed to be completed directly after the full necromancy one...as his body was adjusting to living again. She also chose the one that would keep the orc no more than a furlong away from her. She wasn't taking chances. Iris spoke out loud, but to herself, "First the potion, then the undead spell, then the bind."

"Got it," Quince said from the counter as Iris realized he was stuffing a dried beetle sandwiched between two small pieces of bread in his mouth.

She groaned. "You really shouldn't eat here while I'm making potions. Who knows what you might ingest by accident?"

"Aww," Quince said, his mouth full. "You'd miss me."

Iris gathered the book and the potion then leaned down for Quince to scurry up her shoulder. "I wouldn't say that." But the statement was completely untrue. She and Quince had been constant companions since she was a child. "Now stop distracting me."

Once back by Talon, she placed the open book at her side with the waiting potion, and for a brief second she surveyed the situation. She gulped as reality began to settle in. Necromancy was no small thing to get right, but Iris needed to keep positive. "This will work better if I flip him over."

"You're not stalling, are you?" Quince asked from her shoulder.

"The potion goes in his mouth," she shot back, offended. "Now hang on."

Quince dug his little claws into Iris's top while she bent and flipped the orc over. The spell she'd done to get him into the cottage more easily was definitely starting to wear off, and moving him took more even effort, but Iris managed the task.

The blood was barely visible on the front of his shirt, and other than being pretty dirty he barely looked injured, let alone completely dead. *Well, in a few moments that problem will be solved*, she thought. Her eyes drew to his fierce—but definitely handsome—face. Even if she'd wanted to, Iris was unable to deny that fact. She gulped and pushed the thought aside. It didn't matter.

Iris took a few more breaths to settle her nerves and held out her hands. She'd performed complex spells before. Of course it had been with the help of her sisters. But she was skilled, and Iris needed to prove that to herself.

"Potion first," Quince reminded her. "That's what you said."

Without answering him, she reached for the now slightly thickened potion and held the jar's mouth over Talon's tusk-flanked lips. The liquid drained out of the spout, and she allowed it to drop inside his open mouth until it all was gone.

She held her breath. The orc had interesting teeth too. Straight.

"Now the spell," Iris said, still a little shaky inside, but she did her best not to let on to Quince. *Just keep going*, she thought. She held out her hands and repeated the words from the book, struggling to keep her voice from shaking.

*"Close the wounds and shadows cast,
Your journey onward now impasse.
Rise o rise from your place,
Be your sleep now effaced."*

Quince's body radiated warmth on her neck. And as she continued speaking the words, her mind sank into a near trance, settling all her nerves, as if everything else in the realm had fallen away.

Energy twisted in her chest, then flowed out to her arms. Iris's breath picked up. She still half sensed Quince on her shoulder amplifying the spell. Talon's life force was powerful, angry…vicious. Greedy for the power, Iris reached into the air and harnessed it, pulling it toward herself and then thrusting it down to his body.

Merging their vitality invigorated her. She was capable, energized, as if her goal was so close and within her grasp. A cackle exited her mouth, and she didn't even attempt to stop it.

Knock, knock came from the door.

Determined, Iris snapped her mouth shut but did her best to ignore the interruption. She clenched her eyes as she stretched out her hands over Talon's chest. Sparks appeared from the tips of her fingers and connected to him. His life force danced under her hands, and the power forced a smile onto her lips.

"Hello, dear." A woman's voice through the door broke Iris's concentration again.

"It's Kate," Quince whispered while his whiskers tickled Iris's ear.

"Snails," Iris swore, trying to ignore the second round of knocking coming from the door and her annoying familiar. Despite the effort, Talon's life force dwindled away from his body.

"Are you home?" Kate's voice came again from outside.

Iris stood and whipped around, making Quince fly off and onto the ground into a little pile.

"You're going to have to answer it," Quince said, dusting himself off. "She just looked in the window."

"She *what*?" Iris asked, knowing Talon's time was limited and she wasn't going to fail by allowing Kate to interfere.

The hedgehog sucked his teeth. "They're pretty dirty. I don't think she saw anything."

It was true. Iris hadn't had time to clean the windows for months, and the fact had become a sore spot. "Are you judging me?" Iris asked, her body still tingling with the ghost of the magic.

"Only stating facts," Quince said. "I'm not tall enough to do it."

"Yoo-hoo," Kate singsonged. "Anyone home?"

Iris's fists balled; then she let out a long string of stressed-out curses and whirled around. The ever-present stray tendril of hair flew into the middle of her face, and without a thought Iris blew it straight up.

"Take a breath," Quince called from the floor. "We already have one dead body to deal with."

To get rid of the woman, Iris stomped across the floor, reached for the handle, twisted it, and cracked the door. "What?" she sneered for the sake of appearance.

Iris's neighbor stood out front wearing her typical low-cut cotton blouse, this one with tiny flowers embroidered on the edges. Her blond hair streaked with a bit of gray at the temples was pulled up onto the top of her head, and several pieces cascaded down. Kate's pinkish lips complemented her light skin, which looked as if the woman rarely worked outside. *She probably doesn't… All her suitors do that for her*, Iris thought.

"Oh," Kate cooed in an innocent tone, but it was obvious she was trying to get a peek at what was going on inside the cottage. "You're home. I thought I saw lights. I wanted to make sure everything was okay."

"Yes…I'm home, but I'm very busy," Iris said, keeping the door crack as small as possible, but pointed to the note on the basket. "That's why I left the sign."

Kate's blue eyes crinkled at the corners as she fiddled with something inside of her skirt pocket. "Oh, sorry. I didn't see it." She tipped her head again like she was trying to get a view inside but in the process brought out the top of the item in her pocket. It was the apple.

The poisoned apple.

Iris's mind whirled with the possibility Kate might steal it, take a bite, and meet her own demise. It wouldn't be Iris's fault then. However, she'd still have to deal with the body, since she was *not* raising Kate from the dead. "Did you need something?"

The woman grinned. "Just being neighborly. We girls have to stick together. I thought I saw a stranger wandering around." She glanced behind her and toward the side yard, where Talon had died.

"All good here." A grimace stretched its way over Iris's lips. "But yes. Us girls should stick together. Well…I have someone…em…something…*baking* and I don't want it to burn."

"Oh, yes." Kate said. "Don't want that." She brought the apple fully out of her pocket and unfortunately deposited it back in the basket.

Iris mentally cursed the missed opportunity.

"Is it an apple pie?" Kate asked.

Her patience completely gone, and worried that Talon's spell would be ruined, Iris forced a completely foreign sweet smile. "Yes."

"Perhaps we—" Kate started to say, but Iris had already shut and locked the door.

She rushed over to the window and pulled the curtains shut.

"You should probably hurry," Quince said as Iris scooped him up and placed the hedgehog on her shoulder again.

Of course she was fully aware of the need to make it snappy.

"That woman deserved that apple," Iris complained as she bent down in front of Talon again and tried to refocus. She stretched out her hands and summoned his life force again. It was weak. "I need you, Quince. We're losing him."

Her familiar's body warmed against her shoulder, and in seconds Talon's presence was back in full force. Iris drew it out and the shimmer came again, enveloping his entire body. Iris's gaze focused as his chest rose with breath and his eyes flickered open.

"Don't forget the binding spell," Quince reminded her.

Anticipation built in Iris's chest, and she took a big breath before she leaned in and touched the place where the orc's heart was. Her breath hitched as it beat like a drum under her fingers. She placed her other hand over her own racing heart and spoke the words she'd memorized. "Until the breath leaves your body once more, Talon Gefroy, you will serve and protect me while never going far."

Words spoken, power surged through Iris's body. She gasped, unable to get enough. She wanted more of this. And all the time.

Full-time evil.

Talon groaned and worked to sit up onto his elbows. He blinked open his amber eyes, and within seconds, he locked onto Iris. He bared his teeth, but Iris held her ground ready for the ensuing growl that would forever terrify anyone who wasn't supposed to be around her. She wasn't scared. She was more than ready.

"I hope this goes well," Quince said as he jumped from Iris's shoulder to the floor.

Iris turned to him, confused by his questioning tone. "What do you mean by that?"

"I dunno." Quince puckered his little lips briefly. "That practice mouse ran right up to a cat. Got eaten."

"What?" Iris's voice came out all squeaky, and her attention flicked back to Talon, who was still staring at her.

"I'm sure it will be fine," the hedgehog assured and waved a paw nonchalantly.

Iris whipped her attention back to the orc as he stared at her, blinking.

Something in his expression was not quite as she expected, and a shiver tickled its way over her spine.

Talon reached out and brushed the stray tendril from Iris's face and said in a soft, completely unexpected voice, "You're *so* pretty, Iris Weyward."

He sounded drunk.

Chapter 4

"What?" Iris's gaze dropped to Quince, who sat on the wooden floor next to Talon's leg.

But the hedgehog only shrugged.

The orc's intense gaze changed to almost shyness, and he pulled back his hand. "Um." As he gazed around the room, his eyes suddenly narrowed in confusion as if he had no idea what was going on. "You have a lovely home here."

Everything went into slow motion as Iris's mind whirled and her entire body locked into a state of freeze.

What if this was a mistake? She recounted the steps of everything she'd done, including the events of the morning, while doing her best to avoid actually looking at Talon again.

It had, *in fact*, started out all wrong. Her missed waking affirmation…the tea leaves…just the fact that Talon had randomly died right in her yard, and then she'd gone straight to a big spell she hadn't entirely perfected without stopping to think if doing so was a good idea, since her magic had been so off.

"Snails, snails, snails," she muttered to herself and clenched her fists into balls.

But how could she have known the mouse had something wrong with it after she'd reanimated it? Quince hadn't bothered to tell her before she'd actually gone through with the necromancy spell.

Out of the corner of her vision, Iris watched Talon as he continued to gaze around the room from the floor.

Had he lied to her and wasn't actually a mercenary? Had someone bumped off the orc at random? Maybe that was it.

Or had *she* simply messed up? Iris shook her head, not wanting to believe that it was a possibility.

Oh, what if it was all a bad dream?

Yes. *That was it*, she thought.

Iris pressed her eyelids closed even harder, trying to will it all away. Or wake up from the nightmare.

Either would have been fine.

Only when something touched her shoulder did Iris come back to reality. She blinked several times to find Talon sitting up on his knees in front of her. Quince had crawled back up her arm and clung to her blouse.

The orc really was massive, and everything about him

looked threatening: his gigantic frame, sharp curled tusks on the sides of his mouth, his large hands with nails filed to look like claws…but not his eyes. Those were entirely different from what Iris had expected. Kind.

And Iris did *not* like that. It was all wrong.

What had happened? Then another thought came to her—she might be overreacting.

What if he was confused? That was possible, right? Iris's gaze dropped to his large, mud-caked boots. *If I were in his shoes*, she thought, *I might be confused too. He'd recently been killed. Then whatever happened after that. Then someone came along and brought him unexpectedly back to life. It's a lot to process.*

Yes. That was it. That made so much more sense. What if that's what had happened to the mouse too? If it had had more time to adjust. Someone to guide it. Perchance it wouldn't have gotten eaten.

And Iris *could* guide Talon.

"I think you need to say something," Quince whispered into her ear.

She gestured for him to be quiet. "I've got this." Iris took a big breath in and out, then cleared her throat and forced a smile at Talon. "What *do* you remember?"

"Remember?" Talon said, still staring at Iris intently with a near grin playing at the corner of his lips as if he simply enjoyed staring at her. "Remember what?"

Okay. That wasn't good.

Nothing about the situation seemed right, but Iris kept

her focus anyway. The guy had recently been stabbed, then died. It would stress any normal person out, even an orc.

"Yes, do you remember what you told me not too long ago? In our last conversation?" She didn't want to remind him right away about his death if it was something he didn't recall.

Talon tipped his head as if he didn't quite understand any of what Iris was saying. "Has anyone ever told you that you have the most beautiful voice?"

"Are you sure you put the right guy back inside him?" Quince asked. He was sitting up on his haunches while perched on Iris's shoulder. Then he burped. "Or maybe those beetles are bad. Guess I shouldn't have eaten quite so many."

"Quiet," she said to Quince. "The beetles were fine." Her thoughts waffled between wondering if she had actually drawn the wrong spirit back into Talon and whether that was even possible. It was true, she hadn't quite gotten through the entire book yet. And suddenly her stomach turned as if the apple she'd had for breakfast was about to come back up. But Iris quickly settled herself again and did her best to ignore Quince *and* the ridiculous things Talon was saying.

Stay focused.

Iris started again, stood, and held out her hand to Talon to help him up, since apparently no good was coming of them staying on the floor. "Yes. We just spoke a few moments ago, and you told me something about a…" She paused for the right word. "Scuffle."

The orc took the proffered hand, stood, and stared at Iris.

She craned her neck to get the full view of him, and she was suddenly glad she'd bought a cottage with taller-than-average ceilings. Talon was as tall as she'd estimated, if not taller, and Iris couldn't help staring back at him. Her stomach fluttered and she scolded the feeling in her mind.

"That's an under-exaggeration," Quince snorted. "'Scuffle.'"

Iris growled, pried the hedgehog from her shoulder, and tossed him on the floor. "Go eat some more beetles, okay?"

The little familiar groaned and waddled off toward the kitchen. "Trying to poison me? See if I'm around next time to help."

But he'd be around.

"Scuffle?" Talon asked.

"Yes." She led him away from Quince and to one of the high-backed chairs next to the fireplace then gestured for Talon to sit. Given his bloody and dirt-stained clothes, it probably wasn't the best idea, but she figured the fabric could be cleaned later if necessary.

He sat nearly dwarfing the chair, still with a ridiculous grin on his lips. The orc rubbed his hands on the chair arms. "This is nice."

"It was her family's," Quince called from the kitchen as he ate a second beetle sandwich. "They used to have this big house—"

Iris shot him a glare and suddenly regretted the set of stairs she'd built leading up to the kitchen counter to allow him to help himself at any time without her.

The familiar resumed munching and made a gesture over his lips with his paw, as if he was locking a door.

Turning her attention back to Talon, Iris flopped into the other chair and leaned out on her knees. She needed to make her questioning even more simple. It would work. It had to. After letting out a deep, settling breath, she looked at the orc again, doing her best to maintain her composure. "Let's start with something simple. Do you remember your name?"

Talon tipped his head as if in thought before he spoke. "Yes. I do." He instantly sat up, and a satisfied expression overtook his face.

"Mind sharing?" Quince shouted from the kitchen.

Iris pursed her lips but didn't look in the familiar's direction. "Yes, what is it?"

"Oh," he said. "Talon Gefroy."

"Good, good," Iris said. "Now we're getting somewhere."

An extra-silly grin spread across his green mouth as if he might be incredibly proud of himself that he'd pleased her.

Iris gulped. "Okaaay. What else do you remember?"

"That your name is Iris Weyward."

Iris's teeth clenched. "Yes. We've established that. Do you remember where you were before you came here?"

Talon twisted his lips and looked up toward the fireplace mantle. He squinted. "Looks like you could use a little dusting around here. Would you like for me to do that?"

"Good eye. I've noticed that too," Quince called.

Iris whipped her head around toward his voice and shot

Quince a death glare even though she couldn't see him from her position.

Not a real death glare...more of the figurative kind.

"Quince!"

"Zip it," he said. "Got it. No more yapping for me."

Talon was already in the process of getting up toward the fireplace when Iris reached out and touched his arm. Instantly his skin under her hand prickled up, and she pulled it back.

"No, no," Iris said, her eyebrows raised. "That's not what you're here for."

"What *am* I here for, Iris Weyward?" Talon asked, returning his back end to the chair.

Iris cleared her throat and thought about retrieving the book from the floor to check for any troubleshooting tips that might be inside. But she'd do that later. Instead she smiled and spoke, doing her best to get back on track. "Um. We had a recent conversation...only a few moments ago."

But Iris really had no idea how long it had been. The morning had already drawn on as if it had lasted at least a week.

She continued, "And I...I had offered you a job."

"A job? So I *can* start with the dusting?" Talon gazed around the room. "Where do you store your housecleaning supplies?"

Iris knew they were in her bedroom closet, although it had been an age since she'd really used any of them. She quickly cast the thought from her head. She had more important things to do. "No. It wasn't *that* sort of job."

"Then what was it?" Talon asked, folding his hands on his massive lap, apparently eager to hear what she had to say.

Ugh. This wasn't working.

"Do you remember *any* of what happened to you before you arrived here?" The words came out too quickly and desperately. And again, she didn't want to be the one to remind Talon he'd actually died a somewhat violent death. Who knew how he might react? She really didn't know. The orc seemed so…sensitive.

Talon's forehead scrunched up in thought. "I do remember something."

"What?" Iris leaned out over the chair's arm in Talon's direction.

His face relaxed before he spoke. "*You* were there, Iris Weyward. At least your voice was." Talon paused for a second. "But you are far more lovely than I envisioned." His tone went all dreamy, as did his features.

In an instant Iris shot up from her seat and grabbed the spell book from the floor, covering the title with her hand. She quickly flipped through the pages, searching desperately for what must have gone wrong. But it was like the words were all jumbled. Focus was impossible. After a moment of searching, Iris tossed the book onto the ground and started to pace.

"Was it when Kate came over?" she muttered to herself. "Or possibly it really *was* the damn beetles." Iris knew the problem wasn't the beetles. "Or did I just screw up somehow?"

"You seem stressed, Iris."

She looked up to Talon, who was less than an arm's length away and towering over her. Caught off guard, she took a step backward. Unfortunately, her still bare foot caught the edge of the book and there she went.

But Talon's large, steady hand caught Iris, and she stayed there halfway between standing on her own and falling on her ass, looking up at what should have been her new, terrifying orc bodyguard…who by some stroke of bad luck… wasn't terrifying at all.

Iris squirmed from his grasp and righted herself. She straightened her blouse and her shoulders.

"Are you all right?" Talon asked, his tone surprisingly gentle.

"I'm fine." Iris kicked the book, and it slid across the floor and under the dining table. None of this would do. She drew her hands into her hair and walked toward the kitchen.

Talon unfortunately followed.

When she got there, Quince lay sprawled out and snoring, the jar of beetles tipped over and half gone.

"I could make you a cup of tea if you like," Talon said from behind. "And then we can talk about that job."

Iris whirled on him and glared at Talon, not quite knowing what to say. Or do. Could she shove him out the door and send him on his way? Yes. That was an excellent idea. Iris eyed the front door. She'd give him a few coins and lock the door behind him.

She twisted her lips, turned back to Talon, and opened

her mouth to speak. But the orc was already filling the kettle. "Yes, thank you," she mumbled.

"I'd really like a cup too," Quince said, awake again as he pointed to the spot on the shelves where Iris kept her extensive tea collection mixed in with the poisons and spell ingredients.

"Oooooooh, lavender mint," Talon said as he bent to look at the labels.

"That one is really nice with a few teaspoons of sugar," Quince said, licking his lips, probably just glad someone was willing to make him food and drink.

"Quince!" Iris scoffed. Even though she'd had the same desire.

His little head twisted to her, and he held out his paws. "It is! And you never make me tea."

But he was right and she knew it. Iris pinched the bridge of her nose in complete shock and desperation. "This isn't happening. I've worked too hard to get to where I am."

"How about that one?" Talon said, pointing to one of the jars. "Which one do you prefer, Iris Weyward?"

Her breath hitched. Was someone asking her what she wanted? More than anything, she wanted to tell him a cup of lavender tea with cream would be lovely. But her eyes widened in shock from the unexpected and disturbing desire. Frustrated with herself, Iris threw her hands high, spun on her heel, and marched toward the door. "I'll be back."

She needed something a mite stronger.

Chapter 5

The morning sun beat down on Iris's head, and all the way into Fraywell she checked behind her no fewer than five times to see if Talon had followed her.

He hadn't.

But she'd chewed down both her thumbnails and her mood had gone as sour as a lemon. Her disposition had not improved, either, the farther she got from the cottage. Particularly since she walked out her door still with no shoes on.

And, for the moment, returning for them was *not* an option, since she had no idea what she might say or do. What if she had went as far as sitting down and enjoying a cup with them?

"Lavender tea," she muttered. "What was I thinking?"

It was, for better or worse, a good long walk into the village, and when Iris had bought her cottage she'd made sure that was the case. She didn't want to be too close to other people, since being the witch on the outskirts of town added to her villainous mystery.

At least that had been the goal.

Then Kate had built her cottage across the road, ruining the entire look with her sunny yellow shutters.

Her presence had, however, brought more foot traffic for Iris's potion business.

Iris muttered to herself, the words likely completely unintelligible to anyone listening. Over and over she ruminated on the spell she'd cast on Talon and where it had gone wrong. Maybe she'd miscalculated the potion based on his size and weight. Had she forgotten an ingredient? She should have taken more time and not rushed the process.

She cursed herself.

It seemed Iris spent half her time underestimating herself, then the other half overcompensating. And finally, it looked as though it had really gotten her into trouble.

Then she grumbled to herself some more.

By the time she arrived at the city square, Iris was so deep in thought she didn't even realize she had made it into Fraywell.

The small town boasted a tourist center and a rich population, with people living there from all over the realm. There were elves, dwarfs, humans, sprites, and gnomes as well as Iris…the one witch in town.

That was another reason Iris had moved there after she and her sisters split up…lack of competition. It made starting over easier.

Fraywell was also a booming center of small business, with artisans, craftspeople, and even several well-reviewed restaurants when many other towns had only a single mediocre one attached to the local inn.

The latter was the one she headed to. The Boar's Head.

Truly, the food really was subpar, but the owners, Herman and Lysander, kept the tavern dark and generally left her alone to do business with people passing through.

That was not always the case with others in the village. Fraywell overall was annoyingly cheery, with people always in other people's business and on the tree-lined streets.

"Morning, Ms. Weyward," someone shouted out.

Iris snapped out of her distracted state and looked toward the location of the voice. It was Puck, the local bard. The lanky (for a sprite) musician stood on the corner with their wooden lute in hand and a coin basket waiting on the ground. The blue-skinned, lavender-haired sprite was absolutely terrible. Or at least their singing was. Iris didn't know much concerning their personality since she did her best not to know *that* much about anyone in town unless they wanted an order from her. But it was impossible to avoid Puck's off-key tunes, which were regularly heard by anyone who didn't carry around something to plug their ears. And Iris had also forgotten those back at the cottage.

Thankfully for her, the sprite hadn't begun their set, and Iris kept walking without saying a word.

"Ms. Weyward," Puck called again after her.

Iris winced. The last thing she wanted to do was talk to anyone, unless it was to order a drink at The Boar's Head. She kept walking, pretending she didn't hear Puck.

Alas, small, booted feet padded against the cobblestone street after her anyway. "Ms. Weyward!"

Iris's chest tightened and she gritted her teeth together. "What?" She spun on her bare heel, just in front of the basket shop, Something Wicker This Way Comes, and toward the sprite. Her loose tendril landed and lay over the middle of her forehead. For some inane reason she couldn't help but remember how Talon had moved it off her face. She quickly swiped it off as if a bee had attempted to land on her nose.

Puck skidded to a stop directly in front of her with their mouth agape and still clutching their lute. The instrument looked entirely huge in their sprite-sized hands. "Um—"

Eyes widening and her patience thinner than usual, she stood there waiting for them to speak. "Well, I don't have a lot of time here, so get out whatever you're going to say." A teeny part of Iris, way deep down, did feel slightly sorry for them since Puck had a decent amount of tenacity for their terrible barding, and everyone needed to make a living. An unfamiliar voice in the back of her mind told her to give Puck a coin…to get rid of them, of course. But she shooed the thought away.

Puck looked around as if they planned to ask something

important and didn't want anyone to hear. "I...I heard you make potions."

Iris was taken aback that the sprite would be asking her about *that*. Who did they want to kill or maim? She straightened herself and relaxed her gaze. "Yes?" It came out like a question even though that's not how she'd intended it.

"It seems," they said, looking down at their lute, "that no matter how hard I practice, I don't quite improve. And I've always had this dream—"

Puck continued on about the life dream they had, but Iris was barely listening. All she was focusing on was the fact that someone was asking her to use her skills toward good, and that was completely unacceptable. She gritted her teeth again with annoyance while her skin crawled. What did she look like? *Wait? Do I look like a benevolent person?* "I can't help you, sprite." Then she turned and started walking.

"Are you sure?" they called. "I *have* saved up."

Iris hated turning away business, but she had standards to uphold, and it was obvious she hadn't quite created the reputation she'd hoped since she'd come to Fraywell.

She would need to work on that. Starting right away.

How would Iris ever meet her goals if the corner bard wasn't even convinced she was a menace? Frustration burning in her chest, she flung around, held up her hands like claws, and snarled at the sprite.

Their brown eyes widened, and they nearly dropped the instrument on the cobblestones. Then they spun around and dashed back to their corner.

"Good," Iris muttered and blew out a long breath, ignoring the heaviness pressing into her chest.

If she wanted to be a proper villain, she couldn't let a little guilt stop her from achieving her goals.

Moments after the incident Iris made it up the front stairs to The Boar's Head. A large sign hung outside the inn and tavern of the expected semi-fierce-looking boar's head with the words arched over it. Anger still tingling in her chest, she climbed the steps, flung open the worn wooden doors, and walked inside.

The place smelled of stale food, alcohol, and sweaty travelers.

Just as she liked it.

Immediately, she looked to the left inside the lobby where the bar entrance was located. The doors were shut. Iris pursed her lips, walked up to them, and pulled the worn brass handle. It didn't budge.

"It's closed," Herman Quickly said from the reception desk.

Iris whirled around to him. "Why the snails would it be closed?"

Herman was a short, balding human man with sepia skin. Not moving, he sat on a tall chair at the large wooden desk where he checked guests into the inn. Casually he gazed at the clock on the wall. "It's only nine a.m."

Iris shot Herman the same figurative death glare she had given Quince earlier as the unfortunate morning's events once more took a promenade in her mind. She seriously considered casting a curse on the man simply for telling her the bad news. But that probably wouldn't be the best choice either. Herman's husband, Lysander, would in all likelihood look poorly on such a thing, and the men had always been pretty supportive of Iris. Mostly by leaving her alone.

Plus, her magic obviously wasn't working.

A growl tickled at the back of her throat. "Then open it."

"Can't." The man dressed in an ivory cotton shirt with two strings hanging from the neckline fiddled with some paperwork in front of him on the desk.

Completely out of sorts, Iris straightened her blouse and shoulders. "Why *not*?"

"Lys has the key," Herman said. "And he's out."

That would not do. It would not do at all. Iris didn't want to go back to her cottage. Who knew what was going on there at that point? And whatever it was, she *definitely* didn't want to be a part of it. Or deal with Talon.

"Then where *else* can I get a drink?" she asked in an exasperated tone.

Herman riffled around with the papers and then bent to the side. His head disappeared below the desk. "I might have a little something around here." His voice was muffled, but up he came with a stout bottle of amber liquid. After holding it out in presentation, he plunked it on the desktop and then produced two small glasses. "In case of emergency," the man said and then gave Iris a friendly wink.

She took a step back, and the space between her eyebrows wrinkled. Her villainous nature wanted no part of any friendly interaction. But since it promised whatever was in the bottle, she'd give the man a pass. Plus, in the moment, he was tolerable.

Then he reached back and pulled a stool waiting behind him against the wall up to the side of the desk and patted it.

"Have a seat, witch," Herman said. "Pretty sure I need a drink too." He proceeded to pour two generous portions of the liquid into the glasses.

Iris let out a long sigh, and her gaze drew to the alcohol. What she'd *really* wanted was to sit at the booth in the farthest corner of the tavern looking ominous to anyone who passed, but with the near tragic events of the morning occupying her mind, she hadn't even considered that it wasn't yet lunchtime. At least the drink she'd wanted sat right there calling her name.

It was something that hadn't gone horribly wrong.

She shuffled toward the registration desk as Herman scanned her down to her bare feet.

"Must have been a doozy of a morning if you got all the way into town without your boots," he remarked.

"I don't want to talk about it." Iris collected the drink but didn't sit. There was no way she was staying long…not right there in the open for anyone coming in the front door to see. "What is this?" She couldn't make out the label, since the bottle was turned.

Herman chuckled. "Does it matter?" In one swoop he grasped his glass and downed the contents.

Iris shrugged and let out an uncomfortable little laugh

of her own. "Probably not." She placed it to her lips and allowed about half into her mouth and down her throat. The liquid was whiskey. The slightly sweet alcohol burned her throat a little, but the toffee notes danced on her tongue… and promised a numbing. Almost instantly her nerves settled, and she closed her eyes just to take in the calmness. She tipped the glass to her mouth again and swallowed the rest.

"Some days are rubbish, eh?" Herman said, pouring himself another drink.

"That's an understatement." Iris didn't even know she'd sat on the stool until she found herself holding the empty glass out toward Herman asking for another.

Without question, he obliged and poured her a single. In reality, she wanted more. But it was a bad idea for her own clarity.

Warmth swirling inside and her brain slightly calmer, Iris sipped the whiskey. That time she realized that in addition to the caramel notes it had a bit of cherry on the back end. "This is good."

"Why do you surmise I keep it down here for myself?" Herman's dark gaze lowered, indicating the space below the desk.

Iris snorted and sipped her drink. She hated letting her guard down, but what would a few minutes of it matter?

"So what happened that was so bad you made it all the way into Fraywell with no shoes?" Herman asked, leaning his chin onto his free hand.

She studied Herman. The man was older than Iris.

Probably close to the age her father would have been if— Iris cast the thought aside. She didn't like to dwell on what had happened or admit there were days when she missed the witch and wanted to know how he was getting on. But Herman's fatherly appearance and tone dulled her inhibitions a bit. Or perhaps that was the whiskey.

Iris opened her mouth, about to tell him more than she should, but the inn's door flung open, saving her.

Lysander appeared with his arms full of bags loaded with fruits, vegetables, breads, and probably other food items, but Iris didn't notice. She was only glad for the distraction.

The last thing she really wanted to do was be approachable. Even to Herman and his whiskey.

"I'm out, working my tail off," Lysander complained in a high-pitched, over-the-top tone as he marched over to the registration desk. The tawny-skinned elf had his shoulder-length grayish-white hair secured into a low ponytail. He stared down over his round spectacles at the two of them and finished his scolding. "And you all are having cocktail hour at…" He gazed at the old clock on the wall. "Nine ten a.m."

Herman clicked his tongue. "We only have the two guests, and they're not up yet." His tone was nonchalant. "No one else has come in."

Lysander gasped, and his eyes grew wide. He held up the bags and shook them. "This is why we'll be testing new recipe options for the restaurant today."

"We?" Herman asked, not moving. "This was your idea."

"Yes, *we*." Lysander bobbed his head then brought his attention to Iris, who'd already finished her second pour and placed the glass down. He snapped his fingers and tipped his head to a door to their left, then made his way over and through it. "Come on, Hermy. Morning, Iris."

Herman leaned over to Iris. "Guess the bar is closed."

She almost laughed at the whole scene but kept it to herself despite the alcohol taking a stronger hold. "Probably best." But she didn't quite like the fact that The Boar's Head might not be doing that well, since it was one of the few places in town where she was comfortable. And if Lysander was planning to change things up, would it even stay a place where she felt that way? "I should be going anyway." She stood and walked a few steps.

The innkeeper placed the liquor bottle under the desk and plucked the two used glasses.

"Oh, what do I owe you?" Iris asked and ran her hands over her skirt pocket, realizing she didn't have any form of payment with her either, but she wasn't one to skip out on her bills.

"On the house," Herman said and tipped his head her way.

"Um, thanks," Iris said.

"Use it at the cobbler." He looked down at her bare feet again.

Iris winced. Shoes would not solve her problems. Unless they were enchanted and could whisk her away to another magical land.

Chapter 6

But Iris wanted to prove herself in Fraywell...not somewhere else.

Not to mention moving would be an absolute pain in her backside. Quince would be no help whatsoever with his tiny paws and lack of thumbs.

Her head light, Iris trudged out the front of The Boar's Head and plopped herself down on the hopelessly worn front steps. She placed her hands down beside her and ran her fingers along the rough wood. The place really was shabbier than she'd ever cared to notice before. She gazed back at the door and suddenly found a strange sensation tingling in her middle...worry for Herman and Lysander.

Unfamiliar thoughts rounded in her mind. *What would*

they do if the inn had to close? Where would they go? As far as she knew, they'd lived in Fraywell most of their lives... not that she'd asked. *Would they stay here?* Iris didn't like the thoughts in her brain or the sensation in her stomach.

"Damn whiskey," she muttered and mentally vowed never to drink before noon again.

"Good mornin' to ya," a cheery voice said and instantly drew a shiver up Iris's spine.

Iris lifted her chin to see a gnome who couldn't have been taller than her shoulder height. His first name might have been Morton. The guy wore a bright yellow shirt and pants, and Iris wrinkled her nose at the sight, since the color reminded her of Kate's offensive cottage shutters.

Morton owned the tailor shop in Fraywell, 'Tis Sew Sweet.

To make matters worse than the fact he'd spoken to her, at the same time the tip of her index finger also caught a loose splinter on the wooden step. In a complete overreaction to the injury, Iris jumped to her feet and hissed at Morton while clutching her bleeding finger. "What's so good about it?"

The gnome shot his arms up and tucked his chin in horror.

Despite her painful finger, satisfaction pooled in Iris's stomach at his expression. At least someone was perceiving her the way she intended. And to make the look even better, she bared her teeth a second time.

"Just being friendly," Morton said and shook his head. Seconds later, he scurried off.

Iris cackled in response while the unfamiliar feelings concerning The Boar's Head left her belly. "That's right, you run!"

But as the gnome hurried off down the street, Iris's satisfaction was short-lived. She might have reminded one person (two, if Puck counted) that evil still resided in Fraywell that morning, but she still had her own problems back at her cottage. Plus, the unease from her behavior jabbing at her chest was threating to ruin the entire accomplishment.

What was she going to do about Talon?

Stress tightened the muscles in her neck, and to calm herself, she closed her eyes. Then she took eight breaths, holding each at the top and letting the air out slowly while her muscles relaxed and her mind cleared again. When done, she opened her lids and narrowed them into slits.

Iris knew what to do.

Like any good ruffian, she'd soon shuffle him off this mortal coil again.

He was supposed to die that morning anyway. Iris would simply put things in their proper place. Plus, she couldn't have this version of Talon out there somewhere in Verona wandering around and serving as an example of her work. It would ruin her reputation entirely. Of course the actual deed wouldn't be easy for Iris…since it was something she'd never *actually* done before herself. But it would seal her infamous path…as well as prove to her that she could do hard things.

It was both diabolical *and* the right thing to do.

She rose, straightened her shoulders, and then moved her head from side to side, allowing her neck to crack.

There would be the problem of the body, but it was nothing she couldn't handle under the darkness of night when Kate was asleep or busy inside her cottage with one of her visitors.

"Yes," Iris said out loud. That's what she'd do. She'd brew a potion and send the orc back to the other side.

The burden she'd had since she'd left her house that morning suddenly lifted. It *was* a shame, however, that she hadn't solved her bodyguard dilemma as easily as she'd hoped…but someone else would come along to fill the position.

Iris was sure of it.

To ensure no one else would speak to her on the way out of Fraywell, Iris did her best to put on a terrifying scowl all the way through town.

Once outside of it, Iris took to a jog despite her lack of shoes.

Unlike when she'd left her cottage, all was right in the world again.

Even a storm was rolling in and eating up the pestiferous sunny blue sky.

Perfect.

By the time she got to her cottage, it was already starting to rain.

Big, fat drops. The kind that made everyone stay inside and leave her alone.

So Iris didn't even care that she was already drenched and badly needed a change of clothes. She had a plan. A good one.

She picked up the pace as she reached the short path leading to her cottage. Excited, she flung open the door, ready to get busy.

"Quince," she called, not even getting the door completely open and feet wiped. "We need to talk."

But the second the words exited her mouth, her stomach dropped. Something was wrong, because there were voices coming from inside and not from Quince or Talon.

"Oh, thank you very much," a feminine voice said. "I'm so glad we made it before the storm."

Iris gulped. *Why in the snails are* they *here?* she thought, circling back to the idea she'd had earlier that the entire morning might just be a nightmare. She pinched her arm to check, digging her jagged nails into her skin. "Ouch," Iris said out loud as the door creaked and floated all the way open.

Unfortunately, she didn't wake up, and the skin on her arm now stung.

Her redheaded younger sister, Poppy, squealed and shot up from her place at the eating table, jogging over to Iris with her arms spread wide.

Panicked at the thought of an impending body slam, Iris surveyed the room. Her older sister, Dahlia, with her pin-straight, white-blond bobbed hair cut at the chin, sat at the table with a cup of tea in hand and her left brow arched. Quince was gorging himself on a cream-topped scone, while

Talon was in the kitchen doing dishes, donning what looked like clean clothes and...an apron. She had no idea where he'd gotten it, let alone clothes that were mysteriously clean. Plus, her sisters' familiars had to be around there somewhere, but she didn't see them.

The entire scene was like one out of a nightmare.

At least the broken teacup had been swept away.

Had she been gone that long? She glanced up at the clock on the wall. It wasn't even lunch. Her head spun, but Iris had no time to think about it anymore since Poppy plowed into her, nearly knocking her over and back out the door into the rain.

"I missed you so much!" Poppy threw her arms around Iris and squeezed until her older sister gasped. The woman was petite but had quite a grip on her.

Iris's eyes widened like saucers as she looked out at the ridiculous scene taking place inside her cottage. She was pretty sure she caught Talon smiling before he waved at her, but her gaze trained on her sister.

"What are you doing here?" Iris managed while her Poppy still kept a grip on her middle.

Dahlia, dressed in her standard full-length black robe, reached for something on the table and then held up the unopened letter that had been sitting there for weeks. "We wrote."

Knowing Poppy would not let go unless Iris did something, she gave her younger sister a consolation squeeze and a quick pat on the back. "Yeah, about that." She wriggled from Poppy's grasp and made her way toward her Dahlia.

"It's a good thing someone was home," Dahlia said as she studied Talon with her plum-colored eyes…a shade Iris had always been a little jealous of, since hers were grayish.

"About that—" Iris started, but Poppy appeared in front of her again.

Her emerald gaze intrigued, her little sister whispered, "He's cute." Poppy elbowed Iris in the side.

At the declaration, Iris's heart nearly jumped into her throat, and her attention zipped over to the massive orc humming a jaunty tune at the sink.

It all *had* to be a nightmare! But by that time, she knew it wasn't. It was her life.

Desperate for an excuse to get out of there, Iris announced, "I'm going to change." She tugged at her wet shirt as proof of the need.

Poppy fanned her own blouse, embellished with lace around the sleeves and neckline. It was spotted with water droplets all across the front. "I might need to do that too."

"Maybe you shouldn't have been squeezing me like a wet dishrag," Iris muttered as she rushed down the hall to her room and nearly crushed Quince in the door.

"Hey," he grumbled while he checked himself. "Rude."

With the door shut tight, Iris whirled on her familiar. "Rude? Last time I saw you, you were downing a scone. You didn't even say hello."

"It was a good scone," Quince said.

Iris pursed her lips and pointed to the back of the door. "You're the one who's rude even letting them in the cottage."

Quince reached back, pulled out a loose quill, and used it as a pick for his teeth. "I didn't let them in."

"Who did then?" Iris stomped over to the dresser and riffled through her drawers, where she found the last clean skirt and blouse. She held up the shirt, which was a bright blue and had little embroidered yellow flowers along the neckline and encircling the puffed sleeves. It wasn't even hers. It was Poppy's, and it had somehow ended up in Iris's things since she had moved to Fraywell. "Ugh. Yellow again," she muttered, knowing it was her only option since she hadn't gotten to the washing in weeks.

"Who do you think?" Quince said while climbing onto the bed and turning around in little circles as if he was preparing for a nap.

Iris stiffened her back. "Talon?"

"The orc does make a mean breakfast." The hedgehog twisted his body into a prickly cinnamon-roll shape among the now-extra-rumpled blanket from her unmade bed. "He'd probably do your laundry too."

Fury nearly burned in her middle. "I didn't need a cook… or someone to do the laundry," Iris said through gritted teeth. "I needed a bodyguard."

After sighing and accepting her fashionable flowered fate, Iris stripped off her wet clothes and tossed them into the overflowing basket in the corner. Trying not to dwell on it too much, she pulled on the blouse, followed by the skirt. She and Poppy were shaped a little differently, and while her sister was a few inches shorter, the blouse was baggy enough to fit anyway.

"Couldn't hurt though," Quince said.

"What?" Iris asked, entirely annoyed with her familiar. She checked herself in the mirror and winced. She almost looked...pretty. But she made the best of it and readjusted her pulled-back hair.

"A cook might be nice while your sisters are here," Quince said sleepily but with one brown eye open toward Iris. He untwisted himself, rolled over, and patted his belly.

Iris flinched at the mention of her sisters. "Did they say how long they're staying?" She didn't really want to hear the answer.

"Oh," he said. "At least a week."

"A *week*?" The question came out too loud and shrieky, and Iris threw her hand over her mouth.

The hedgehog yawned and laid his head on the blanket. "They did write."

With that Iris deadpanned, "Why do I keep you around?" Without waiting for an answer, she spun on her heel toward the exit.

"You love me," Quince said.

She did. But she wasn't going to say it.

Even so, Iris flung the door open and stepped out into the hall to escape her familiar. The door cracked, she immediately stopped and leaned her back against the wall when she heard her sisters' cackling in the front half of the cottage.

Apparently the two of them were getting along. But she didn't know if she was ready for any such thing. She enjoyed being the only witch in town. What if Dahlia and Poppy decided they liked Fraywell too? And stayed? There wasn't long to dwell on it before something furry wrapped around and tickled her leg. Iris's breath hitched, and she looked down at a gray-and-black striped cat.

Her intense green eyes stared up at Iris.

"I wondered where you were, Ursula," she said to her sister's familiar.

The two of them had always gotten along better than Iris had with Dahlia. Her older sister was always bossy and forever telling her what to do. The cat never did that. At least not to Iris. Now Quince was another story.

"Checking out the place," Ursula purred. "Who's the orc?"

"That's Talon," Iris said. "Found him in my yard this morning."

The cat sat and kneaded the wooden floor, her sharp claws extending and retracting. "I don't like him. Too cheery. All the incessant humming."

"Right?" Iris said and bent to scratch Ursula's chin. The cat was good at keeping secrets, and Iris almost told her of her plan to eliminate Talon but decided to keep it to herself for the time being. She needed to think about what Quince had suggested. "I've missed you," she said instead. It was true.

The cat stood and rubbed her face on Iris's leg then trotted off down the hall to the second bedroom and disappeared through the open door.

Iris could only assume her sisters' belongings were inside and ready to stay there for a week. She sighed at the sound of Quince's snores coming from the opening in her cracked door. Then her sisters cackled again.

What if he was right? She should keep Talon around for a little while. At least for the week. She could always go through with her plan after her sisters left.

Chapter 7

Iris slunk from the hall, but instead of heading out to her sisters, who were still having breakfast at the dining table, she made a right into the kitchen. If she planned to keep the orc around for a bit, then some things needed to be handled.

Talon was in the process of cleaning the counter with a wet dishrag and humming a new little tune Iris had never heard. His back was to Iris, so he didn't notice her.

For a brief moment, she just stood there staring at him as he cleaned and then around at the space. Her kitchen hadn't looked so good since…well, now that she really thought about it, never.

She hadn't noticed with all the commotion when she'd

walked in, but the place smelled great...like sugar and freshly baked treats. The trash had even been taken out, since her apple core from the morning was gone.

All of her teas were organized alphabetically, as well as her potion ingredients. There were no dirty dishes in the sink or any stray hedgehog quills lying about (which was a regular occurrence). Out the moisture-specked kitchen window she could see the rain had stopped, which was both a good and bad thing. It meant her sisters might leave her house for a while to check out Fraywell. Even torment some of the residents...which seemed like a nice thought after the morning's debacle.

A plate of Talon's scones lay out on the counter, and Iris mindlessly picked one up and took a bite. The vanilla-flavored pastry melted in her mouth. It was the best thing she'd had in weeks...months maybe.

Then her eyes traveled over Talon, all the way from the top of his head down the outline of his muscular back and everything below that point.

Iris bit her lip and thought about the last time she'd had a relationship...too long ago.

She at least found her fate a solitary existence. Which was mostly good...but not always.

But that was not something to think about someone who worked for you. A witch or otherwise, she needed to maintain a professional relationship...even if it was only for a week.

Talon kept humming while he wiped the counter with a new dry cloth. His voice was deep and soothing, and the entire scene made Iris's body relax as if a spell had been cast over her.

But she quickly realized what was happening to her and dropped the half-eaten scone back on the plate. Iris shook herself from the daydream and spoke. "Talon?"

The orc flinched and turned. His amber eyes instantly brightened. "Oh, Iris Weyward. I didn't see you. Can I get you anything?" He rubbed the cotton dish towel over his massive hands while he continued holding her gaze.

For about a blink, several things revolved in Iris's mind, including the size of his hands and the fact that the orc did not look as if he'd been dead only hours before. He looked *entirely* healthy...but she squelched the thoughts, since his mind was obviously not the same. As interesting as Talon might be, he did not belong in her house long-term...or even on the current plane of existence. At least not after her sisters left.

Until then, she could offer him a short-term job. Not that he had to know that.

Iris lowered her shoulders, which were creeping up around her ears, and said, keeping her voice low so her sisters wouldn't hear, "We should have a conversation."

Talon grinned and placed the dishcloth on the counter. "I'm available anytime you need me." He regarded her. "You look lovely."

Iris felt her neck heating, and she pulled at the blouse to fan herself. She'd need to have another talk with Talon about saying such things.

"Hey, I've been looking for that shirt," Poppy's voice came from behind. Iris turned and saw that her sister was leaning out from the table to get a view of her.

"Then you can have it when you leave," Iris said, hoping that would be sooner rather than later so she could get back to her normal life. "I'm out of clean clothes."

"I—" Talon started, but Iris rushed into the kitchen and pulled him toward the rear door. "Where are we going?" the orc asked with great interest.

But Iris said nothing until after she had the door open, she was through it, and he'd ducked out the opening. She could only ever surmise a gnome must have installed the back door, since it was even a mite too short for her.

"We need to discuss the details of your employment," Iris said while she kept pulling Talon across the yard and past the henhouse. One chicken with a tuft of white feathers on her head bobbed at them and continued pecking at the ground for worms.

"Ooh...chickens," Talon said, as if the common birds were somehow infinitely fascinating.

"They need to be fed," Iris muttered, looking back to make sure Poppy or Dahlia hadn't come out the back door.

"Right now?" Talon asked and lightly pulled away from Iris toward them.

Iris scoffed and was seriously considering the wisdom of keeping Talon on for the week. "No, not now." She grabbed his shirtsleeve and tugged him toward the barn.

The ground was squishy with mud, and once again she

realized she *still* didn't have any shoes on. A growl tickled at the back of her throat. But finally she got the orc inside the barn.

Talon gazed around the place with a look of awe, but, out of patience, she snapped her fingers at him to get his attention.

"Over here," Iris said.

Talon's demeanor became shy. "I don't know if I've ever been in a place like this before."

"You've never been in a barn?"

The orc shrugged. "Not that I remember. But I'm certainly glad to have the experience with you, Iris Weyward."

The memory loss Talon had experienced from the spell must have been worse than Iris had even imagined. "It's just Iris," she managed. "And what do you remember?"

Talon twisted his lips for a few blinks. "You?" He paused a bit more, and then his eyes lit up. "And that talking hedgehog—"

"Quince," Iris said in a flat tone as a vision of her familiar—likely asleep and snoring—came into her thoughts.

"Yes!" His eyes lit up even more and he pointed at her. "I like him." Talon pursed his lips and looked up in thought. "Then you left for a while… That wasn't great, but I cleaned up." He gripped the side of his shirt and pulled the fabric out for Iris to see.

You mean the evidence that only about an hour before you were entirely dead? Iris thought. After turning to pace, she crossed her arms over her chest. Mostly she was entirely frustrated with herself for botching the spell *so* badly. It seemed like nothing of Talon's former self still remained. Not that she'd gotten to know him very well in his spirit state. But as a witch, she was completely off her game.

He continued, "Then I started to make breakfast for when you'd come back. Quince said you always come back."

Iris groaned. "Remember anything else?"

"Then your sisters arrived and the older one…" He tipped his head to the side.

"Dahlia."

"Yes, Dahlia," he echoed. "She told me I was really *something*."

"That was nice of her." Iris didn't really know why those words came from her mouth. It wasn't like her at all to say such a thing.

"It was!" Talon grinned a lopsided grin.

Iris's eyes widened at the sight of him. She should have just re-unalived Talon right then and there, but looking around, she saw there was nothing to do the job. Not even a pitchfork. Only hay and her boxes of spell books she apparently should have been reading more of. And chicken feed. She made a mental note to buy more items that could be used as weapons in case of emergencies like the current one.

"Well then." Iris clapped her hands together but kept her back to him. "As for the job offer. We'll need to…test things out. For a week. While my sisters are in town, I'll need you to keep the house clean, make meals…and generally take care of the household chores." She pointed to the place where her ogre bodyguard had slept in the corner. "That will be your bed at night or when you're done with household duties."

She turned on her heel toward Talon and looked up at his face. The ridiculous smile on his lips had at least doubled in size.

"And less smiling." She added the requirement to the list of responsibilities.

Instantly the expression flattened but Talon still stared at her, his irises dancing with joy. "Yes, Iris Weyward."

Iris sighed and turned for the exit. It was going to be a long week. For more reasons than one. But she didn't want to be the one waiting on her sisters and if Talon could do it happily then more power to him.

Plus, what he didn't know wouldn't hurt him.

"Can I feed the chickens now?" Talon asked.

"Sure," Iris said. "Why not start with that?" She gestured to the grain storage on the way out. "Please don't feed them too much."

Talon made a beeline for the grains and scooped several portions into his apron, which Iris was just realizing must have been hers at one point, since the fit on the orc was tight and the ties barely made a bow in the back.

But she left him to his business and walked outside into the sun. The clouds had all but receded. Iris got about halfway across the yard and stopped. Normally the sunny weather seemed too pleasant…almost too happy. But at that moment, the morning rays on her face were warm and relaxing. Standing there in the beams in the middle of her yard meant not dealing with her sisters or Talon.

She closed her eyes and took in the warmth.

"Here chick, chick, chick." Talon's voice ruined the moment.

Iris kept herself from looking at the scene while the chickens squawked happily behind her... It was probably the earliest in the day they'd been fed in at least a week.

The sounds got her walking again to the house, but her stomach roiled, knowing what waited for her inside. Iris's gaze traveled to her roofline, where Poppy's golden-eyed raven sat pecking at a large seed.

"Morning, Oberon," Iris said, not wanting to be rude.

The raven only lifted his head and cocked it then returned to seed pecking. He didn't talk much. At least to her.

"Come sit with us," Dahlia called out as Iris opened the back door.

Just hearing her voice made Iris want to backtrack, but she walked through the kitchen instead.

The two sisters had made themselves comfortable on the pair of chairs next to the fireplace. They both had cups of tea in hand, and Ursula lay curled up on Dahlia's lap, her tail draping down the side of the chair.

There were only two chairs in the living area (purposely on Iris's part, since she was averse to too many visitors, but this was one occasion where the choice was regrettable). She sighed and dragged a chair from the eating table over to them. Being the middle sister never made life easy.

As Iris approached them, she could see Poppy was doing needlework. Iris looked over her sister's shoulder at the work. Delicate purple flowers and leaves were arranged like a wreath around the words *I Am More Than Capable of Being Evil Today*.

It was a good reminder.

Instead of saying so to make small talk, Iris plopped into her wooden seat, folded her hands into her lap, and opened her mouth to say something else.

"So when did you hire Talon?" Poppy asked, looking up from her needlework.

A growl rumbled at the back of Iris's throat. That was not what she wanted to talk about.

"He is rather an *interesting* choice," Dahlia said while Ursula jumped off her lap, stretched, and lay next to the fire.

Poppy giggled. "But he makes a great scone, and he *is* cute."

"You said that earlier." Iris twiddled her thumbs, wishing they'd get to the point.

Her younger sister shrugged and pulled her purple thread through the fabric in her hands. "I'd like someone that cute working for me."

"I *don't* really care how cute he is," Iris insisted. But she had noticed, of course. "Why are you both here?" She decided to spill the question to get off the topic of Talon as soon as possible.

Dahlia sipped her tea, turned in her seat, and then drew her attention to Iris. "If you had read the letter, you'd already have this information."

A frustrated sigh left Iris's lips. This was the thing about Dahlia and one of the reasons Iris hadn't spoken to her in a year. "Well, we're all aware by this point that I didn't. So perchance you could take the time to fill me in."

"Something's wrong," Poppy blurted as she pricked her thumb with her needle. "Ouch!" Several drops of blood fell onto the needlework. "Oh snails," she complained and placed aside the work.

"Just put a few more flowers over it," Dahlia advised.

Iris scrunched her brow. Yes, getting as far away from her sisters had been the right choice. "What do you mean, something is wrong?"

"I noticed it about a month ago," Dahlia said. "But I didn't think much about it at first."

"But then I showed up at her door, since I was having the same problem." Poppy pulled out a strip of fabric and wrapped it around her finger.

Iris stood and walked around to the back of her chair. She hated it when her sisters were cryptic. "And would you care to share this *problem* with me?"

"If you had read—" Dahlia started.

Iris threw up her hands. "Yes, yes. I should have read the letter." She stomped over to the dinner table and grabbed the letter from the top. She ripped it open and flung the paper from the envelope. "Happy now?"

"You haven't actually read it," Poppy said, holding up her injured and wrapped finger.

"Ugh," Iris scoffed and brought her attention to the

words on the page. It was Dahlia's perfect penmanship. She scanned down the words to find the part letting her know they'd arrive on that very day. But near the end it stated something alarming: *Our magic is failing.*

The second Iris finished, Talon walked by the front window. Even in its dirty state she could make out the ridiculous parade of chickens waddling behind him.

Chapter 8

Iris tossed and turned all night. She didn't sleep a wink.

At one point it was mainly due to Quince ending up underneath her and poking her in the back. But that wasn't that out of the ordinary, and in normal circumstances she could sleep through the jabbing. Getting skewered by her familiar while sleeping had happened at least once a week for decades.

Mostly her mind had bounced between the fact her sisters were asleep in the other room (with no idea yet what was wrong with their collective magic) and that Talon was in the barn and his current state was likely due to Iris's spell malfunctioning. And she would have to off the guy in a few days, despite the fact he'd made the most amazing dinner for them. Then there were the flaky vanilla scones he'd made, and Iris hoped there might be more in the morning…since after her sisters told her the bad news Iris had gone and eaten the entire plate of them.

Plus…she was still worrying about Herman and Lysander losing their inn, which was entirely ridiculous. Since when did she care about such things?

The sun hadn't even come up when the smell of cinnamon had wafted under her bedroom door. Iris's mouth watered at the scent. Somehow it smelled even better than the vanilla scones.

She didn't know if that was possible.

There was no way at that point she'd ever fall asleep, so Iris sat up in her bed and threw off the covers. Quince lay on the pillow next to her curled into a spiral. The little guy looked so cozy, Iris couldn't help but feel a little jealous of his ability to sleep through most anything.

After giving the hedgehog a scratch on his ears, she twisted out of bed, lobbed her feet on the floor, then shuffled her way to the door and out of the room, not bothering to change from her nightclothes or put on a robe.

Too much bother.

The aroma of cinnamon and yeast only grew stronger in the hall, and the anticipation of what Iris might find in the kitchen amplified with it.

When she got there what she found didn't disappoint.

A tray of jumbo cinnamon rolls lay out on the counter cooling as coffee percolated on the stovetop. But Talon was nowhere to be seen. Relief settled over her. Maybe he'd left the breakfast as an offering and then gone...wandered off far away, leaving Iris to her current problems, sans the one he was causing.

Iris took a plate from the cupboard and helped herself to a cinnamon roll drenched in a thick, rich icing. Then she poured a cup of coffee and topped it off with a splash of cream from the little white vessel shaped like a cow sitting on the counter.

After she'd poured the cream, she held up the little cow-shaped container and stared it in the face. "Where'd you come from?" she said out loud. Iris wasn't sure she'd ever seen the cow in her life. And why was there cream? That was another mystery. She didn't have a cow.

"I was getting eggs," Talon said from behind her.

Iris twisted around, nearly dropping the cow-shaped container on the floor, but somehow kept a grip. "Snails. You scared me."

He wasn't gone after all.

The orc's face drooped. "I'm sorry, Iris Weyward."

Iris's face deadpanned, and she set the cow on the counter. "It's *just* Iris." She turned back to her coffee and cinnamon roll but didn't leave the kitchen.

"I hope you like those," Talon said softly and placed a basket of eggs next to the sink. He was still dressed in the apron he'd worn previously and didn't look any less ridiculous.

Iris sighed and glanced down at her breakfast, taking

solace in what awaited her. If they were even a quarter as good as the scones Talon had made the day before, she thought she would like them, but she was unwilling to admit that fact. "How was the barn?"

"Oh, very comfortable," Talon said as he reached for a cast-iron skillet in the cupboard. "I had at least two hours of sleep."

"Two hours?" Iris asked, wondering how he could be so perky. She took a sip of her coffee, knowing it would help remedy her own sleepy condition. The rich, lively flavor filled her mouth, cut with the sumptuous mouthfeel of the cream.

"Mm-hmm," he said and reached for an egg from the basket. "How do you like them?"

Still lost in the coffee deliciousness, Iris muttered, "What?"

"Your eggs."

"Over medium," Iris said with barely a thought. She picked up the gooey cinnamon roll and admired the bread's rise. The cinnamon sugar scent traveled into her nostrils, and her mind traveled to a place it had not been in too long… to relaxation. The kind of relaxation where everything was taken care of for her.

As Talon fiddled with the eggs at the stove, Iris took her first bite of the cinnamon roll. Her knees almost went weak for the luxury, but she held out her hand and caught the edge of the counter to keep herself from toppling backward. The first taste that hit her tongue was obviously the spice. The earthy flavor somehow grounded her, and, mixed with sweet sugar, the entire sensation brought her to another level of headiness. If she thought too much about it, the experience made no sense. Then the buttery, yeasty bread was like an edible pillow in her mouth. It was almost as if Iris found herself outside her body. She moaned.

"I'm so glad you like them," Talon said while he placed the eggs in front of her and set a fork beside them.

"They're amazing, Talon. You're a really good baker." When she realized what she'd said, Iris instantly snapped from her relaxed state and plopped the cinnamon roll onto its plate and coughed. It was important for her to never let her guard down, particularly around anyone she didn't know very well.

The orc's eyes grew in size, and concern tensed his jaw. "Are you well, Iris Weyward?"

The compassionate look stirred something in Iris…a buried emotion she didn't want to confront. She coughed several more times, grabbed her coffee, and took several sips. "Um. Yes," Iris finally managed. But she had no idea if it was true. "Down the wrong pipe."

Talon nodded, apparently satisfied with her answer.

"Where did you get cream for the coffee?" Iris asked to change the subject.

"Across the road," he said as he scraped bits of eggs stuck to the bottom of the pan into the trash.

Iris's forehead wrinkled and she coughed again. "At Kate's?"

"I only know the cow's name," Talon said. "Speckle. She seemed nice and didn't mind if I took some milk."

Iris twisted her lips in interest. "So you stole it?" And he'd found out the cow's name too. She had no idea what to do with that information.

Talon's face scrunched for a second and then he stuffed his hands into his pockets. "We needed cream for the coffee."

Something about the gesture resettled Iris's nerves. She hadn't been feeling particularly herself that morning…but at least Talon had performed a criminal act. And if it was by stealing milk from Kate's cow…all the better. Plus, if Talon was willing to steal from the neighbor for her, what else was he willing to do?

She picked up her plate and coffee and moved to the table. "Would you like to join me for breakfast?" Iris figured he would.

The orc's lips arched into a wide smile as he placed the skillet back on the stovetop. "Really?"

"Yes," Iris said. "Take a break. I'm not sure we truly finished our conversation yesterday. Might be a good time to do that while everyone is still asleep."

As Talon arranged two portions of cinnamon rolls onto his plate, Iris noticed an enormous pile of her folded laundry on one of the chairs in the living room.

"You did my laundry?" Iris asked, her heart skipping at least twice.

Talon placed his breakfast on the table. "I didn't get to put it away in your room, since you and Quince were asleep and I didn't want to disturb you."

Iris shook her head, not quite sure how to respond to the

fact Talon was taking care of everything around the house. "Um, thank you."

Un-aliving him at the end of the week was not going to be easy. She couldn't quite remember the last time anyone in her life had taken care of her so well.

Basically never.

But that was an issue for another day. After pulling out her chair, Iris sat and decided to refocus on the moment and on the gooey cinnamon roll. Attention it rightly deserved.

Talon sat, the wood creaking under him, and he looked entirely too big for his chair. After he settled, he cut off a small piece of cinnamon roll with his fork, then put it in his mouth. "Oh. These *are* good." The orc looked taken aback at his own work.

A chuckle left Iris's mouth as she swiped her finger across the top of her cinnamon roll and gathered a dollop of the sticky frosting. "You're so surprised?" She licked the sweet topping and smacked her lips. They were undoubtedly delicious.

Talon took a second bite, then answered, "I guess I am?"

Iris still didn't know much about Talon other than he'd likely been sent to bump off someone before they'd actually gotten to him first. "Have you ever made cinnamon rolls before?"

The orc leaned back in his seat, making the wood groan more than it should. "I really don't know."

Iris still wondered if she'd accidentally drawn the wrong spirit back into Talon's body.

The wheels, if he had them, really seemed to be turning in Talon's head as he considered Iris's question. But while she waited for the answer, Iris dove into the eggs on her plate. They were perfectly cooked and somehow seemed tastier than they should have been too.

"My mother may have taught me," Talon finally said as if he'd dug up a memory.

"To make cinnamon rolls?" Iris asked, suddenly finding herself more interested in hearing his answer than she had anticipated.

He bobbed his head. "I'm pretty sure she was a baker."

A slight twinge played in Iris's heart. She hadn't known her mother, since she'd passed away when Iris was only about four. Most of what she knew about her was through her father or Dahlia, who'd been a little older than Iris when it had happened. But her father was gone too. All she had were her sisters…and even they hadn't spoken with each other for a long time until the day before.

Iris couldn't help but wonder how things might have turned out differently for her if her mother had lived. Maybe she and her sisters would get along better? Maybe they would have created an empire together and ruled the realms? She gulped and pulled herself back into the present. "I know I've asked this before, but do you remember anything else before waking up on my floor?"

Talon's eyes landed on the spot in the middle of her living room, and he squinted. "Possibly?"

"What?" Iris was suddenly hopeful. In the end it would

be easier not to need to rid herself of Talon soon if he actually remembered who he was. She took the last bite of her cinnamon roll while considering heading back into the kitchen for a second serving before she'd even chewed and swallowed it.

"I was supposed to…" He paused, and the space between his brows knit so tightly it could have churned out an entire sweater.

As Iris leaned closer, partially to learn more but also to distract herself from the pastries nearly calling her name from the kitchen.

Talon finally spoke. "I was supposed to find someone." His tone brightened. "What if it was you, Iris Weyward? Since I came here."

She sighed and flopped back in her chair. "Iris." But she almost wondered if she should propose a compromise and let him call her Ms. Weyward.

"Either way," he said as he finished off his cinnamon roll, "here I am. Like serendipity."

Iris rolled her eyes at his sudden big word. "Serendipity, indeed."

With a smile on his face Talon reached for Iris's plate. "Are you done?" he asked.

Strangely disappointed their breakfast was already over, Iris nodded and took her coffee cup. The creamy liquid inside wasn't hot anymore, so out of habit she commanded heat into her hand to warm it up and watched Talon take their dishes.

But of course the magic didn't come, and she'd have to drink the coffee cold and without Talon's company.

"I noticed you don't actually have a lot to eat for lunch," Talon said from the kitchen as he riffled around searching the cupboards and the cold box.

Cinnamon rolls are fine, Iris thought as she sipped her cold coffee. "I haven't had time," she said instead.

He poked his head around the corner. "I'd be glad to head into town to pick up a few things. The market is open today. I saw it on your calendar."

Iris nearly choked on her coffee just imagining Talon all alone in Fraywell. "No," she blurted. "How about you make a list and I'll go?" She didn't really want to venture into town either, but it might be better than hanging out with her sisters. Plus, the fresh air might provide some time for her to think about their magic problem.

Talon walked completely into view, stared at her for a blink, and began rattling off the list. "Tomatoes, sugar, flour…chicken—"

"Chicken?" Iris asked. "We have plenty of chicken outside."

Suddenly a horrified look overtook Talon's face. "We could never eat Viola, Valentina, or Valeria."

"You named my chickens?" Iris had never bothered, since she'd end up eating them at some point down the road.

Nonchalant, he shrugged. "They told me their names."

Iris wrinkled her nose, then spoke. "The chickens talk?"

"Quince talks," Talon said matter-of-factly and listed at least twenty more items on his grocery list.

Overwhelmed and still dwelling on her chickens, Iris flapped her hands in the air for him to stop. "Fine, fine… we'll go together. I don't want to carry all that stuff back anyway."

Talon grinned.

Chapter 9

Iris dressed in a clean blouse (which actually belonged to her instead of Poppy) and a pair of brown cotton pants, held up by a belt with her money purse attached. Thankfully, laundry was another issue she didn't need to worry about for the week.

Before they left for the market she made sure to flip her shop's Closed sign so she didn't have to make any potions until her sisters left.

So that was another stressor off her plate.

But as they walked to Fraywell, Iris couldn't shake the idea that Talon might have *something* going on in his mind other than naming chickens, making pastries, and calling her by her full name. For the time being, though, it didn't matter, if it meant additional mornings of breakfast deliciousness and a clean cottage.

He'd be gone soon anyway.

And she needed to worry about the present.

Trying to get her mind off the problem, she gazed upward. There was no trace of the clouds and rain from the day before, meaning the market would likely be crowded that morning. Iris brought her attention to Talon, who she had been able to convince to leave his apron behind.

His clothes had been entirely mended, and despite what came out of his mouth, the orc at least looked fierce enough to be her bodyguard. Never mind the fact he had a woven wicker basket hung over his arm and looked a bit like a child headed to Grandma's.

Iris pulled it from him. "No talking at the market," she said and held the basket in front of herself.

"Oh. Why?" Confusion pulled at his features.

Iris dug her fingers into the basket handle. "Because I said so."

Talon nodded several times then asked, "How am I supposed to tell you what we need? Since we didn't write the list down." His brows furrowed, and he looked at his palms as if life without the basket was suddenly meaningless.

Clutching it tighter and fighting the urge to give it back to him to wipe the sad look off his face, Iris said, "Just point and grunt."

A confused grin overtook Talon's green lips. "Grunt?"

As Iris stared at him, two thoughts fought for dominance. The first was she currently needed a bodyguard for the optics. The second was the pesky one Poppy had planted that Talon was cute. He was. There was something about him…an innocence. Add that to his square-cut jaw, amber eyes, and black hair that had the tiniest wave to it (she begrudgingly noticed), and a teeny, tiny part of her liked having him around. But she quickly forced the first thought to the forefront of her mind, since the second was unacceptable for her lifestyle. "No smiling!"

"Oh." Talon rubbed at his mouth, and when he lowered his hand the smile was gone. His lips were exaggeratedly turned down. "Like this?"

Iris balked at the absurd expression and halted on the path. "*No*. That looks ridiculous."

It did. That much was true.

"Then how?" Talon asked with frustration in his tone, then stuffed his hands into the pockets of his pants. The orc looked like a lost puppy begging for a home.

Iris studied him intently, wondering if she should off him then and there out of pity. "Show me your teeth."

Again, Talon gave her a wide, welcoming grin.

"Ugh. No!" She recoiled and shook her head violently. "Even if you're only making food for me and cleaning, I need you to at least *look* like my bodyguard, not a court jester."

Talon's lips pressed into a straight line and his irises shone. "You want me to protect you, Iris Weyward?"

Iris! The word screamed in her mind, but it wouldn't do any good to say it again. "*Yes*. Your job is to protect me."

"Why didn't you say so," Talon said, obviously working not to smile but completely failing as the left side of his mouth quivered then lifted upward.

Iris rubbed her thumb over her index finger's ragged nail while her shoulders tensed. "Let me see your teeth…as if you're growling."

Without question, Talon did as she asked, but the expression didn't quite make its way to his amber eyes, which were still half smiling.

"Now *actually* growl," she said.

"Grrrrrr…" The sound came from Talon, but he sounded more like a cranky puppy tugging on a rope than a lion on the hunt.

Still holding the basket, Iris crossed her arms over herself and evaluated. The sound was weak, but she was unlikely to run into any *actual* threats at the Fraywell market. "Needs work, but it will do."

Talon's expression immediately broke into one of joyous pride, entirely breaking the fierce facade.

And Iris scoffed out of frustration. "No smiling."

"Oh, sorry." He wiped the grin from his lips again and growled back at her.

After a quick scoff, Iris said, "Fine." It was the best it was going to get.

By the time they'd breached the outskirts of town, Iris had chewed off the pesky rough nail on her index finger and the ends of two others that hadn't even needed it to assuage her anxiety.

But once they walked to the center of town, the smells of the market hit her nose and some of the nervousness in her middle dissipated. Spices, smoky meats, and greasy sausage mixed with candles and fresh produce. And the market wasn't quite as packed as she'd thought it might be.

At least that was something. They could get in and get out.

Iris looked down the aisles of vendors and said, "Where should we start? I don't really want to be here very long." But when she turned back to Talon, he was gone. "Talon?" she said, then gulped, feeling entirely unlike her normal self. Her mind raced back to her fight with her sisters at Hillock and the strange needling in her gut she'd felt there too. To make herself feel better, she held out her hand to ignite her magic, but sadly nothing happened. Quickly she spun around to find her missing "bodyguard."

Already she completely regretted saying yes to the trip as her heart thudded in her chest.

Finally, when she saw him standing at the bakery table, Iris blew out a quick breath and straightened her back. Before she got far, Puck's singing and lute playing accosted her ears, but she remained focused on her beeline to Talon.

"These all look incredible," Talon said with genuine enthusiasm to Gerti, the owner of Sweets to the Sweet bakery.

Gerti stared up at the orc with a wide-eyed, pleased

expression on her face. "These are the special for today, Mr....?" She held up a wooden board filled with fancy sugar cookies and was obviously fishing for his name.

"Oh, Talon," he said. "I just moved here to Fraywell and am working for—" He turned as soon as he said it and Iris arrived at his side.

"What happened to grunting?" Iris asked, keeping her voice down but not nearly enough for Gerti not to hear.

In a blink, Talon's expression drooped. "Sorry," he whispered. "I forgot." The orc turned back to Gerti and "bared" his teeth at her. It was a completely halfhearted effort. Imminently worse than when they'd practiced.

Gerti drew her chin back in confusion. "He's working for you?" The baker raised her brows in surprise, her eyes wavering between Talon and Iris.

"Yes," Iris answered shortly. "He's my new bodyguard." She pointed to the sourdough rolls, not sure she wanted to buy anything from the woman, but ended up saying, "We'll take half a dozen of those."

Still looking confused, Gerti briefly stared at Talon, then moved on to bag up the rolls. "I heard Jamy left you."

Iris narrowed her eyes at the bakery owner, though Gerti wasn't actually looking at her. "I *let* him go," Iris said. Of course that wasn't how it had happened, but she did not want the town baker to butt into her business. She needed to maintain some air of mystery.

"Ah." Gerti handed the bag to Iris, obviously not believing her.

Iris considered a few hexes she might cast on the baker when her magic was working properly again.

But for the moment, she dug out several coins from the purse on her belt. Before Iris had the chance to hand them off, though, Talon grunted and pointed at the cookies. Again, the orc looked more like an overgrown baby animal standing there next to her than a vicious protector.

Iris took a frustrated breath and blew it out. Her affirmation passed through her mind. *Love the life you live…and destroy those who get in your way.*

A hex on Gerti was definitely on the horizon.

"Plus six sugar cookies…and hurry it up." She put on her best stare-down while Gerti bagged up the cookies and handed them over. Iris blew out a deliberate breath and gave the woman a solid sneer…to keep up appearances.

"Have a nice day," Gerti said with plenty of sugar in her tone.

Iris didn't reply.

"What's next?" Iris said when she and Talon were far enough away from the bakery table.

Talon gazed around the market. "You should set up a booth here for your potions business," he mused, not answering her question.

"What do you know about my potions business?" Iris asked, keeping a frown on her lips. "You've known me for a day."

The orc's eyes gleamed as he addressed her. "I rearranged all your herbs this morning and saw your stack of past orders. Seems like you could get more business if you advertised more."

Advertise? What kind of villain needed to advertise? Iris shuddered at the thought of herself with a market table and a sign listing potions and their prices. Off your husband—two coins. Hex a neighbor—one and a half.

"Living so far out of town must put a real damper on foot traffic," Talon said.

"Less talking, more snarling," Iris muttered halfheartedly. But as annoying as it was, he was right. Not about the idea she should have a booth at the local market but that she'd been thinking too small. How could she really establish herself while living on the outskirts of a town like Fraywell?

Talon leaned down to her. "We need produce." He paused for a blink. "Grrrrrr."

His close proximity made butterflies loop in Iris's stomach, but she squashed them, grabbed Talon's shirtsleeve, and tugged him in the direction of the produce tables.

Along the way they picked up several items from Talon's list, including poultry he hadn't formally made acquaintances with as well as some dried herbs, since he reminded Iris she was running low on a few ingredients.

By the time they made it to the produce section, Iris spotted Lysander perusing the selection, and she walked up next to the elf because he was more familiar than anyone else around the market. His grayish-white hair was pulled up on the top of his head, showing off his pointed ears. Lysander looked tired and, from the looks of his tight jaw, frustrated.

Iris knew the feeling and kind of wanted to talk to him but decided it was a bad idea. She and Talon needed to get back to the cottage. And making what might be construed as *friends* with anyone in Fraywell was a terrible idea.

Enthusiastically, Talon waved one hand to the lettuce, and Iris gathered two enormous heads of the greens while the orc piled tomatoes into the basket.

"Surprised to see you here this morning," Lysander called out, a cotton bag looped over his shoulder.

Iris sighed and turned to the elf, but before she could say a word, Talon loomed over her, partially baring his teeth.

"Grrrrrr," Talon guttered, attempting to growl.

A groan left Iris's mouth, and she turned her head to glare at her bodyguard. "Not at him."

Talon scoffed. "How am I supposed to know? You are so confusing, Iris Weyward."

The elf raised his brow, his expression somewhere between that of utter confusion and amusement.

Iris pushed the heavy basket into Talon's hands and returned her attention to Lysander, deciding it wouldn't hurt to talk to him for a few minutes. "I'm training my new bodyguard, Talon, and I have guests back at the cottage."

"Cupboards were almost bare," Talon piped in. "Although I found an adorable little cow pitcher way at the back."

Iris shot Talon a look, and he instantly closed his mouth. But his blabbering had solved the mystery of the cow-shaped container. That was something of a win.

"New bodyguard, huh," Lysander said, looking Talon up and down. "You've needed one for a while, right?"

Apparently *everyone* in Fraywell knew about Jamy.

"I have," Iris admitted and chose a basket of strawberries. She handed it to Talon. And Talon showed up right on time.

"Well," Lysander sighed, picking up a basket of blueberries and setting it down again. "I *must* figure out the new menu for the inn." He leaned closer to Iris. "The tourists are getting picky these days. But our cook…I don't know if he's up for the job."

Iris felt bad for Lysander. And as before, she still didn't want The Boar's Head to go out of business. But there wasn't much she could do about it.

"What did you buy?" Talon asked, eyeing the bag Lysander held. "For the new menu?"

Iris flicked her attention to him, but Lysander held out his open bag to the orc before she could hush him.

"We're trying to come up with a new stew recipe today," Lysander said. "But all the other attempts were just tasting like the old one."

Talon pursed his lips. "Are you searing the meat before adding it to the liquid?"

Iris stood there, words completely eluding her. How did Talon remember those sorts of things but not the fact he'd been a mercenary?

"Only boiling it," Lysander said.

Talon shrugged. "Try searing it in oil first, and make a good broth with the bones."

A surprised Lysander stepped back and closed the bag. "Not just water and salt?"

"Snails, no," Talon said with a rich chuckle. "It's all about the flavor." He leaned in like he was revealing a secret. "A bit of red wine might be nice too. Costs a bit more, but worth it."

"Red wine?" the elf said. "We never thought of that."

"Maybe you need a better cook," Iris muttered, but neither Talon nor Lysander seemed to hear her. She looked around at the market and the place was filling up. It was time to go.

"I'm Lysander." The elf held out his hand to Talon, and the orc shook it.

Not sure how she felt about the friendly turn of conversation, Iris paid the produce vendor and turned her attention back to Lysander. "Surely you'll get everything worked out." Then she looked up at Talon. "We need to go back to the cottage. My sisters are probably up."

Lysander's bespectacled olive-green eyes gleamed with hope, and he brought his hand up with a flourish. "Do you think Talon might have a few moments to spare to come and advise us on the menu? Hermy is no help either. We really need to get this worked out for the sake of the inn."

Iris's stomach dropped, and suddenly heat flustered in her chest. A feeling she hated. "I'm not sure if he'll have time. But possibly." After she'd said it and regretted the last part, she signaled for Talon to follow her. "Let's go."

"Bye, Lysander," Talon said, and Iris grabbed his arm and tugged him away from the produce stall.

As they hurried away, Iris knew she couldn't get out of there quickly enough.

"That was fun," Talon said, and from his tone she was positive he was grinning from ear to ear, but she didn't look behind her to see.

Chapter 10

"Damn sun," Iris complained and squinted while struggling to stay ahead of Talon on the path back home. But the orc's stride was twice that of hers, and the attempt was completely useless.

The top of her head burned, and her stray tendril kept falling into her face. Iris swiped it away for the fourth time while a growl rumbled in her throat.

"Are you unhappy, Iris Weywa—"

"Iris!" She flipped around and stepped directly in front of him. Her arms flew out to her sides. "Just *Iris*!"

Before she had barely gotten the words out, Talon's eyes widened, and he nearly dropped the basket on the ground.

"You don't need to call me by my entire name!" she

shouted, and several speckled, brownish birds flew out of a bushy patch on the side of the road from all the noise.

Talon stood there motionless, his eyes fixed on Iris while her fists balled at her sides.

But it wasn't long before she started to feel entirely ridiculous for getting worked up about something so meaningless, when there were so many more important things going on. In truth, Iris had no idea why she was so frustrated with Talon. By her own doing, the guy had been literally born yesterday. So instead of saying another word or waiting for Talon to speak, Iris turned on her boot heel and started marching home again.

"I don't mean for you to be unhappy…Iris…" He didn't say her full name that time, but Iris could tell it was on the tip of his tongue.

"Happiness is overrated," she muttered and kept her pace. "There are much more critical things in life." (Like living up to expectations.)

As she walked, Talon continued trudging behind Iris and not saying anything. And that fact fussed inside her chest. Compelled, she turned to see him, and the orc looked entirely glum. Against her better judgment Iris signaled with a tip of the head for him to come up beside her.

Of course the gesture brightened his features, and he sped up and met her pace. "Happiness is a good thing… especially if you enjoy it with the right people."

"And who are the right people, Talon?" she asked, despite her preference for silence and avoiding her own issues. Iris wiped a bead of sweat trickling down the side of her brow.

"The people who see past all our insecurities and take the time to stick around to find out what we're all about," he said, holding the basket with both hands and swinging it slightly from side to side.

"I don't know what you're talking about." Iris wrinkled her nose, but it was mostly to hide the fact that she knew exactly what he was talking about. How could someone so different from herself see her so clearly?

"I did like going into town with you," Talon said, not expanding on his previous statement. For all Iris knew it was gone from his brain completely. "Your friend Lysander seemed nice."

"Lysander is *not* my friend," Iris insisted, irritation grinding her insides. "I only eat at the inn he owns with his husband, Herman, sometimes."

Talon tipped his head. "You didn't want me to growl at him, so I only assumed…"

"*Now* you remember who you are supposed to growl at or not?" Iris interrupted and planted her hand on her hip. But now Talon had made her wonder why she'd done that. Did she like Herman?

The orc lowered his chin slightly. "The market was a little overwhelming."

Iris shook her head, knowing she should be angrier at him, but something inside her wouldn't allow it. Where the anger should have been was instead replaced with concern for Talon's well-being. Which was completely annoying. She figured it had to do with the defective spell she'd cast on Talon. Could be it had affected her too.

Iris cursed herself internally. She needed to get back on track.

"When we are out and about, what I really need is for you to focus on being my bodyguard, Talon," she said. "You said you were willing to protect me. So you need to be the silent type… unless you're growling at someone. Look tough…you know…" She stopped in the middle of the road and planted her feet in a wide stance then quickly crossed her arms over her chest.

Talon halted, watching her intently.

While she gathered her strength down deep, Iris twisted her features into her best glower, raised her eyes to Talon, and growled. The sound that came out of her mouth was low and ferocious.

Not missing a beat, the orc lifted the shopping basket chest high and took a step back. "Ooooooh, you're good at that!" He quickly bared his teeth, mirroring Iris's fierce expression to a much lesser degree. "Grrrrrr."

Ignoring how absurd the orc looked holding the basket the way he was, Iris said, "You have to put more diaphragm into it." She reached out and patted directly under his belly and the basket. The muscles there were defined and tight. His body temperature was much warmer than hers. Unexpectedly, a strange sensation looped in her own stomach from the touch. Iris gulped and quickly drew back her hand like she'd been bitten.

"My what?" Talon lowered the basket down toward his hips.

Iris, still trying to get over the sensation from touching the orc, cleared her throat and said, "Put the basket down."

He immediately did what she asked.

The tingling in her middle inexplicably moved up to her chest, making it incredibly difficult to breathe. But working to clear her head, she decided to follow her own advice and took a deep, low breath, pushing her diaphragm downward. "Your diaphragm," she repeated slowly. "It's down here and can help get big sounds out, like singing…or yelling." Iris touched the spot below the curve of her round belly. "Take a big breath and fill it up."

Talon put his hand in the right spot, but when he took a breath it was all in his shoulders. Which was entirely wrong.

"No." She extended her hands but stopped short of touching him this time, although something in her really wanted to. "The breath needs to fill the space here." Iris pointed to the spot. "Then you'll get enough air in your lungs for a respectable growl."

After a head bob, the orc tried again and failed. His brow crumpled with frustration. "Show me again, Iris."

At the sound of her name, Iris's stomach did another loop. She blew out a quick breath to rid herself of the emotion and placed her hands on her chest and lower belly. Iris filled her lungs with air and imagined the breath moving downward. When satisfied, she allowed a fearsome growl to emerge, and more birds flew out of the bushes beside them.

"You're very clever." Talon took a step backward, and his lips arched upward toward his tusks. "If you can do that, I'm not sure why you need me."

The freeing nature of the noise did something to Iris. She felt better. Confident. A smile curled onto her own lips, and a laugh left her mouth. "That was amazing!" The words spilled out as if she were a silly child, but she didn't care, because she was so invigorated. For good measure she let out another growl and then tipped her head up and howled.

"Show me!" Talon asked.

Still amused, Iris laughed again. "Show you what?"

"Show me where the air goes," he said, giddiness in his tone.

Hesitantly, she glanced down at her hand on her belly while Talon reached out to her.

"Can I feel how you breathe?" the orc asked, genuine curiosity dancing in his expression. "I want to do that too."

"Umm." Iris dropped her hands, not quite knowing what to do with them. Everything in her wanted to say yes *and* no at the same time.

Talon drew back with genuine concern. "I'm sorry, Iris Way—." He stopped himself. "Iris."

Her mind settled with the sound of her name coming from him. "It…it's fine." Iris reached out for his hand.

Without hesitation he extended it to her. "Are you sure?"

Iris waved dismissively at the air. "I'm sure. Yes." She shrugged. "I'm not used to people touching me. Thank you for asking."

Villainy was indeed lonely work.

She directed Talon to the spot below her belly, and when his hand settled there, Iris had no problem taking in a deep breath, since it happened all on its own from Talon's touch. His warmth seeped through the fabric of her shirt instantly.

"Feel it?" She somehow managed, but it came out a tad croaky.

Talon nodded vigorously, drew back, and straightened.

"You try it now," Iris said, both relieved he'd moved on and missing his touch at the same time.

He lowered his shoulders, opened his mouth, and took in a huge gulp of air. But that time his belly expanded.

Iris's eyes grew and she raised her voice in anticipation, "Now growl!"

Taking a wide stance, Talon balled his fists, bared his teeth, and somehow released one of the loudest, most impressive growls Iris had heard in an age. Considerably better than her last bodyguard could manage.

At least ten birds launched from the bushes into the sky.

"Yes!" She threw her arms up into the air with joy. "You did it!"

Uninhibited, Talon tipped up his head and howled at the sun.

Then they both broke into belly laughs that continued for several minutes.

"You finally found it in you," Iris congratulated while happiness from her own accomplishment surged within her.

He shook his head vigorously. "Not sure where it came

from." Talon collected the basket from the ground and looked around. "But too bad no one else heard."

"Oh, well the birds did," Iris said with pride. "And I'm pretty sure you'll be able to do it again." Her hands were clasped together, and warmth spread through her fingers. Aware of the heat, she glanced down and opened her palms to the magic. Her heart leaped. Was it back?

"I do have a question though," Talon said and looked back the way they had come.

"Sure," Iris said, and the magic dissipated, her skin returning to normal.

Talon squinted as if in thought. "Who is it I need to protect you from back in Fraywell? Everyone there seems pretty nice."

The smile on Iris's face fell away at the sudden gain and then loss of her magic, but she wanted to remain patient with the orc. Talon didn't know the answer, and it was obvious he could learn. "When a witch is in my line of work, they have to maintain a certain type of *reputation*." She signaled him forward.

Talon picked up the basket and followed her, seeming to hang on every word. "And what kind of reputation is that?"

While his growl had been decent and was a good start, she didn't really know if Talon was ready to hear the tale of her and her sisters' treacherous past. It might have been too much for his still sensitive mind and spirit. He wasn't going to be around forever anyway.

"You saw the receipts for my potion's business, right?" Iris asked.

"Yes," Talon answered. "The one I mentioned getting a table for at the market."

Certainly, the topic wasn't one Iris wanted to discuss, but she decided to meet him where he was. "The very one."

Talon grinned, then seemingly remembered to form his expression into more of a grimace.

It was something.

Iris continued as her cottage came into sight down the path. "The potions I make are sensitive. And the people who I make them for need me to maintain a sense of…" She paused to think of the right words. "Mystery and expertise."

"Ooooooh." Talon nodded as if he got it, but Iris was not entirely sure he did.

She resumed anyway. She was in a good mood. "And not everyone is always happy with my business." There were a few people in the past who'd escaped her and her sisters' magic and who could have a grudge or two against them. But Iris tried not to dwell on such things. "And I need protection, so it's important my bodyguard is a certain…" She looked over to Talon. "Type."

"Am I your type?" Talon asked, his tone entirely sincere.

As if on cue, Iris's stomach twisted into a knot. Of course she knew what he was saying, but her mind went completely elsewhere. Did she have a type? Over her twenty-seven years

Iris had had a handful of flings…but never anything serious. "I…I guess so." But why was her mind even on Talon in that sort of way?

Unseen in the bushes, birds started chirping as if to taunt her. Iris whipped toward them and snarled. None flew out, but they seemed to shut their beaks as she walked on.

She turned back to Talon, and his brows were raised. Despite Iris's mediocre outburst, he seemed impressed.

"But I'm not really sure why you even need a bodyguard, when you can do that," Talon said while swinging the grocery basket with one hand.

Not completely used to compliments, Iris felt her cheeks heat up, but she didn't want the orc to notice. "Let's get moving." She wasn't exactly excited to get back to her sisters, but she also knew if they could work out their magic dilemma, they'd probably go back to their own homes, leaving Iris to her business.

Almost at the cottage, Iris picked up her pace as they passed Kate's garden.

"Oh, yoo-hoo." Kate suddenly popped up from a tall patch of tomatoes.

Unfortunately, Talon let out a little scream and dropped the basket, but Iris groaned.

Kate giggled. "So sorry. Didn't mean to scare you."

Tomatoes rolled out from the fallen basket.

"You didn't," Iris said flatly, still thinking about Talon screaming and wanting to bury her head in the dirt.

Completely ignoring Iris, Kate turned her attention to Talon and scanned him up and down. "And who are you?"

With the screaming and produce-dropping incident, Iris didn't really want him to say he was her new bodyguard. "He's training as my employee," she got out quickly before Talon spoke.

"Oh. Well, I'm Kate," she said, flicking her loose hair over her shoulder, still not looking at Iris. "How about I replace those tomatoes, Mr....?" She lowered the pitch of her voice while holding out several plump, juicy vegetables to him.

Talon just stood there like he was frozen.

Filled with sudden jealousy, Iris flung out her hand and knocked the tomatoes on the ground with a splat.

"Whoops," Iris said. "We need to go." She grabbed Talon by the shirtsleeve to get them both out of there as quickly as possible.

But before they moved, the orc bent down and swiped all the fallen produce back into the basket, then pursued Iris to her doorstep.

"You can stop over any time, Mr....?" Kate called in a singsong voice.

"Talon," the orc said.

"You can't pilfer my employees!" Iris called, but she'd been pushed entirely off-kilter again. In an attempt to regain her composure, she blew out a quick breath, hoping no one would notice. Only then did Iris reach for the door handle, but before she turned it Talon leaned to her, his breath tickling Iris's hair.

"I would never go to work for her," he whispered.
Iris blushed. But she chalked it up to the heat outside. It had to be that.

Chapter 11

"Where've you been?" Quince's voice was peppered with stress as he scurried across the floor, meeting Iris and Talon at the door as they walked inside. The hedgehog's quills stuck out straight like he'd been hit with a lightning bolt and still survived.

"In Fraywell"—Iris indicated Talon's basket—"getting groceries at the market."

The orc grunted and pointed to it.

Iris groaned at Talon's uncanny ability to *still* not get her instructions right, just as the sound of her sisters' agitated voices carried to her ears from their room down the hall. "What are they arguing about?" she asked Quince.

The little hedgehog sat up on his haunches and held his

paws out to his sides. "What *aren't* they arguing about? Even Ursula and Oberon escaped an hour ago. But this is *my* house, and the thought of catching my own snacks in the wild is completely unacceptable."

After a blink, Iris bent down and presented her hand to him. The hedgehog dashed into her palm and made his way up her arm. Seconds later, he nuzzled her neck as he clung to her shirt.

"So cozy," he murmured. "Never leave again."

She winced. Her familiar's spines weren't comfortable, but she said nothing, since the feeling was…well…*familiar* if nothing else. "They're only here to figure out what's going on with our magic," Iris said, mindlessly stroking his head. "When we do, they can leave."

"What's wrong with your magic?" Talon said with alarm at the edge of his voice.

Nearly forgetting he was still there, Iris turned toward him and looked the orc up and down. She couldn't help but remember meeting his spirit before the dead-raising spell… brutal and ready to do her bidding. The person standing in front of her was *not* the same.

He was a stark reminder of what was wrong with her magic. But they'd had such a pleasant time on their walk that she didn't want to say anything to hurt his feelings. Plus, her broken magic was also the reason there was a good chance he wasn't even going to exist next week. And a tiny part of her almost regretted the fact.

"Don't you worry about that." Iris shooed Talon toward

the kitchen. "How about you start making something for lunch?"

He kept his attention on Iris for a moment, and she swore she caught an extra air of concern, but then he brought his gaze down to the food. Talon grunted again, hiked up the basket, and did as Iris said without any more questions.

Ignoring her current issues, Iris watched him as he walked into the kitchen and started unloading the basket one item at a time. Lost in the moment, the witch's thoughts rounded in her mind. What if she kept Talon around just to take care of the house? Even though he really should have passed on, it was a shame to waste such an employee. She could always hire another real bodyguard, and they'd share the barn.

As she had the thought, a whisper of a smile curled at the ends of her lips.

"That must have been some market trip. Something going on between you two?" Quince's words barely met Iris's ears when he asked the question a second time, followed by a prick in Iris's neck with one of his spines.

"Ouch," Iris complained, then nabbed her hedgehog and moved his body to the edge of her shoulder. "What? No!" Somehow she kept her voice down and twisted her head toward the living room. "But look at this place!" She cleared her throat.

The entire house *was* nearly spotless. Iris even checked the window to her side, and all the smudges had been wiped completely clean.

But clean windows might allow nosy neighbors a

glimpse inside. She and Talon would have to have a chat about that.

"And I don't have to worry about cooking," Iris said as Talon pulled the white apron over his head and tied it in the back. Admittedly, her gaze lingered a little too long, and she couldn't help but think she might have changed her mind about how the orc looked. Particularly the *look* of him in her house.

"Hello?" Quince waggled his paw out in front of her face. "Why are you doing that with your mouth?"

Iris's breath hitched when she realized her mouth was agape. She snapped her lips shut and then licked them out of nervousness. "*A lot* has happened since yesterday."

"You're telling me," Quince agreed. "Talon…your sisters. But I will agree the food's better around here."

"Ugh," Dahlia interrupted. Her voice was strained. "You're finally back."

Iris looked up at her sister, and despite her desperate tone, everything about her looked perfectly draconian. The hem of her pressed black robe swished against the wooden floor, and her blond bob was as straight as a pin. At an early age, Dahlia had perfected the skill it required to maintain such a constant presence…on the outside at least. Sometimes the not-so-refined emotions would creep out, although she always did her best to stuff them back inside quickly if they appeared.

Poppy tagged behind her wearing a frilly purple dress and a red stain on her lips. Iris's youngest sister used her looks to her advantage for her evildoing. Her motto was *Use your honey to attract the bees.*

Looking down, Iris evaluated her own pants, which had somehow gotten wrinkled from the market and the walk home. But who cared? Iris had always found being underestimated was her best defense.

Even so, she let out an enormous sigh before speaking. "What's going on?"

"*I* wanted to wait for you," Poppy scoffed. "But Dahlia didn't. She said it didn't matter. But it did."

"Wait for me for what?" Iris asked, not sure it was actually wise.

Her older sister made her way into the living room, sat on one of the chairs, and folded her hands neatly on her lap. "The clarification spell we cast while you were gone."

With a flourish, Poppy flopped onto the other chair, making her full skirt fluff out before her behind hit the cushion. "But because you weren't here, and since our magic isn't one hundred percent, the vision was unclear." She flicked her fingers, and weak magic flickered over her palm. Poppy scoffed.

Dahlia only flared her nostrils and looked straight ahead. "I couldn't have known. It should have been fine."

"Of course you could have known." Poppy threw both her hands up, and Iris noticed her pointed fingernails were colored purple to match her dress. "*I* told you."

"Why would I listen to you?" Dahlia said flatly while staring at Poppy, who was still trying to light fire in her palm.

"Because I'm your sister!" The youngest twisted to Iris, pleading with her eyes. "You agree with me, right?"

She was already tired of their bickering and definitely reminded why she'd left them back in the cave at Hillock. Who had time for wickedness if all the time was spent arguing with her sisters?

Iris bit her lip. "I'm going to need a few more details."

"You always take her side," Dahlia said and crossed her arms over her chest.

Iris certainly did not. She'd always made her best effort not to take either side.

"See what I'm talking about?" Quince whispered into Iris's ear, his whiskers tickling her neck. But the commentary was entirely unnecessary, and Iris waved at him to be quiet.

Around the corner Talon clanked and banged in the kitchen and for a second Iris thought about leaving her sisters to help with whatever he was doing. The orc *was* frustrating, but not nearly as much as her sisters.

Instead she decided to be the grown-up, grabbed the wooden chair from the dining table again, and dragged it along the floor to them. She didn't even care about the scraping sound it made, since she was pretty sure it would annoy them both.

Iris's adult persona only went so far.

She released the back of the chair and let the legs drop on the wood, then sat. "The faster we figure this out, the faster we might never have to see each other again."

Iris didn't know if she *entirely* meant that statement, but it felt good at that moment.

Unable to light the flame in her hand, Poppy huffed and grabbed her unfinished needlepoint off the floor in front of the fireplace. She'd stitched several flowers over the spots where her blood had stained the fabric the day before. "*You* can tell her," she spat to Dahlia.

"Since you disappeared this morning, we decided to go ahead and cast a clarification spell," Dahlia started.

"*You* decided." Poppy didn't look up from her needlepoint.

Dahlia shook her head. "You went along with it."

"Why'd you do that without me anyway?" Iris grumbled.

"We got a bit more amplification with Quince here," Dahlia said. "So while we were waiting for you, we decided to give it a go. Plus, Poppy was bored."

"*You* were bored," Poppy shot back.

"Fine. Please get to the point," Iris said, somehow keeping her calm, but as she spoke, the most enticing smell of garlic and onions came from the kitchen and made it difficult for her to think.

His nose twitching, Quince slid down her arm and into her palm. Iris placed him on the ground, and the hedgehog scurried away.

He was the lucky one.

"As I was saying," Dahlia said, "we performed a clarification spell and did receive some information from the result."

"Not enough," Poppy complained.

Dahlia whipped her head toward their youngest sister and hissed. Poppy stuck out her tongue.

Iris's cheeks puffed out with air as she pursed her lips in annoyance at her sister's lack of maturity. And she decided that yes, her never seeing them again was probably the best idea. "The clarification spell!" she demanded.

"Someone is probably demanding revenge," Poppy blurted out.

Probably? Iris thought, while her oldest sister only glared at Poppy.

"Revenge?" Iris asked. "Who'd want revenge on us?"

Of course, it was a rhetorical question. There were people all over the realms who wanted revenge on the Weyward sisters. There was the incident with the Scottish king, the prank they'd played on that realm the year prior, then the debacle with the old woman down the street when they were growing up (let's not mention what actually happened there), the little thing they'd done to an entire town maybe six years back... and the list continued. Not to mention all their own individual deeds someone might have had a *tiny* grievance about.

But evil is as evil does.

Dahlia's golden brow shot up. "That's all we know. But it looks like someone might have cast a little spell against us... and they *could* be trying to take us out one by one."

Suddenly agitated, Iris stood and rounded to the back of her chair. She clasped the back and squeezed. "But how can we put a stop to it if we're not sure who cast it?"

"It *was* fuzzy," Dahlia admitted.

"Exactly why we should have waited for Iris," Poppy insisted. "We're all apparently half-assing our magic here. If we're going to get anywhere we need to work together."

"Language, sister." Dahlia growled and folded her hands in her lap. She was forever trying to make it look as if she was the most mature out of the three, but to anyone who knew her, the facade was entirely transparent. "We must focus."

Clanking came from the kitchen again. And more of the wonderful smell.

Unable to help herself, as well as to escape the conversation with her sisters, no matter how important it was, Iris leaned back to get another glimpse of what Talon was doing.

The orc stood over the stove with a cast-iron skillet in hand. Steam wafted over the top of what must have been whatever was making the savory smell. He tossed in a sprig of rosemary.

"We *could* make a list of all the people we've orchestrated torture against, maimed, or caused to come down with a bad case of the pox and then just cast a little spell to get rid of all of them," Poppy suggested as she pulled on a length of purple thread. "You know how I hate leaving loose ends."

Dahlia narrowed her eyes, and Iris was pretty sure Poppy would find one of Ursula's cat turds in her shoe in the near future. "You think we can do all that with our *half-assed* magic abilities? Anyway, that would take an age."

Attempting to divert their bickering, Iris said, "Why don't we try the spell again?" She turned her full attention back to her sisters. "We can recast the clarification spell with me involved. Maybe it will be enough."

"About that—" Poppy started, but Dahlia cut her off.

"We'll need to figure out a different way," Dahlia said. "It wasn't only that the spell didn't *work*. We were actually cut off."

"What do you mean by that?" Iris asked, half wondering if anything they were saying was true.

"Everything went poof," Poppy replied and fidgeted in her seat. "Dahlia got a little zap."

"I don't want to talk about it," Dahlia growled. "But it was definitely a warning."

A sinking feeling settled in Iris's middle. She'd heard of that kind of thing before. "Could there be a witch with stronger magic involved?"

"Precisely my thought," her oldest sister said. "Maybe word got out about our success at Hillock last year."

Iris really didn't want to revisit Hillock.

"Yeah." Poppy jumped from her seat. "Like they could have been jealous of our power. That has to be it. It's definitely a sign that word must be getting around Veronian."

Iris really, *really* wasn't so sure of that. But who knew? The Scottish King Project had gone off well. And there was a villainy pecking order that some definitely wanted to maintain. So another witch causing their magic loss was a solid theory.

"You still have Dad's old books, right?" Dahlia asked.

Iris had had them sent from Dawndale, along with the

rest of her things after she'd gotten settled in Fraywell. And since they'd arrived, she had kept them in her bedroom on the bookshelf. But she hadn't had the heart to look at them in an age. "Of course." She inhaled deeply and held it.

If she didn't have to, Iris never thought about what had happened to their father. It was another good reason to have distance between herself and her sisters. Iris could think about it less.

"Then it's about time for us to revisit them again," Dahlia said.

"Lunch is served," Talon called as he poked his head into the living area.

Iris blew out the breath, glad for the reprieve. "I'm entirely famished." She popped up and dragged her chair to the table before her sisters sat down with her.

Chapter 12

Frustratingly, the day ended with no more answers than it had started with. Despite having their bellies filled with two amazing meals from Talon, including dessert, the sisters were barely closer to solving the problem of their defective magic, finding out who'd cast the curse, or learning who'd had it out for them in the first place.

They'd even made a list of potentials who could have cast the spell: Sycorax, Jupiter, Diana, and a few others. The sisters had had run-ins with them all, but none of them were a sure thing. So they'd have to scour the books for possible spells then cross-reference all those with all the potential witch's particular magic. It really could take an age. And even if they found the right culprit and the right spell, would they even be able to break it without their full powers?

On top of that, Iris still hadn't even admitted to them that *Talon* was a part of her magic problem. She didn't know why, but for whatever reason it didn't seem like it was their business. Plus, he was taking care of almost everything while her sisters were there, and she didn't want to get in the way of that.

She watched her older sister, who seemed deep in study with her inkwell in front of her and a feathered plume in hand, which she'd been using to take notes in an open notebook. Dahlia had always been meticulous; not only did she have perfect penmanship, she had everything ordered from most to least likely to be important. In contrast, Iris's note-taking was sparse, messy, and disorganized.

She couldn't focus at all.

"I never liked school," said Poppy, who sat with her bare feet on the edge of her chair and peeked up over a large tome titled *Creating Trouble*. Her face wasn't even visible, and from Iris's vantage point it looked like a mop of curly red hair was sprouting from the edges of the book.

Dahlia tsked with judgment. "And your marks reflected that, sister."

"My marks weren't that bad," Poppy insisted and pulled the book down from blocking her face.

"If you had spent more time inside your spells class," Dahlia said, "instead of out back kissing—"

"That was only once," Poppy said, but her eyes shone

with humor and fond recollection while she played with the corner of the book.

"Once?" Dahlia raised her left brow, obviously questioning her sister's honesty.

Her skepticism was likely founded.

Apparently reliving something long forgotten, Poppy said, "I should look him up again. Haven't seen Fredrick in years, but he was a great tutor."

"Tutor?" Dahlia sneered. "I do *not* remember him tutoring you on any subject."

"Oh." Poppy bit her lip and slipped into a dreamy tone of voice. "He *did*. Snails, I might have liked school more than I remembered." The corners of her lips pushed up at the corners.

"I thought you hated Fredrick?" Dahlia said. "Didn't you turn him into a worm once?"

Poppy swept her hand in the air. "Oh, it's a fine line."

"Ugh," Dahlia scoffed and pointed the end of her plume at Poppy like a wand. "You need to focus, sister."

Poppy narrowed her gaze at Dahlia. "Some days I think you'd be easier to get along with if you had a little more *tutoring* in your life."

Of course, Iris had been doing her best to ignore them, but she snickered at the jab as her oldest sister shot her a look. To avoid her wrath, Iris quickly glanced outside the newly cleaned window. Not that she saw much, since darkness was coming soon. But the sky was mottled with pink and blue. She rose from the dining table, where several more of her father's books filled with his own notes lay sprawled open along with the notes she and her sisters had taken.

"I need a break," Iris said to change the subject and snapped her own journal shut, since she hoped to avoid Dahlia casting any judgment on her sloppy penmanship.

"This can't be like the last time, Iris," Dahlia insisted while pushing one side of her blond hair behind her ear. "We have to work together."

How long has it been since we've been able to do that? she thought. Too long.

"We've been at this since after lunch," Iris said as she stuffed her hands into her pants pockets. "I understand how important this is just as well as the two of you do. But we also need clear heads."

Poppy flopped back in her seat and twirled a red curl around her finger. "I could use a break too."

"I think there's one more piece of the apple pie Talon made in the kitchen," Iris said, her mouth watering at the thought of how the perfectly cooked fruit balanced by the spices had tasted at lunch.

Her younger sister's eyes shone. She slammed her book closed and shot up out of her seat. "That's mine then."

"Ugh," Dahlia groaned as she flipped through the book she held. "The two of you are *such* distractible children."

Iris pursed her lips, wanting to argue. But she indeed was distractible. Instead she waved a dismissive hand at her older sister and made her way past Poppy, who was already eating the pie out of the tin.

"This is so good," Poppy said, stuffing another bite into her mouth. "I need to find a bodyguard who also does the cooking around my place."

"Is Fredrick available?" Iris asked.

Poppy looked up from her pie, her eyes wide. "Ooooooh. I wonder if he can cook."

After a deep breath followed by a chuckle, Iris wandered out the back, closed the door, and leaned on the wall next to it, happy for the fresh air. The sun was just falling behind the horizon, and the sky above it slowly morphed into a purple canvas.

The brief moments before darkness fell were Iris's favorite time of the day. But that day the experience hit differently. She rubbed her temples, frustrated not only with her sisters' surprise visit (yes, she should have read the letter) but also with the entire magic-loss situation. Of course, maintaining her lifestyle always had its risks, but up until that point she'd mostly been confident in her choices. At a young age, she'd recognized her father was a powerful witch, and she wanted that for her life too.

But reading his books and seeing his writing in the margins unfortunately brought back memories she was disinclined to think about.

Iris needed to be careful, since life could change in an instant. She knew that all too well and strongly disliked the reminder.

As she was about to go for a short walk, rustling came from the bushes not too far from her, and she twisted, her heart pounding. "Who's there?" Iris managed a fighting stance and called her thermal magic in her hands, but the magic only popped and sparked, then fizzled out.

"Snails," she cursed.

While Iris's life flashed before her, she thought about calling her sisters, but nothing came out as her breath hitched. A dark figure rose, holding something that looked long, sharp, and very much like a knife. Her mind reeled. Was this an assassin sent to snuff her out? Was it the end of her existence? Would her sisters attempt to raise her from the dead? She shrugged. Probably not. "Who are you?" she demanded, knowing those might be her final words.

But before her imagination got too far away from her, the silhouette spoke.

"It's only me," Talon's voice came from the figure.

A few more curses rolled around in Iris's mind, and she blew out a quick breath. *Get a hold of yourself, woman*, she thought and dropped her back to the wall again for support. "What the realm are you doing?" Iris managed out loud, not expecting him to be directly outside the door, and then her eyes dropped to whatever he was holding.

"Pruning." Using both hands, he held up the "knife," revealing the blades of a large set of pruners. The orc reached out with them and snipped a portion of unruly bushes lining the back of her cottage. "I found these in the barn." Talon held up the pruning tool. "Your landscaping looks a fright."

Confused at what she was both seeing and hearing, Iris felt her jaw tighten. "You're *gardening* in the dark?"

Talon tipped his chin up to the sky as if he were evaluating the stars beginning their nighttime dance. "It wasn't dark up until a few minutes ago. But I do have excellent night vision."

Iris had read once that orcs saw extremely well in the dark. It's what made them excellent hunters and mercenaries. But night gardeners? "You really don't have to do that." She shook her head in disbelief and suppressed the desire to tell Talon what she knew about him and how far he'd fallen. There was no point.

The chickens clucked lightly outside the henhouse.

"You and your sisters seemed like you had important things to work out," he said. "And I didn't want to be in the way. Plus…" He turned back to the bushes. "It doesn't appear you have the time to take care of the plants around your cottage. It's a real shame."

That was the understatement of the age. There was also the fact a well-manicured garden wasn't exactly the vibe Iris was trying to exude. But it really didn't matter. As soon as Talon was gone, the plants would go back to being a snaggy and dead mess.

She unpeeled herself from the wall and walked over to Talon. "As long as you have time to patrol while you… garden, I guess it's fine." She wanted him to keep busy and was still a tad hopeful he'd work out as a bodyguard. Keeping him on would be less of a bother than "firing" him.

Talon snipped several more branches, and the leaves tumbled to the ground. "Oh good. I have a bunch of ideas for both the front and the back."

Iris crossed her arms over her chest, half of her wanting to know what those ideas were and the other half knowing she should probably go back inside. She blew her cheeks out like a chipmunk and gazed around the dark yard.

"You told me you thought your mother was a baker?" Iris asked instead of leaving. She probably shouldn't inquire about such things, but it was somehow better than going back inside and making an excuse to go to bed early to avoid her sisters. Reminding Talon of his past also might spur on more recent memories if her defective magic hadn't damaged him too much. Plus, if she would admit it to herself, more than a small part of her wanted to know more about the orc.

Before he spoke, Talon moved to the left to work on the next set of bushes. "An excellent cook too," he said while snipping.

"Lunch and dinner *were* very good." Iris thought back to the herb-roasted potatoes Talon had made earlier, and her mouth watered. "Was your mother human? Can you remember?"

"No," Talon said, keeping his focus on his gardening. "My father is human. Mother's an orcess. A quite lovely one too."

"They're still alive?" Iris raised her brows, somewhat surprised. She didn't know why, but she hadn't ever pictured vicious mercenaries with parents who baked.

Talon reached into the bush and snipped off a leaf with his sharp nails. "Oh yes. I try to visit them at least once a year."

"Your father too?" Iris clasped her hands together, suddenly liking the fact that she was getting somewhere. Talon *did* have recent memories...although they were different from what she'd expected.

The half orc chuckled. "Of course. Why would I visit my mother and not my father? They live together."

Iris's mind reeled at the thought of Talon spending a holiday with his orcess mother and human father. *What did they do together? Other than baking?* "Have you seen them lately?" she asked, rightly curious.

Talon stopped pruning and held the tool out, as if he was thinking. "I believe so. Right before I had my last job." He went back to pruning the second bush, and a clean, fruity scent wafted to her nose from the leaves.

Iris's breath hitched. Talon's spirit form had told her about the job he'd been performing when he'd unfortunately met a sticky end in the process. *Did his parents know what he did?* "And what job was that?" She tried to keep the questioning nonchalant.

He kept snipping and moved down to the next bush while he hummed a little tune.

Iris followed him. "Do you remember your last job, Talon?" she asked as the chickens happily clucked some more from inside their henhouse.

"It's funny," Talon said without looking her way. "I don't. But I keep telling myself the memories will probably come back. Do you think we might be able to go back into Fraywell tomorrow?"

Iris couldn't help but think Talon might be deflecting. What if he already remembered more than he was saying? She cast the thoughts away. "Why? We bought plenty of food today." And she had been into town more times that week than since she'd moved to Fraywell.

"Your friend Lysander—" Talon started.

"He's *not* my friend," Iris insisted, crossing her arms over her chest again.

Talon stopped clipping for a second. "Okay, the elf who owns the tavern you eat at sometimes. Your not-enemy."

Iris tightened her arms across herself while she let out an exasperated breath. She was glad it was dark, but she quickly remembered Talon's excellent night vision and cleared her throat. "What about him?"

"I'd like to pay him a visit," Talon said as he went back to clipping.

Iris groaned. "This isn't about the inn, is it?" She looked up to the full moon low in the sky illuminating the side of Talon's face.

"He said they were having difficulty with the menu," Talon said, still working. "I know I can help them."

The memory of the extra-crispy garlic potatoes and apple pie from dinner came to Iris's mind again. And there was no doubt she knew the same. Talon could help Herman and Lysander...and they did need the help. But her lips pinched. "With my sisters here, I'm not sure there's time for me to take you." She definitely didn't want him heading into Fraywell alone. Iris gazed around at the yard. "And there is a lot for you to take care of around here." She almost felt guilty saying it.

Talon turned his attention back to Iris and smiled. The moonlight highlighted half of his face. "You're right. We might have more time next week."

"Next week," Iris repeated, guilt definitely sinking in her belly. He wasn't going to be around next week. Not if the sisters solved the problem with their magic.

The half orc leaned toward the bushes and reached for something on the top. When he turned back to Iris, he held out several white flowers to her.

"Oh." She took them and without even thinking held the flowers up to her nose. The scent was sweet, almost heady. "I didn't even know those were there."

"When plants get the proper care, they'll bloom more often," Talon said with a grin.

Iris blushed and was glad he probably couldn't see the color of her cheeks. But she couldn't help but wish he wasn't talking about plants.

Chapter 13

"What are these?" Quince had already pulled a flower out of the vase (the same one she'd planned to defend herself with before Talon collapsed in her side yard) and gave it a big whiff. To avoid any questioning from her sisters, Iris had managed to sneak it and the bouquet Talon had picked for her the night before into her room.

Iris rolled over to get a better look at the familiar perched on her side table. The flower in his paw was nearly his size. "Apparently we have those out back."

Quince chewed a petal, then pursed his little lips. "Well, I've always known we had those scraggly rose bushes, but why do you? Unless a flower is poisonous or good for a spell, you've never seemed that interested."

"Talon pruned them last night," Iris admitted and pulled the blanket over her head, hoping it might block the sound of Quince's voice. She made a mental note to find a spell that could do that on demand.

"*Talon* gave you these?" The hedgehog's voice raised in pitch, and he jumped onto the bed then picked up the cover to get a look at Iris. "You sure there's nothing going on there between you two?"

Unwilling to respond to the question (since she didn't want to know the answer herself) and tired from another night of tossing and turning, Iris didn't say anything. Instead, she rolled over to avoid blurting something she might regret.

Undeterred, Quince grabbed the top of the blanket and began to pull it off Iris. As quickly as possible, Iris attempted to yank it back, but the familiar already had it halfway off her face and had crawled up on her neck.

"No one has *ever* given you flowers before." Quince's normally beady eyes were wide as he stared at Iris.

She didn't exactly like the painful reminder, but she hadn't wanted flowers before either. "I should have just tossed them."

"But you didn't," Quince said. "Are you thinking of keeping him around?" His voice trilled with excitement as he rubbed his paws together.

Yes... No! Iris only scoffed.

"What did Dahlia and Poppy say?"

"They didn't say anything," Iris answered, but her sisters hadn't actually seen the roses. Quince had already been curled up asleep on the bed, so he hadn't seen them until then either.

Confused, Quince tipped his head, but Iris refused to talk about it anymore, and she threw off the covers, completely covering the hedgehog in them. She scooched to the other side of her bed and escaped his questioning.

But Quince was faster at unraveling himself than she expected. "And what happened to that phrase you say to yourself every morning when you get up? You haven't said it in days."

Love the life you live…and destroy those who get in your way came to the forefront of her mind. Iris flipped around to Quince. "You looking for me to destroy *you*?" But she also knew she'd been too distracted the last few days. She hated it when the familiar was right.

Obviously annoyed, but not taking her threat too seriously, the hedgehog perched up on his back legs and crossed his arms over his chest. "Just making sure you're okay. It's kind of my job."

Iris held out her hand and called magic into it. A weak shimmer popped and fizzled, then extinguished. "Do I look okay?"

Quince dropped his stance and fell onto all fours, not saying anything for once.

Frustrated with both the situation and herself, Iris hurried to the neat stack of fresh clothes on top of her dresser that she hadn't put away. Jaw tight, she riffled through and found what she wanted, wriggled from her nightdress, then tossed it onto the bed to pull on her fresh blouse and skirt. Somehow they both smelled like lilacs, but she pushed the thought aside. Afterward she brushed and pulled her hair into long bunches on the sides of her face and secured them with twine. She tucked in the one piece that didn't want to stay behind her ear.

"Good enough." Iris caught sight of herself in the mirror and then reached down to gather and pull on her boots. There was no way she was getting caught without them again.

"You'll get this fixed," Quince finally said and hopped off the bed to follow her out the door. "We've always made it through in the past."

Iris twisted to the hedgehog. He had concern pulling at his little features. She both expected her familiar to be supportive and hated it at the same time, but she muttered, "I hope so."

It wasn't like Iris to be *so* unsure of herself. She'd worked for years to get past any insecurities, but some days took a bit more effort. And these last few days were no exception. It wasn't her fault a curse had been cast on them, but knowing that didn't make it any easier. Old wounds had a way of festering when one ignored them.

"Morning, sleepyhead," Dahlia said, sarcasm in her tone the second Iris walked into the living room. She already had books spread out on the dining table and floor while scrawling notes into her journal. Ursula lay asleep on one of the chairs in front of the unlit fireplace.

"No one said I needed to be up at the crack of dawn," Iris said as she breezed past her sister toward the kitchen, trying to sound confident. The clean window revealed that the morning had brought on another cloudless day. The sun shone brightly, casting rays across the living room almost like a kaleidoscope projecting on the ceiling and walls. A rainy day would have made everything easier. Put her mood at ease.

Poppy had pushed a stack of books away from her and sat eating a plate of pancakes slathered with creamy butter and syrup. "Oh, Dahlia's just crabby because she hasn't eaten yet." Oberon sat perched on her shoulder, and Poppy held up a bite of pancake on her fork toward the raven's beak. He quickly snatched the sticky morsel and downed the bite in one swallow, making smacking sounds with his beak.

"You'd be crabby too if you had to fight a bird for the blankets all night," Dahlia said, not looking up from her notebook.

Oberon let out an annoyed squawk toward Dahlia and puffed out his wings.

"He couldn't help it," Poppy insisted. "He was cold."

Renewed annoyance at her sisters built in Iris's middle as she made it to the kitchen, where Talon once again stood over the black stove and flipped a pancake with a wooden spatula in the cast-iron skillet.

Seeing him there relaxed her nerves.

On the counter was a waiting vessel of syrup...at least it looked like syrup, judging by the brown sticky liquid trailing down the side of it and onto the wood. Beside it was another bouquet of roses inside a vase. There had to be at least a dozen flowers, and Iris couldn't believe she'd never really noticed them before.

"Hungry?" Talon asked.

At his question, Iris's heart and stomach fluttered. But before she answered, Quince had already scurried up his stairs onto the counter, held out his little paws, and said, "Yes!"

Talon grinned and turned out the latest pancake, which was entirely too big for Quince, into his open arms. Even so, the little hedgehog grasped it with two paws, fell over backward onto his rear, and took a bite. Then he ripped a piece off and swiped it through the syrup pool on the counter.

"I haven't had pancakes in years," Iris said, picking up a waiting plate and moving over next to Talon, where he had a stack ready to eat. They smelled so good that she nearly forgot about her responsibilities waiting in the other room. And before she knew it Iris had piled the pancakes four high and covered them with butter and syrup.

"I'm so glad you like them," Talon said as he poured the batter, forming another pancake in the skillet. His eyes crinkled at the corners.

Iris's chest warmed at the sight of his expression, and magic heated in the center of her palms. She shivered and the sensation quickly disappeared. With a wrinkle of her nose she held out her hand and focused, trying to ignite the magic again…but nothing. "I haven't tasted them yet," she managed before she cut off a thick slice with the edge of her fork. But they were going to be good. And a pleasant distraction from her frustration over her magic.

And indeed they were. The scent of buttery vanilla wafted into her nose, and then, as she placed the bite in her mouth, the strong taste of maple overtook her taste buds. The pancakes were the lightest and fluffiest she'd ever had. Iris's eyes fell closed as she savored her breakfast, wishing it would never end.

The experience was nearly magical.

"I've got to meet your mother," she said as she swallowed.

Talon let out a chuckle as he wiped the cast-iron skillet clean. "She makes a mean pancake. And I think she'd like you."

"She would?" Iris asked, surprised.

Talon straightened his shoulders. "Yeah, I'm pretty sure she would."

With a gulp, Iris stuffed another morsel into her mouth, not sure what to think or say about his comment. Part of her wanted to be liked by his mother…but Iris was not a good person…so… Did she want to be a good person for someone like Talon? She quickly cast the horrible question out of her mind like a dirty old rag. Of course she didn't want to be good. Did she? Ugh. She cursed herself under her breath.

Still on the counter, Quince watched the exchange while rolling a dried beetle up in a pancake. He took a crispy bite. "Even better," he declared with a toothy grin.

Iris winced from the crunch but was most definitely glad for the diversion and the chance to dig into her own plate for a second round. Thankfully, hers was sans beetle and as good as the first, and while she was reveling in it, Talon pushed over a cup of tea he'd poured for her.

"Cream?" he asked.

Iris nodded, with her mouth full of pancake. "Yes, please. No sugar."

The orc obliged and poured a generous amount of cream from the cow-shaped container, but before Iris had a chance to enjoy a sip, Dahlia called from the living room.

"You know we don't have all day for pancakes," she said. "This is kind of a life-or-death situation."

"We kind of *do* have all day," Poppy answered. "And no one has died...not yet, anyway."

That last part made Iris cringe. Talon had died...

After a sip of her tea, Iris sighed, looked up to Talon, and kept her voice down. "I guess I have to do this." She also noticed a basket on the end of the counter on the other side of him but didn't ask about it.

Talon shrugged. "Looks that way." He gave her a soft smile. "You'll figure out how to fix your magic."

Iris chewed her lip. She'd avoided talking to Talon about the topic, but it was impossible for him not to see with his own eyes what was going on. Possibly his brain wasn't as damaged as she thought. "Thanks." Iris allowed a deep inhale to settle into her lungs while Talon bowed his head and resumed cleaning up the breakfast spread.

"Hey!" Quince said to Talon as he polished off the last of his beetle-pancake roll-up. "I'm not finished."

"Sorry," Talon said and put the stack of pancakes back down in front of him.

"Oh, I think you are finished." Iris had already noticed his overfilled belly and balked at the thought of the hedgehog complaining to her later about his tummyache. Avoiding his quills as much as possible, she carefully plucked her familiar from the counter and plopped him onto the ground.

"Rude," Quince complained, then looked toward Talon while holding his paw up to the side of his mouth. "I'll be back when she's not looking."

Iris shook her head. "I can hear you, you know."

The hedgehog shot her a quick grin.

"He will *not* be back," Iris insisted and, taking her plate, turned to walk to her sisters.

"I will," Quince whispered.

Iris turned back around and insisted. "You won't."

"She's the boss," Talon stated and raised his hands, palms up.

Something in her stirred, enjoying the entire ridiculous exchange, but after an eye roll, Iris made her way to the table again.

From behind, Quince groaned like a disappointed teenager, but Iris heard his little feet scampering along behind her.

Holding her plate and tea, Iris took her seat across from Poppy, who was finishing her last bite of pancake. Dahlia was still frantically taking notes, and Ursula had moved from the chair to the floor, splaying out her striped body across two open books. Oberon cawed and flapped his wings while still on Poppy's shoulder.

"I gave you half," she complained to her familiar. "I'm sure there's more in the kitchen."

But the raven didn't budge, and Iris didn't mention Talon cleaning everything up. Instead she grabbed a book off the stack on the table, without even looking at the title, and opened it.

"Do you mind?" Dahlia stopped writing to say to her familiar.

"Not at all." The cat stretched and flicked her tail over a third book. "I'm helping."

Dahlia scoffed. "You aren't."

Attempting to focus with all the chaos around her, Iris slid her plate and steaming drink onto the table and plugged her ears with her fingers (not that she would be able to eat or take notes in that position). Even so, she dragged her attention to the pages in front of her, but as soon as she did, Quince pulled at the hem of her skirt, asking to come up. Sighing, she quickly reached down, carefully grasped him, and placed him on the table.

He scurried over to the stack of books and flopped down beside them, leaning his back against the closed pages. He rubbed his paws over his extended belly and then opened his mouth to speak, but Iris cut him off.

"Don't you dare tell me it hurts," Iris warned.

Squinting, Quince closed his mouth, then sucked his teeth.

Iris returned to her book and unplugged one ear. She cut and took another bite of her pancake stack, and while it was still incredible, the words on the pages in front of her seemed to jumble as Dahlia said something to Poppy and they started bickering again.

The whole thing set Iris's teeth on edge. What they were doing was important, and they needed to figure out a solution sooner instead of later. Plus, it meant her sisters would leave.

But she couldn't get anything done here.

"I'm going to take this elsewhere." Chest vibrating, Iris stood and in doing so pushed her seat back, the legs scraping the wooden floors. "There's something I need to do."

"More important than this?" Poppy asked, her forehead wrinkled.

"What do you mean, 'elsewhere'?" Dahlia faced her sisters and paused her note-taking again.

Iris closed her book and gathered two others off the stack without even looking at them. "Just what I said. I can't think around here."

"I don't have a problem thinking." Poppy said.

Agitated, Iris had things she wanted to say to that but held them inside her brain. Instead she pushed her stray hair out of her face and gave a smile that didn't extend to her eyes. "Then you should stay. I'll be back later."

"Can I go too?" Quince asked while getting up.

But she didn't want him tagging along either.

"It's your job to watch the place," Iris said, leaving her

teacup behind but piling the plate of unfinished pancakes on top of her books, then turning for the kitchen. She didn't even really know where she was headed, but *anywhere* was better than her suddenly extremely cramped cottage.

"Please?" he whined and hopped onto the chair, then the floor.

She didn't look back but said, "You can have the rest of these." Iris tossed the plate onto the kitchen counter to distract the hedgehog.

"Really?" Quince ran up his stairs to the counter and started nibbling on the pancakes. His tummyache was a problem for later.

Behind him, Talon had finished the dishes and was wiping his hands on a dishcloth. The sight of the orc gave Iris an idea. Her excuse for an escape, not to mention it would give Talon the chance to do what he'd asked.

"I'm going into town," Iris shouted. "Talon has to meet a…friend, and I can study these while he's busy." She was pretty sure she'd be able to find a quiet corner at the inn.

"Talon has friends?" Poppy asked. "I thought he just moved to Fraywell."

Talon's head tipped in question but he said nothing.

"Come on," Iris said and hiked up the books in her arms. "Before I change my mind." But she wasn't going to.

Talon grabbed the basket behind him and squeezed out the back door behind Iris.

"Get back here! You have responsibilities," Dahlia called in a huff before it shut, but Iris didn't slow down.

Chapter 14

By the time they'd made it into Fraywell, exhilaration moved through Iris's veins like a flash flood. She'd been chattering the entire time, with Talon mostly listening. But what she'd been talking about, Iris barely even remembered, except that she had shared what she knew about her magic malfunction.

And doing that felt good. Having someone other than Quince to talk to was, well, nice. *Talon* was nice to have around.

Despite the sunny morning, she'd actually enjoyed the trip into town. In all honesty, being tortured in a dungeon probably would have been preferable to staying back at the cottage with her sisters, so maybe that had something to do with it.

She was never going to get anything done with them around. And maybe she liked Talon's company.

Finally she glanced over at the orc and really noticed the basket he'd been toting the entire way, as well as the books he'd taken from her hands when they were barely past Kate's cottage. Luckily she hadn't been outside tending to her garden yet that morning.

"What did you bring?" Iris asked as they followed the street to The Boar's Head, doing her best to ignore any villagers.

Talon dropped his attention down to his arm. "Oh, this?" He raised the basket slightly but didn't answer the question.

"Yeah," Iris said. "That."

He lowered it again. "I brought some...samples for Lysander."

Iris scrunched her brows with suspicion while most of the good feeling she'd had shriveled. "Samples?"

A half grin tipped the side of Talon's mouth as if he was trying to avoid saying something, but he did anyway. "After I finished with the gardening last night and all of you had finally gone to bed, I still couldn't sleep. So I baked a few things."

"For *Lysander*?" Iris raised one brow into a perfect arch.

"Yes?" Talon answered as he adjusted Iris's books to his other side.

Iris paused walking and planted her hand on her hip. "But we weren't coming into town."

Talon clicked his tongue. "After I saw you escape your

sisters last night, I figured you might want to this morning too." He wrinkled his nose in innocence.

Truthfully, Iris couldn't help but notice it was a fairly cute nose. Slightly round at the tip, and it somehow suited his face.

After a moment he continued, "And if you didn't, I'd serve them up back at the cottage to you and your sisters."

Iris didn't know if she appreciated Talon reading her so well. Was she that transparent? Without a response, and slightly annoyed with herself she'd even noticed his nose, she started walking again, and Talon followed. But she crossed her arms over her chest to block out the world around her.

With a couple of streets to the inn to go, they passed the market, which seemed extra busy to Iris and reminded her a little too much of the scene back at her house. The muscles in her neck tensed. And after all the excitement, she realized she was tired.

"Are you mad at me?" Talon finally asked as the inn came into sight.

The question tensed in her chest. "It's fine," Iris answered and picked up her pace, not really wanting to talk about it. "I needed to get out of the house. You wanted to help Lysander. We both win."

A moment later they were outside The Boar's Head, and Iris hurried to open the door for Talon, who had his hands full.

"Thanks," he said. Iris wasn't entirely sure if it was for holding the door or inviting him to come along.

"You're welcome," she answered to either of the possibilities.

"Greetings, travelers," Lysander said and stood from the seat behind the registration desk, although he wasn't looking their way. His voice swung fairly glum until he gazed up at them and his expression lit up. "Talon?" He bowed his head a tad when he saw Iris. "I wasn't expecting either of you."

Iris cleared her throat, then spoke. "Yesterday, you mentioned needing help with your menu." She held her empty arms out to Talon for the books. "And I needed a quiet place to study since I have...guests." She really wanted to add the word *annoying* in there, but she held that part back.

Talon handed over the stack.

"Well," the elf said in a dry tone, "if you wanted quiet, you came to the right place." He raised his hand and gestured at the empty room.

Iris twisted her lips. A twinge vibrated inside her, and although she didn't want to admit it, she felt bad for the Quicklys. And it wasn't *just* for the possibility of losing the place where she occasionally stopped in to eat and pick up potion business. She actually might have sympathized with their plight... She wasn't entirely sure, since the sentiment was a little unfamiliar.

She shook her head. It wasn't like her.

"I brought some samples to try," Talon said as he held up the basket.

Lysander's breath hitched, and he stood and came out from behind the desk. "Samples, you say?"

"What's going on in here?" Herman came through an

open door behind the desk. "I thought I heard—" His gaze landed on Iris, and the skin between his brow wrinkled. "I thought that was your voice, Iris."

Her neck muscles throbbed, and she held up the books to distract herself from the irritation. "I have research to do. Talon's here to help with your menu."

"Oh." The innkeeper's attention flicked to his husband, then to Talon. "We're most grateful. Lys mentioned your suggestions, and the cook gave them a try. The stew was much better."

Talon's lips formed a wide grin, and delight nearly radiated off his body.

Without asking, Lysander lifted the top and peeked into the basket. "Those look *wonderful*. I can't wait to try them!"

Iris still couldn't see what was inside, but asking seemed silly.

The elf clapped his hands together, looking much more invigorated than when they'd walked in. "See, Hermy?" He unhooked the basket from Talon's arm and brought it over to Herman to show him.

The bald man tipped his head and nodded. "I'm expecting you to save one of those for me."

"Of course, dear," Lysander leaned in, pecked the man on the cheek, then handed the basket back to Talon.

Iris's curiosity was piqued, and she wished she'd looked inside the basket before they'd arrived. But she declined to appear too interested. "You think I can study in there?" Iris indicated to the closed door leading into the tavern.

Lysander's hands were clasped together at chest height as if he were about to sing some kind of aria. "If you promise to let Talon come back, you can study anywhere you want in here."

"Let's not get carried away," Herman said dryly while eyeing his elf husband. "But yes, the tavern is fine."

Iris hiked up the heavy books dragging at her arms and looked at Talon. "See you in a few hours. Don't want to leave my sisters alone for too long."

"Good luck with the studies," the orc said to Iris.

"Okay, no more dillydallying." Lysander piped before Iris could answer and pulled the orc through the door behind the desk. "I can't wait to try the..."

But Iris still, unfortunately, didn't catch what might have been in the basket before the door shut with a *thunk* behind them.

"I'll be here," Herman said and unlocked the tavern door, then planted himself in the registration desk chair.

As soon as he sat, Iris hurried into the tavern. When the door swung shut behind her she stopped and looked around. There were several windows near the ceiling letting in some light, and her vision quickly adjusted. The place was, of course, completely empty. But she'd never seen it in that state before. Round wooden tables and chairs were dispersed around the room, and the bar was positioned ahead of her. The dark walls gave the place a moody atmosphere she appreciated, and the smell of stale food and drink permeated her nose. That, paired with the quiet, instantly calmed her.

"Finally," she said out loud. "I'll be able to think." In seconds her interest moved to her favorite corner booth. She walked to the familiar spot and slid onto the bench against the wall.

Carefully Iris slid the books and journal with her pencil inside onto the table. She leaned her back against the wall and scanned the titles. *A Codex of Non-Magical Gardening*, *The Proper Care of Wands and Broomsticks*, and *A Midsummer's Guide to Enchantment*.

Iris sighed. "Gardening?" Why hadn't she looked at the books before she'd left? Surely she'd have made better choices. Then she remembered the commotion back at her cottage. That was why.

A Midsummer's Guide might have something, though. It was a beginner book from childhood, but the spells inside were solid. Plus, she'd have time to go over the notes she'd already taken. It wouldn't be a complete waste of time. Iris opened the notebook to get to work.

But then a glass filled with amber liquid glided across the table in front of Iris, and she looked up to see Herman standing in front of her.

How did he get in there without Iris hearing him? She really was off her game.

"You looked like you could use this again," the innkeeper said as he studied the titles of the books and raised a brow.

"It's barely past breakfast." Iris sat up and quickly closed her notes. But she was most definitely considering the contents of the glass.

Herman shrugged. "Didn't bother you last time. But your choice. No judgment either way." And then the man spun on his heel and walked out of the otherwise empty tavern, leaving Iris alone again.

She kept her focus on the door, half expecting him to come back, but he didn't. After a few blinks Iris leaned back to the wall again and made herself comfortable and reopened her notebook. She reached out for the drink, grasped it, and brought it to her lips. The liquid warmed her tongue and only briefly burned before the sip trickled down the back of her throat. It was the same whiskey he'd given her the last time she was at the Boar.

Iris considered Herman. Why was he being so kind to her? The man had to be aware of exactly who and what she was, but it didn't seem that he was afraid of her or hoped to impress her in any way. She shook her head, uncertain of what to do with that information. Before doing anything else, Iris kneaded her neck and shoulder, particularly one stubborn knot she couldn't work out, and she decided to focus on her drink.

She randomly flipped open *A Midsummer's Guide to Enchantment* and gazed at the page. The first line of the spell read, "Sisters, sisters, come one, come all."

Without her permission, her stomach flopped. It was the first spell she and her sisters had ever completed together… binding them as lifelong best friends. It had been so long ago, and she'd nearly forgotten about it.

Without thinking, she found her hand copying the spell

into her notebook, word for word. When she was done, she doodled a little art of the three of them as children around a cauldron. It wasn't very good. Iris gazed down at the page, dropped her pen, and ran her fingers over the pencil marks, smudging the words. There was a part of her that missed the days when she and her sisters were close. She thought what had happened to her father had been too much for them all.

All the good that spell had done them then. Iris gulped and took another sip of whiskey. Then another.

Before she knew it, Iris was leaning on one hand and downing the last drop of whiskey, wanting another pour, but she had no intention of heading out of the empty tavern to ask for one.

She gazed down at the notes, and all the words and illustrations she'd made started to move in a twirling pattern, then danced on the page.

Iris shook her head. She really needed some uninterrupted sleep.

And before long, her eyelids drooped and she was getting some.

Laughter and the rumble of people chatting woke her. Iris's eyes flickered open and she found her face smashed directly onto her notes. She gulped and sat up, and the pencil came with her, stuck to her cheek. Iris blinked several times while she worked to peel off the pencil and then plopped it back into the spine of her notebook.

Mouth as dry as a desert, Iris turned her attention to the sadly empty glass in front of her and to the notes, which she hadn't expanded on at all. On the page was the childish spell.

Again voices came from outside the tavern door. Something was afoot in the inn's foyer. How was she supposed to get anything done?

With a scoff, she ran her hands over her hair and found it still mostly in the two bunches under her ears she'd fastened them in after she'd woken. Iris worked up a good scowl on her lips, slid out of her seat and marched her way over to the open door, and flung it open, ready to tell anyone out there to pipe down.

But nothing came from her mouth when she found at least a dozen new people, not including Lysander and Herman, from the town inside crowding the foyer and the door slammed behind her. Iris reached for the handle, but it was locked.

"Snails," she groaned under her breath.

Lysander held out a tray with bite-size samples of food with picks stuck in the middle. A man wearing a knitted cap picked one up and tasted it. By the delight in his eyes, the sample was apparently tasty.

No one even noticed her. Which was both good and terrible at the same time.

Frozen, Iris looked quickly around the room for Talon,

but he wasn't there. Instead, more laughter came from a group in the corner, standing by the unlit fireplace.

"Will you be open for lunch today?" A tall man with dark, curly hair asked Herman, who sat behind the desk munching on an assortment of samples laid out on a small plate. Even he was too engrossed in trying the food to notice Iris.

"Oh," he said. "We hadn't planned to, but I think we can serve dinner." His eyes caught Lysander's.

"Yes, yes," said the elf. "I'm headed to the market soon for more supplies."

Behind all the commotion, Talon appeared from the door with another wooden tray filled with tiny chocolate cupcakes.

Lysander quickly handed his own tray to a random halfling—who stuffed three sandwiches in their mouth—and said, "And the finale!" The crowd made a beeline for the orc.

Talon gave a shy grin and passed the tray to Lysander. But his attention zipped to Iris, and a look of concern for her tensed his features.

Iris's mind whirled, but her feet felt as if they'd been turned to brick.

"Ah, Talon. He's brought the most amazing dessert with him this morning!" Lysander said while holding up the tray.

Cupcakes. That's what Talon had brought from the cottage.

Eyes lit up all over the room, and the crowd gathered around the elf, still completely oblivious to Iris's presence.

"Is this your new cook?" a medium-height elf with sepia skin asked and latched on to Talon's arm.

Towering over everyone, Talon waved his free hand in the air. "Just helping out." But he sounded distracted. Then he looked back at Iris.

"He's being modest," Lysander said with a click of his tongue.

"Well, these are amazing," a stout human woman with chubby cheeks said. "You'll be serving them tonight, right?"

Nodding to the elf holding his arm, Talon gently pulled away from him. The orc made a beeline over to Herman and asked him something. Talon's expression was down turned with concern.

Iris internally scolded herself for not walking over and asking Herman to open the door, but her feet still seemed to be nailed to the floor.

"I think I saw that orc at the market yesterday," the chubby-cheeked woman whispered, nabbing a cupcake from the tray and popping it into her mouth.

Beyond her, Herman took something from his pocket and tucked it into Talon's palm. Then he pointed Iris's way.

Afraid to be seen, she ducked behind a large potted plant next to the tavern door.

"He's Iris Weyward's new bodyguard, Talon," Lysander said.

"Really?" a dwarf with a long, red, braided beard said, still not even noticing Iris was steps from them. "The *witch* outside town?"

"Yeah," a woman said, turned toward Iris, and pointed at her. *So much for my foliage camouflage*, Iris thought.

Her neck tensed again. She couldn't tell by their tone of voice how they felt about the fact she was there. But so much joy and excitement even slightly connected to her was not the reputation she was going for. She needed the people of Fraywell to take her more seriously. To save face, she started to give them her best sneer, and the human and dwarf recoiled.

"Oh my," the dwarf said, drawing her hand to her mouth.

But before she said anything else, Talon stepped between Iris and the human woman. The orc bared his teeth, and a half-respectable growl came from his mouth, reverberating around the inn's foyer.

Iris's pulse quickened, and the two patrons backed up.

In seconds, Talon had unlocked the door to the tavern, opened it, and pulled Iris from her terrible hiding place and out through the door. He closed it directly behind her.

"What's going on?" Iris managed, all the while processing that Talon had *actually* done his job.

Talon bit his lip. "That whole thing got a bit out of hand."

"You think?" Iris said, vulnerability seeping through her body. "This was supposed to be a quiet one-time thing."

"I know, I know. I should have been growling at *all* those people the entire time," Talon said, entirely sincere.

Iris let out an unexpected giggle, caught off guard by his statement. "Yes, you should have." Her insides were flipping and flopping. First, due to what had happened and then, second, because Talon had changed in her mind. She should have been angry at him, but she wasn't.

And then something else happened. Talon tipped his head and reached out to her.

Oh, snails. What is he doing? The thought ran through her mind as giddiness bubbled into her chest.

His fingertips gently brushed her cheek, and she shivered at the touch.

"You've got a little something right there," he said, keeping his voice low.

Iris's eyes widened and she took a step back. Her hand flew to her face. "What is it?"

Talon leaned in closer as if to get a better view. "It says *Sisters, sisters—*"

"Oh, snails." Iris gulped and quickly rubbed her face. She'd been out in the foyer with part of a spell inked on her cheek. "Is it gone?"

Talon bobbed his head. "Yep. All gone."

Even so, Iris felt completely ridiculous, and only a portion of that was Talon's doing. She was to blame for the rest of it. She needed to get it together.

"You look good," he said and smiled.

Just seeing and hearing that made her feel a squinch better, but her mind was off with the stars. She cleared her throat. "Thanks, but I really need to leave."

"Oh, Herman told me there's a back exit," he said, pointing past her. "We can take it without going through all those people."

As ridiculous as it was, considering they hadn't even known each other for more than a few days, Iris realized at that moment that Talon saw her. No matter if he remembered who he truly was, she needed to keep him around.

And yes. Even more growling and grunting were necessary if this would work. But he was getting there.

Iris Weyward would not be re-unaliving Talon Gefroy.

She liked him too much.

Chapter 15

Iris wanted to tell Talon the good news right away…not the part where she'd originally planned to re-unalive him, of course, since that would be rude, but that he could stay on as a permanent employee.

(Not to mention she wasn't entirely sure she could have gone through with it anyway. But moving on…)

Excitement buzzing in her chest, Iris opened her mouth to let him know, but after he picked up her books from the table and grabbed her hand, her mind immediately turned to mush.

After that, all she could really think about was how good his grasp felt in hers. His warm skin, the pressure, the light calluses, likely from weapon use. Even more, for once in a long time Iris actually felt safe to trust someone other than herself or Quince.

In the course of a second, her thoughts shifted to a dreamland where the current curse was broken. Her sisters had left and gone home, and it was just her, Talon, and Quince. She'd prepare potions and cast hexes on deserving troublemakers (like pretty much everyone who'd been in the foyer) while Talon made her a cup of tea, gave her a back rub, and helped her work on eventual realm domination.

The perfect scenario.

At some point, though, she might actually have to tell him about her original plans for him. It seemed the honest thing to do.

"Let's go," Talon said, only partially snapping Iris from her thoughts.

"Oh, okay," Iris managed, her pulse beating fast as she continued to wish she had time to finish out the daydream. She was glad Talon couldn't actually read her mind, but she remembered her neck ache and wished he might.

Just as she drew her free hand up to the sore spot, Talon yanked her forward and they made it out the back door into the alley. The surrounding buildings on each side shaded the space, casting shadows even though it couldn't be much later than the lunch hour.

At the realization and despite the smell of sour garbage in the alley, Iris's belly rumbled, and the sound finally brought her completely back to the present. Talon didn't seem to notice the noise, but at that moment, she regretted having given Quince the rest of her pancakes that morning…even if it did get them out of the cottage.

"That way, I think," she said and pointed to her right, but both Herman and Lysander rounded the corner before she and Talon got far.

The orc whipped his attention their way, growling and baring his teeth at the couple.

Iris was immediately impressed.

Undeterred, Herman gestured to Talon and continued toward them. "I really am sorry about all that," he said, huffing and puffing as if they'd rushed. After a blink, he turned his attention on his elf husband and gave him a scolding look.

By that time, the orc had stopped snarling but kept a partial scowl in their direction.

Lysander gritted his teeth. "Don't look at me like that," he said. "You got a little carried away too."

"Those sandwiches *were* really good," Herman admitted, rubbing his belly. "I could go for another."

Talon relaxed his stance and clasped his hands together, seeming more interested in the conversation.

Lysander nodded enthusiastically, and as if they'd forgotten why they were even in the alley. "Someone back there said they were the best they'd ever had in the entire Veronian Region."

"What is it you want?" Iris finally asked, hoping the men would get to the point soon. Impatiently, she shifted her feet. She and Talon really should have gotten going already.

But Talon's scowl completely melted, and the edges of his lips turned up while he rubbed his palms together excitedly. "I *told* you the melted cheese and creamy garlic spread would be perfect with the sliced roast beef."

"And the thin-sliced rye?" Herman brought his pinched fingers to his lips and gave them a kiss.

Annoyance set in as the three of them remained engrossed in the social gathering she'd escaped from. That said, and against her will, Iris's mouth watered from the talk of food. For a second, she almost wished she'd walked up and grabbed one of those mini sandwiches off a tray. She should have snatched the whole thing and run off with it… *That* would have been the most beneficial *and* wicked thing to do if she'd been in her right mind. Then there were the cupcakes. They were likely yummy too, since everything Talon made was.

Her stomach growled again, and Lysander's eyes shot to her.

Iris eased backward and right into Talon. "What? It's lunchtime." They *really* needed to go.

The elf cleared his throat as if the sound had snapped him out of his state. "You were kind enough to bring Talon to the inn to help us. We should have at least told you not to come out of the tavern until everyone was gone. We were too caught up in it all." He held out his slender hand with slightly pointed nails. "Please accept our apologies. We are well aware you like your privacy."

Iris froze, completely caught up in one word the elf had

said. *Kind.* She was kind. Her back muscles tightened, and tingling fizzed over her chest. Not only that, but Lysander also seemed to respect her feelings.

"We haven't seen people that excited over anything at The Boar's Head in..." Lysander turned his head in thought. "I'm not sure ever."

Part of Iris was really glad to hear that Talon had been helpful to them. She did actually like both Lysander and Herman...although she never actually wanted to admit that out loud. But something, a little voice in the back of her mind, compelled her to take his hand and quickly shake it. Instant regret drew her hand back as quickly as she'd offered it.

But he didn't seem to mind.

"Do you think you might have time to come around again?" Herman asked Talon, hope peppering the question.

Iris quickly shot her gaze to the orc, the pressure building in her chest. "I don't think he'll have time for a while. We've only just come out of our trial period. Talon has a lot of body guarding to do in the future."

The orc gasped. "You mean I have the job, permanently?"

"Yes," Iris said, holding back her impatience and grabbing his lower arm. "But we should go. Now."

Seemingly unable to read body language, Lysander clapped his hands, then reached up to pat Talon on the shoulder. "We're so happy to have you as a permanent resident of Fraywell." He slipped his arm around Herman's waist. "Aren't we, Hermy?"

"Me too," Talon said and placed his hand on top of Iris's and patted it.

Iris's focus trained on the spot while the skin underneath his touch tingled. What was happening?

"Either of you," Lysander said to both Talon and Iris. "Come in anytime for a free meal."

"Anytime?" Herman groaned at his partner, who sometimes seemed to be a little too freewheeling with his promises. But he might be protesting too much, since it was the human who'd given her the free whiskey more than once.

"Oh, Hermy." Lysander chuckled with mirth and swayed into Herman. "We like the edge you bring to the Boar, Iris." He leaned in close and lowered his voice as if he were telling her a secret even though everyone could still hear. "A little danger every now and again spices things up."

Herman elbowed his husband. "There you go again, running your mouth."

"You like it," the elf teased.

Herman only shrugged. But it was obvious his human spouse did indeed like it.

Once again, her emotions dithered between complete annoyance and genuine concern about the inn's fate. Iris's heart warmed at the goings-on…and she had no idea what to do with that fact.

"Ooh." Talon drew Iris's hand from his arm. "Getting a little toasty there."

Iris yanked her hand from his and turned it over. Her palm heated to a vivid red, but it quickly dissipated. She shook her head and immediately tried to conjure the heat into her palm again, but it didn't come. The curse was still in place. "We *really* do need to go."

"Yes, yes, but fair warning," Herman said and looked up at Talon. "Everyone inside the Boar left, since we ran out of the samples. But I think you gained a few admirers, so you might want to watch out on the streets."

Talon handed the key he'd dug from his pocket to the man. "Thanks for that. I also do have a few more ideas for your menu." He gazed down at Iris. "Seems I'll be pretty busy from here on out, but I might be able to write out some recipes for your cook."

"Oh," Lysander said, his eyes lively with genuine hope. "We'd be most grateful if you'd manage that."

Iris studied the elf's expression and couldn't help but get sucked in again. The words that came out of her mouth even surprised her. "He stays up all night. I'm sure he'll have time."

When had she ever been so accommodating without an ulterior motive?

"Fantastic!" Lysander said and gestured the way they'd come into the alley. "Then we'll see you soon."

"I don't know if I'd go that far." The words that were most definitely voiced in a joking manner slipped out of Iris's mouth, echoing what Herman had said earlier. What was wrong with her?

The innkeepers both chuckled.

Iris gazed around. Her chest and cheeks were warm, and she was not quite sure what to do. But luckily Talon placed his hand on her upper back and eased her forward and out of the alley, leaving Lysander and Herman behind.

"You have a knot right there." Talon pressed his index finger into the spot that had been bothering Iris earlier.

"Don't remind me," Iris said and rubbed at the spot again. But it was no use. Unless she rid herself of the stress currently in her life, the knot wasn't going anywhere either.

And the situation out on the street wasn't helping one bit. Since it was midday, it was crowded, and the cobblestone street was especially bumpy under her feet. Plus, she couldn't get out of her mind how unlike herself she'd been with Lysander and Herman back there in the alley.

Almost like a regular person…and not an evil witch at all.

The horror! She shuddered, but doing so hurt her neck again.

"Ouch," she said and drew her fingers up to the sore spot.

"We've got to do something about that," Talon said. "How are you supposed to work and get your magic sorted if you're in pain?"

Iris pursed her lips. "I'll manage." Normally she'd brew a potion to apply to it, but who knew how many tries it would take with her magic on the fritz? She didn't want to waste the ingredients until the curse had been broken.

But she had little time to think about it when a well-dressed halfling made a beeline for them, and Iris was pretty sure they were the same one from The Boar's Head foyer. The one taking more than their share of sandwich samples.

"Excuse me!" they shouted and stuck their hand up like they were summoning a horse-drawn cart for hire. "Mr. Orc."

Iris suddenly wished she'd bothered to grab a hooded cloak before she left the cottage that morning for better anonymity. But Talon would have needed a giant one as well, and she didn't have that. It was something to think about for the future though.

The halfling continued, "I wonder if you might be interested in a catering job? I'm hosting a party next week."

But Talon stuck his arm out and stopped the halfling. "I'll mind you to stay back," the orc let out in a halfhearted sneer.

The halfling stopped in their tracks and shut their mouth.

Without another word, Talon ushered Iris forward, but something compelled her to turn back to the halfling. "I'm sure The Boar's Head could help you." After the words came out she slapped her hand over her mouth. What was she saying? She didn't even like the guy!

"Do they even cater?" Talon asked as he kept her going.

"They do now," Iris answered as they escaped the halfling.

The two of them burst into laughter, but when an old woman looked their way, Iris wiped the smile from her face. She was still smiling on the inside, although she wasn't sure why.

Chapter 16

"So," Talon said, excitement in his tone as he carried Iris's books like a precious bundle down the street. "You really want to hire me for good? Your permanent bodyguard? Even after what just happened at The Boar's Head?"

The incident back there *had* been a problem, but Iris could see the potential in Talon. And *potential* was better than starting with someone brand-new. Beyond that, she didn't know if she might like some random troll or ogre bodyguard as much as she liked Talon. She and Jamy had never quite gotten along as well. Plus, he never took care of the house or made flaky pastries.

Perhaps it was a good thing that the ogre had left on holiday and never come back.

"I do." Iris gave him a soft smile, then quickly flattened her lips so as to not look *too* happy about her decision. But her stomach was doing those flip-flops again at the idea of getting to know each other better.

"We should celebrate then," Talon said, looking around the street as if trying to figure out their exact location.

"Celebrate?" Iris didn't exactly know what that might entail, and she really did need to get back to the cottage. Both her sisters were likely to be angry at her, though, since she hadn't actually done any work. So a diversion might not be such a bad idea.

But she didn't get to say any of that to Talon because he was already ushering her into an empty alleyway behind an old wool yarn shop called The Merry Skeins of Fraywell, which had stood empty for a few months.

"You wait here." He placed her books down and gestured to a wooden crate for Iris to sit on. "No one should bother you."

"I—" she barely got out before he cut her off.

"Give me a few," he said and held up a finger. "I'll be back." And with that he hurried off, leaving Iris in the alley.

Of course Iris had no idea what he was doing, but she went ahead and sat on the crate. It was a good time to take a few minutes to herself before facing her sisters, and the alley bothered her much less than a more public place (although alleys were never the freshest smelling, and this one was no exception).

Remembering her magic had come back outside the Boar, she first checked to make sure no one was around. She held out her hand and focused on it. After a moment, she closed her eyes and visualized her heat magic coalescing in her palm. Almost immediately, the magic tingled, and Iris watched as a small spot in the center of her palm changed from pink to orange to red. Staring down at it, she narrowed her brow and did her best to block out the world around her to grow the magic, but no matter how hard she tried it only dissolved, and her skin returned to its usual pink. She sighed, disappointed but not surprised. What had happened at the tavern had only been a glitch. Her expression drooped.

Moments later, heavy footsteps sounded, and she looked up to see Talon, who, unlike her, had a big goofy grin on his face. He also held a large paper bag in the crook of his arm.

"What have you got there?" Iris asked, pushing off her frustration. She couldn't fix her magic problem right then anyway, so she might as well focus on something else.

"A few things from the market," he said, clutching and crinkling the bag. "I know you have to get back to work. But you have to have lunch anyway, so I figured we'd get out of Fraywell and stop for a little picnic."

"A picnic?" Iris's brows raised. She couldn't remember the last time she'd been on a picnic. Or, for that matter, if she'd ever been on one.

Still holding the bag, the orc bent down and scooped up

Iris's books from the ground. "Yeah. It'll be fun. I have the perfect place for it."

Iris stood, wavering between befuddlement and interest. "Fun?"

But he'd already strolled from the alley and disappeared around the corner.

Iris gritted her teeth. Despite her questions about the whole thing, she followed him, and they quickly headed out of town.

"I enjoyed helping Lysander and their cook with the menu," Talon said while they walked along the dusty path. "It only took a few tweaks to what they were doing, and everything was so much better."

"About that," Iris said. After those townspeople had seen them at the inn, it wasn't a good idea for Talon to go back there and help out again…particularly now that he'd be representing her full-time. She started to say so, but Talon cut her off.

"He and Herman seem like friendly folks," Talon said.

Iris twisted her lips. After they'd offered her a place to study and Herman had given her free drinks twice, Iris couldn't really deny that fact. They *were* friendly folks.

But nice people weren't a regular part of Iris's existence.

Iris opened her mouth to mention it but considered the fact that *although* Talon was nice and he was growing on her, a lot, the thought set her teeth on edge.

"How about over there?" The orc pointed to a large dead tree that had fallen over not too far off the path. It was cracked in half, the lower part turned upside down and the roots reaching for the sky…kind of like the hand of a demon thrusting up through the earth. Perfectly horrifying. Next to it was part of the fallen tree, lying flat on the ground and making a suitable place for sitting.

Iris appreciated the suggestion. It was both creepy *and* inviting.

She looked up at the bright sun and held her hand up to shade her eyes.

"It would probably be more terrifying under the moon or on a drizzly day," Talon said. "But we take what we can get, right?"

Her mouth went dry. "How did you know?" Iris asked, bringing her attention back to Talon.

The orc's eyes crinkled at the corners. "I've seen the things that interest you." He lifted the books, as if to indicate them. "And I noticed this spot on the way into town this morning." He tipped his head to gesture toward the tree. "But you were talking, and I didn't have a chance to mention it. So I kept it right here for a later time." Talon tapped the edge of his forehead.

Strangely, on all her walks into town Iris had never noticed the tree before. But in truth, all of her trips into Fraywell had always been about pure function…getting food, stocking up on potion supplies, securing clients. Never about enjoying the scenery along the way. And definitely not about having a picnic or taking in the view. Get in and get out.

But her middle warmed at the idea that *Talon* had noticed it...and for *her*.

She trudged after him, and soon they were past the scraggy grass on the side of the path and at the tree. Once there, Iris admired the dead gray bark, running her hand over the rough surface.

"It's an old oak," she said. "I use the bark in my potions sometimes."

"Then we should bring some back to the cottage," Talon said as he pulled several items from the bag and placed them on the top of the fallen trunk. One of them was a tan woven basket of juicy, ripe red strawberries, and they looked absolutely incredible.

"Are we low?" Iris asked, remembering Talon had organized all her teas and potion ingredients.

"Mm-hmm," Talon said and pulled out a wedge of white cheese. "Scale of dragon is low too."

She rolled her eyes. Scale of dragon was expensive and hard to come by, but she couldn't quite get over Talon's attentiveness.

He placed the cheese on top of the empty bag he'd spread out on the trunk. "Sorry we don't have any plates."

Potion ingredients aside, Iris's stomach rumbled at the sight of the food. She hadn't realized quite how hungry she was until that moment. But looking up at the trunk, she noticed it was a little too tall for her just to hop up on.

"Need a lift?" Talon asked.

As soon as he asked, Iris struggled to gulp, since she had

already pictured his strong hands around her waist. Her attention immediately trained on them the moment he asked. "Um, sure," she barely got out.

Without hesitation, he extended his arms and wrapped his fingers around her, and Iris couldn't help reaching out for Talon's broad, muscular shoulders to steady herself. His skin under his shirt was warm. Too warm. Her breath hitched. "Oh," she said as he easily plucked Iris from the ground and gently placed her on the fallen tree trunk next to their picnic lunch.

Suddenly lightheaded, Iris tried to calm her buzzing nerves by checking out the food. A basket of ruby strawberries she'd already admired, the hard white cheese, seeded crackers, and some freshly sliced sausage with little specks of pepper inside of each piece. Aside from the food, there was also a small jug of cider with a cork on the top. Iris didn't care there weren't any utensils…or plates and cups, for that matter. The spread looked mouthwatering, and her stomach rumbled again.

"How'd you even buy this?" Iris was pretty sure Talon didn't have any coins on him when she'd brought him back from the dead, but she hadn't exactly checked his pockets.

Talon reached into his pocket and pulled out one copper coin. "Lysander wouldn't let me leave without something for my time in the kitchen. I told him no and that I did it as a favor. But the elf wouldn't hear it."

Iris brought her hand to her chest, moved not only that Lysander had paid Talon but also that the orc had gone and spent most of it on *her*...well, for both of them in celebration. She coughed nervously, completely unsure what to do with the new affectivity of someone doing something so... *nice* for her. It almost made her wonder what she could do for him. "Well. It looks amazing. Shall we dig in?"

Talon gave a nod and hoisted himself up onto the log. The action made quite a jostling motion under Iris, and the dead wood let out a mighty crack. But the log held.

"Ladies first," Talon said and motioned to the feast.

Iris was impressed by his manners and reached for the cheese. She broke it into several manageable pieces and placed one of them on a cracker, then topped it with a piece of sausage.

All the while she was keenly aware of Talon watching her every move. She didn't quite know if she liked it or didn't. So far the orc didn't seem to cast judgment on people. She certainly had made a spectacle of herself in front of him multiple times, and yet he still seemed to enjoy being around her. And Iris couldn't help but wonder what he was thinking.

When her creation was complete, she admired it for a second and then held it out to Talon. "Cheers." Then she took a bite. The savory concoction tasted like heaven... The slightly sharp cheese and peppery sausage popped on her taste buds, while the seeded cracker rounded out the flavors.

As she chewed, Talon opened the cider jug and passed it to Iris.

"Why not?" Iris chuckled and took a drink to wash down the rest of her bite.

Talon popped a piece of cheese into his mouth, then leaned back on his hand and turned his face up to the clear sky.

As he did, Iris chose a berry. She took it straight from the top of the basket, but it had to be one of the largest strawberries she'd ever seen. With anticipation, Iris bit into the fruit. The sweet tart juice filled her mouth, and she groaned, barely even noticing that a dribble of it had spilled down her chin until Talon was wiping it away.

Iris's eyes popped open, and her cheeks flushed. She retreated in embarrassment. It was the silly mark on her cheek all over again.

"You looked so lovely," Talon said in a slightly dreamy tone.

Iris sucked in a breath at his words as she held the half-eaten fruit in her fingers. "With strawberry juice on my face?" Nervously she finished it, barely tasted the strawberry going down.

"I'm sorry I startled you." The orc shook his head. "You were enjoying it so much."

Iris almost regretted her ability to let her guard down around Talon, but before she could even work through it he looked down and patted his pants pocket.

"I almost forgot." Talon said, light shining in his eyes. He drew out a small package wrapped in a piece of brown paper. "I hope it's not ruined." He slowly unwrapped the paper to reveal a tiny chocolate cupcake. The same one from back at the inn. Somehow the frosting swirl was still in a perfect miniature twist. "For you."

Shocked and completely forgetting about the strawberry juice incident, Iris looked up from the cupcake to Talon, then reached out and took it. She popped it into her mouth, and it was indeed the richest, most delectable thing she'd eaten in quite some time. The dark, rich chocolate enveloped her senses. It was even better than the other foods Talon had made.

"That's absolutely incredible," she said, fully meaning the compliment.

"Demon's food chocolate cake," Talon said.

And without thinking, Iris said, "You really know the way to a girl's heart, don't you?" All she could think about was kissing Talon… She'd worry about him being her employee later.

Then she leaned out over the picnic spread to him, but before anything actually happened, she placed her hand down on the log and directly into the cheese.

"Oh snails," she said, her pulse zipping with embarrassment at her mess. Had she nearly kissed Talon?

He chuckled, seemingly oblivious to the fact Iris's lips had nearly been on his, and reached for her hand. "That good, huh?"

Iris didn't answer, but she also didn't pull back from him as he turned her hand over, palm side up, to reveal the cheese completely melted and dripping onto the worn oak. And the skin underneath still burned a brilliant red.

Chapter 17

After Iris had explained to Talon why the melted cheese even mattered, they'd packed up the picnic and hurried all the way back to the cottage. Iris fully admitted the story sounded a bit ridiculous…that she'd accidentally melted cheese with her magic.

But it was a positive sign, at least, and Talon didn't seem to judge.

Had the spell been broken somehow? Iris's pulse raced the entire journey, and she couldn't wait to show her sisters. Hopefully they would go home.

The magic still ignited, Talon and Iris burst through the front door, both of them huffing and puffing.

"Oh." Poppy looked up from hunching over stacks of books at the table. "You're back."

Iris skidded to a stop and announced, "Something is going on with my magic."

"You think?" Dahlia sneered. "Ours is getting worse too." She flourished her hand in front of herself as if to conjure her water magic, but nothing happened...not even a dull aqua glimmer. She grumbled under her breath.

Iris's brow furrowed. "Worse? No. I thought maybe the two of you had done something while we were gone." She thrust her palm toward them and drew magic into the center, confident it would work again. But it was gone, and her skin was pale pink again. Iris turned to show Talon.

He shrugged. "I'm not a witch. I don't know anything about this stuff."

"If only you hadn't run off to snails-know-where with your cook." Dahlia wrinkled her nose at them and gave Talon a judgy once-over. But Iris didn't like the look one bit and instinctively stepped between her sister and the orc, fully willing to defend his honor if necessary.

"Oh, Dahlia," Poppy groaned. "You just wish you had a *cook* to take care of *your* business." She winked at Iris.

Iris's eyes widened as big as saucers. What did Poppy think Talon did for her? Although...yes. She had thought about it. "Talon is my *bodyguard*," she insisted, fully ignoring the memory of the failed kiss, and gazed back up at Talon. Her belly whirled at the sight of the handsome orc and she managed, "Who also happens…to cook. Nothing wrong with that."

Her younger sister eyed them for a second, then moved back to her book. Poppy's curly hair looked a fright, sticking up all over the place as if she'd been constantly running her fingers through it in frustration. Very unlike her. "*And* we haven't even had lunch."

With Talon right beside her, Iris stood there inside the doorway, entirely confused and deflated. And if the burning of her cheeks was any sign, embarrassed.

To make things a hundred times worse, Quince tore from the hall like a bat out of the underworld with Ursula hot on his tail.

The gray-striped cat yowled behind the little hedgehog, baring her sharp teeth. "You get back here, you paunchy swag-bellied rat!"

"Iris!" the hedgehog screeched and slid across the wooden floor, slamming directly into her boots and then flipping over, landing upside down and playing dead. His legs stuck straight in the air like an overturned turtle's.

Completely befuddled, although not entirely surprised by the situation she'd walked into, Iris bent to rescue her familiar from his expired position (he even had his tongue lolling out to complete the gruesome look). She glared at the brindle-fur cat, who only then sat and stared at the two of them.

Iris turned to Talon and crumpled her forehead. "It's not always like this."

"I'm not a rat!" Quince demanded and stuck out his little pink tongue at the feline while Iris held him in the air, doing her best to avoid his spines. "Or paunchy!"

"Could have fooled me," Ursula sneered from the floor. "Watch yourself," she threatened, then turned and sauntered back the way she came, as if nothing had ever happened.

The hedgehog turned his head back to Iris, and his pupils grew two sizes. "Don't leave me with them again," Quince pleaded in a whisper.

A sigh left Iris's mouth, and the reasons she'd left the cottage in such a hurry that morning came flooding back to her. "Were you insulting Ursula again?" The three familiars acted like siblings at their worst when together too long. Apparently barely three days was too long.

Iris could relate.

"No!" Quince's voice shot up in what was obviously faux offense. "Why would you even ask that?"

Dahlia raised a brow, shook her head, and looked back at the book in front of her. "He's been a menace all morning. Ursula is nothing but a sweet baby girl."

Iris had no doubt her older sister was being truthful about her hedgehog, and she did like Ursula most of the time, but nonetheless she shot Dahlia a glare of solidarity with Quince.

At a minimum that was Iris's duty.

She set him down on the floor, but the hedgehog didn't move.

"Snails, I'm famished," Poppy announced as she raked

her hand through her red curls. When she pulled it back, one tendril had a tiny flame on the end. She gasped and stood. "Oh, zounds!"

Dahlia, barely reacting, picked up the teacup in front of her and thrust the contents at her sister, immediately putting out the flame.

Poppy screeched, her chin, the bottom of her hair, and her shirt wet with tea. "What are you doing?"

"Putting out the flames," Dahlia said and tossed a cloth napkin from the table to her dampened sister. "Did you want your entire head to catch on fire?"

"No," Poppy said in a pout and dropped back into her seat. She dabbed at herself and her burned-off curl.

Talon groaned and handed Iris's books off to her. "I'll get something going in the kitchen. Everyone seems a little too hungry."

Quince rubbed his little paws together. "I have a few suggestions," he said to Talon and tailed the orc.

Iris gritted her teeth, but the stack of books sank heavily in her arm, and she quickly deposited them on the dining table, then plopped herself into the open chair between her sisters. "I know what happened to me." She lifted her hand up and tried conjuring again, but her palm remained its regular color.

"The magic seems to be in and out." Poppy picked up a slightly burned and wet tendril, then motioned to Iris. "I also burned Oberon's tail feathers by accident this morning after you left."

"But it worked before," Iris said out of desperation and turned to eye Talon, who she could just barely see already slicing bread in the kitchen. "All the way to the cottage."

"It did," Talon agreed without looking up. "I saw it."

Iris's lips twitched at the corners wanting to turn upward from his support, but she didn't dare around her sisters.

Without warning, Dahlia reached over to Iris and snapped up her hand. "Please share what exactly happened. Maybe it's different from Poppy being a danger to herself."

But at that point Iris realized that it probably wasn't. Even though she really didn't want to talk about it anymore, the morning's events rolled through her brain anyway... How she'd fallen asleep in the tavern and not actually gotten to any studying, then how Talon had impressed everyone in Fraywell with his cooking and baking skills, her embarrassing stint in the inn's foyer, how she'd actually been halfway cordial, if not downright nice to some of the people in town. Then the picnic...and the melted cheese. Not to mention hiring Talon full-time because of some connection she thought they might have after knowing the orc for less than three days...and the near-kiss.

Iris gritted her teeth. It all sounded completely ridiculous. As ludicrous as Poppy setting her own hair and Oberon's feathers on fire...like a curse had been cast on her. Which, of course, it had.

She cleared her throat and took a settling breath. "It's nothing. You're probably right and I was just getting my hopes up for no reason."

"Of course I'm right," Dahlia said and dropped Iris's hand onto the table with a thump, going right back to her work. "It's always up to *me* to fix these sorts of problems," she muttered.

"Hey!" Poppy piped up. "What am I? Chopped liver?" She withdrew in complete indignation.

Dahlia flipped the book page, not looking at her sister. "Yes. In fact, you are. Burned chopped liver."

Poppy scoffed and twisted in the chair away from her sister with a huff.

As Iris watched the exchange, she pulled her hands together onto her lap. At the current rate, two things were likely to happen. Either some darker force was going to find and end them all…or her sisters would never leave her home.

She wasn't sure which was worse.

"I think we should try again," Iris said out of desperation.

Dahlia slowly closed her book and brought her attention to Iris. "And what do you suppose we try again, my dearest sister?" Her tone was dry as unbuttered toast.

In an instant, Iris's mouth went dry as well, but she spoke through it. "The clarification spell."

"It didn't work," Dalia said. "And it made the situation worse. Are you looking to make *everything* worse? What are we all going to do if we completely lose our magic? Integrate into society…give up our goals and get jobs selling fruit at the market?"

Iris hadn't even thought of *that*. What would she do? She grimaced but ignored the last question. There were enough problems already. "Of course not. But you didn't wait for me. If this spell was cast on all three of us, then it makes sense that clarification wouldn't work if we didn't do it together."

"Our sister could be right," Poppy said, twisting her wet curl.

"You're just mad about the tea and taking her side," Dahlia growled and plunked her finger on the notes she'd taken sitting in front of her. "I've been coming at this from every angle, and nothing is working."

"You'd be mad about the tea too," Poppy said, crossing her arms over her chest. "If I threw it at your face."

Dahlia ignored her annoyed sister and trained her attention on Iris. "Look, we're not ready to try again. There has to be a different way to break the curse in one of these books. We need to find it." She narrowed her eyes at Iris and Poppy and then returned her gaze to her work.

Iris let out a huge sigh but said nothing. As prickly as Dahlia was, Iris suddenly saw right beyond the facade. Her sister was scared. Not only for herself but also for Iris and Poppy. She'd made the mistake of trying the clarification spell without Iris, and it had gone poorly. Admitting mistakes had forever been difficult for her older sister.

Dahlia was the oldest and had always protected them. She'd taken on the mother role, even when they were kids. And what kind of kid is great at that? Even if they want to be.

And now it was just the three of them. Their father was out of their lives, and all they had was his old books to guide them.

Trying to think of what to say next, Iris clasped her hands together and focused on them. For a brief second intense heat built between her palms. Excited, Iris pulled them apart, hoping for the magic inside, but whatever had been there was gone. She pursed her lips in frustration. "I don't want to argue. It's getting us nowhere."

"You're not the one getting tea thrown at you," Poppy complained and pulled at her still wet shirt.

"I was putting out a fire on your head, for snail's sake," Dahlia shot back. "Did you want your entire head to burn up?"

Frustration building in her chest, Iris scoffed and stood. The chair legs scraped across the wooden floor. "How about I get you something for that stain?" She turned on her heel and walked toward the kitchen.

"Escaping again, sister?" Dahlia called.

Iris's fists balled and she twisted back to face the table. With everything in her, she fought the urge to say what she wanted to say. She wanted to out her older sister concerning the fears Iris knew she had. She wanted to tell her that trying to be so strong was only driving them all apart—the exact opposite of what Dahlia likely truly wanted. But instead she held her tongue. At least for the moment. If the three of them saw this curse from the other side, she was definitely going to speak her mind.

"No. You're right," Iris said. "What we're doing is important, and I need to resist that urge. And Poppy also needs something to clean her shirt right now." With that Iris turned again and walked toward the kitchen.

"You were on fire," Dahlia said in a hushed tone. "What else was I supposed to do?"

"I don't want to talk about it anymore," Poppy shot back.

To get some space, Iris picked up her pace, hoping to get out of earshot. But the cottage wasn't that big.

All she knew was that for once in her sisterly relationship, she needed to be the grown-up.

She needed to lean in for once…make herself vulnerable. Not run away.

Or they'd never break the curse.

Chapter 18

The next morning came all too early, and Iris still didn't know what to do. She'd actually forced herself to sit with her sisters, read through multiple books, and take notes. Poppy had gotten bored more than once, and Iris was convinced Dahlia was simply unwilling to be wrong again. She'd even done her best to be a good middle sister and mediate...extend more than a tolerable level of patience...and they still couldn't agree on a solution to break the curse. It had gotten so bad that Iris just wanted to send them home. Sure, their powers were diminished, but that might have been preferable to spending more days together without a solution to the problem.

Most everyone else seemed to live without magic.

Iris's head pounded at the memory of the night before, and she rubbed at her temples in an attempt to reduce the pain while the same sore spot in her neck throbbed.

The stress was too much.

After throwing on her robe, she shuffled from her bedroom to the front door to check for any orders left in the basket outside. She still had her Closed sign up, but everyone knew people never actually read those kinds of things.

Along the way she ignored the stacks of books on the dining table, but she did notice Talon had left raspberry-filled pastries on the kitchen counter for breakfast next to the white roses.

Before Iris made it to the door she grabbed a pastry from the plate and took a bite. And the act of tasting the crisp exterior offset by a luscious seedless raspberry jam gave her hope that the day would only improve. If nothing else good had come of the last few days, at least the food Talon made was amazing…and she'd hired him to stay on. As she leaned one elbow onto the counter and closed her eyes, Iris almost lost herself in the pastry. Almost…until she remembered what she'd come out to do.

She eyed the pastries again but decided to leave them for her sisters and the familiars, since she loathed the possibility of hearing any complaints over the matter, and then she made it over to the door. Before going outside, Iris checked the weather through the window, and as if a good omen, the sky was an overcast gray.

At least that and the morning pastries were something positive.

Iris shrugged and opened the door.

"Aaack!" Puck shouted as they shrank back, holding a paper in their small cornflower-blue hands. The sprite wore a pair of tweed knickers and a flowy gray shirt with a missing button at the top. Puck's mop of lavender hair flopped into their face, and Iris imagined that must have made seeing a challenge.

Iris furrowed her brows and sucked in a quick breath at the unexpected sight of the bard on her doorstep. She hurried outside and snapped the door shut behind her as quietly as she could. "What in the snails are you doing here?" Suddenly suspicious, she wished her magic were working on any sort of consistent basis to ward Puck off. She flicked her gaze around looking for anyone else.

"I...I," they stuttered and took two more steps back.

Iris crossed her arms over her chest while wondering where Talon was—he should escort Puck off her property. "You what?" she demanded just as the sun broke through the clouded sky. The sight brought a growl into the back of Iris's throat, and she regretted even asking Puck a question that could keep the sprite from leaving a second sooner.

Eyes cast slightly downward, the sprite held out the paper. "I'm here to request a potion to improve my singing."

Iris scoffed. "We've already had this convers—"

But before she finished, the sprite had dug into their pocket and produced several coins. It wasn't much but generally enough to cover the fee for nominal potions. "I've saved up my tips."

In her past excursions into Fraywell, Iris had seen Puck's tips as she'd hurried past the sprite. The handouts weren't much, and logically so, since she was pretty confident she wasn't the only one who found their barding intolerable. Any coins they'd received were likely for pity.

As Puck held out the coins, Iris stared at the sprite, her mind turning automatically with the possible potion recipe to help them. The base would include licorice and honey… but she wasn't sure of the rest since she'd never made something like that before. But no sooner had she thought about that than a twinge jabbed at her chest.

Why am I even considering something so ridiculous?

"I need you to leave," Iris growled out loud and lunged at the sprite, who by that time looked as if they'd been magically frozen. She took them by the shoulders and spun them around to face the road back to Fraywell.

"Talon mentioned something about using the diaphragm," Puck squealed as Iris pushed them forward.

She gulped and twisted them back around. "Talon? When did you talk to Talon?"

They pointed to the side of the house. "He's out there. I talked to him before I came up to put my request in your ordering basket."

Iris's shoulders tightened and tweaked her neck again. "What else did you talk to him about?" Again, she didn't even really know why it mattered, but what if Talon had said something about her business she didn't want anyone from Fraywell to know?

"Nothing, nothing." Puck shook their head vigorously. "He just mentioned the dia...dia...dia*gram* and something about using it for singing before he fed the chickens. I don't even know what it is."

Irritated, Iris narrowed her right eye at Puck and leaned down closer to the sprite's eye level. "You make a living singing and you don't even know what the *diaphragm* is?"

In all truth, Iris had only come across the information by accident one day when she was about ten years old. She'd been reading through one of her father's anatomy books and had run across one all about the body and internal organs and such. The diaphragm had been of special interest, since it helped one project their voice more...which was always an asset in scaring off annoying people and using one's voice effectively to give off a fierce appearance. Only years later had she made the connection to singing. Not that she sang much.

Puck shook their head, making their messy hair flop back and forth on their forehead. "No. But I'd like to make a living with my singing. And it seems like you could help me."

Good luck. Iris almost said the words out loud but somehow kept them inside her head. Even thinking about the insult brought on a tinge of immediate guilt, and what she did next was only to assuage it as quickly as possible.

"It's down here," Iris said, as if her previously intense desire to show Puck off her property had vanished. She indicated the spot under her own belly and explained to them much the same thing she had to Talon.

Puck stood there, eyes wide watching her, and by the end they gave it a go. And what came out of their mouth wasn't exactly good but also wasn't the worst thing Iris had heard either. The notes to the first line of "It Was a Lover and His Lass" were only *slightly* off pitch.

When they finished, Puck's blue lips spread across their face in a smile wider than Iris had ever seen…not that she paid much attention to Puck's expressions when she'd seen or heard them barding in Fraywell. She'd always done everything in her power to get away from their singing as quickly as possible.

But that morning, Iris tipped her head in interest as warmth bloomed in her chest. Then reality came tumbling back and she quickly shook it in disbelief over what she'd just done and the emotion she'd allowed. She'd helped Puck. *Puck*, of all people. Yes…of course she'd helped Talon the day before with his growling…but that was in her best interest.

He was her bodyguard, for snail's sake.

Puck was a thorn in her side. And now she'd pushed it in deeper on purpose. Yet somehow, helping them actually felt good.

As quickly as possible she forced her mind back to its senses. "Lesson over." She reached out for Puck's shoulders and spun the sprite around again. "You need to leave."

"I think a potion might help the situation even more," Puck insisted while Iris shoved them toward the road back to town.

She'd suddenly become quite aware of the fact her sisters were likely up by then and might have heard or seen the exchange through the window. Iris twisted to see if she spotted them, but no one was there. Even so, she only pushed harder to get Puck going that much more quickly. "No, no, it wouldn't. All the potions I make only make life worse…or snuff it out altogether."

"What if you tried the other kind?" Puck insisted. "You could test it out on me. I wouldn't mind."

"Oh, I think you might mind," Iris said, thinking about all her clients' victims. "Now get out of here before I turn you into a newt."

Puck didn't have to know that turning anyone into anything was not one of Iris's go-to skills…even when she wasn't cursed. The threat was entirely empty.

She kept pushing, concerned her sisters might still come out of the house and realize she was losing her touch.

"Ouch, ouch." Puck picked up speed and escaped Iris's grasp. They turned and clutched their shoulder. "I'm leaving! No need to burn me."

Iris turned over her hand and gazed at it. Her palm was intensely red. But immediately upon her noticing it the magic disappeared, only to be replaced by an unfamiliar sense of guilt in her belly. "Sorry." The word slipped out and she wanted to slap her hand over her mouth. To compensate, she wrinkled her forehead and lowered her voice. "Don't tell anyone what happened here."

A confused look scrunched Puck's delicate features, then narrowed them further. "Only if you make me the potion I want."

"You little misbegot," she snarled and threw out her arms, hoping a little heat might come from them to ward off the sprite. But it didn't.

Even so, the action did the trick. Puck waved at her and started walking away.

"Fine," they muttered. "I'm going."

And although several much more wicked ways of *solving* the problem (that weren't just letting the sprite go) came to the forefront of Iris's mind, she couldn't bring herself to consider any of them. Instead, she only took in a grounding breath and watched him disappear down the road.

"Morning," a scratchy voice came from behind and slightly above her.

Iris flinched and turned to see Oberon perched on the edge of the roof. His feathers were puffed up and ruffled as his golden eyes stared down at her.

Her pulse picked up. Oberon was the quietest of the familiars in her family, and Iris often didn't know how to read him. "How long have you been there?" she asked, trying not to sound suspicious but also fully knowing that asking the question made her sound suspicious.

"Not long," the raven said and tipped his head.

Iris stuffed her hands into her robe pockets, unsure of how to respond. "What are you doing, then?"

"Oh, morning flight," Oberon said. "Getting fresh air." He flicked his attention toward the road. "Fraywell is an interesting place, don't you think?"

Iris had no idea what he was getting at and whether his chatter was only small talk. "You've been there?"

The raven bobbed his head multiple times. "Every day since we arrived."

Iris's heart clenched and she couldn't help but wonder if he'd followed her into town and seen any of her recent interactions with the people there. And if so, what had he told her sisters? Iris bit her lip, trying to keep her thoughts imperceptible. "I visit as little as I can."

Oberon just stared at her for a moment, then spread his wings and flew off to a nearby oak tree.

Left alone, Iris contemplated the front door and decided against going back inside yet. Instead she walked around the corner to deal with Talon. It wasn't long before she found him sitting on the wooden bench in front of the chicken coop, facing away from her. His large muscular frame took up a good portion of the space, and he didn't seem to be doing anything but sitting there.

The chickens pecked around at the ground where he must have spread seeds for them, including a variety of leftovers like apple cores and carrot tops from dinner the night before.

As she watched the happily pecking chickens, which had never had names before Talon arrived, the almost comforting sounds they made brought on a sense of calm that relaxed her entire body. But it wasn't long before she corrected herself and tensed. She was *not* the kind of witch who took even a little joy in something like the sounds of chickens in her backyard…was she?

Iris quickly gazed around for Oberon, but unless he was being extra sneaky, the raven didn't seem to be around.

She continued to Talon and rounded the bench to face him. The orc's eyes were closed, and his breathing seemed slow and deliberate. And seeing him almost made her wonder if that was what she'd looked like a moment before.

Iris reached up to the tender spot on her neck and rubbed at it. But the spot stayed tense. Could be that was how it was supposed to be. But after a moment of standing, and still not wanting to go back inside, she quietly lowered herself to the small, open space beside Talon and closed her eyes.

The world still felt entirely out of sorts. But somehow it was a little better sitting next to him.

Chapter 19

"Oh, good morning," Talon's deep voice said.

Iris's eyes flickered open to the sun unfortunately shining brightly overhead. She had no idea how long she'd actually sat there. It could have been a minute or an hour, but all traces of the overcast sky she'd come outside to that morning were gone. The day was getting worse by the minute.

The thought that came to mind first was reminiscent of *What's good about it?* In addition, it also included several colorful and interesting curses she heard in The Boar's Head tavern, but she said none of it out loud to Talon, including the curses.

Doing so was too vulnerable.

Instead she asked, "Why were you talking to Puck?" The question was the real reason she'd come to find him anyway.

The orc twisted his lips for a moment as if he were considering his answer. "Because they were here," Talon finally said and turned his attention back to the chickens. "Not talking to them would have been rude."

Iris pinched her mouth at his answer and decided it probably didn't matter. Puck had gone back to town, and that would be the end of it.

"I've been trying to come out here to think every morning." Talon sighed and kept looking out toward the chickens. "Valentina likes it."

Valentina? Iris thought and then remembered Talon had named the chickens the first day he was here…which seemed like years instead of days. She surveyed the hens. One had a tuft of white feathers and looked like it was wearing a tall, puffy hat, one was brown and black, and the third was sort of a rust color. Iris wasn't actually sure which one was Valentina or if she cared. What she did know was that she hadn't actually spent any time since she'd moved to the cottage the year before doing much of anything outside unless she had to. And she'd never *had to* sit on the bench in front of the chickens.

"And what is it you're thinking about?" The question even surprised Iris, but she couldn't take it back.

"Life," he said simply and rubbed his right hand over his leg. "And how I ended up here."

Iris was pretty sure Talon wasn't asking an existential

question, but truly she wasn't entirely sure. "In Fraywell? As my bodyguard?" she asked, unsure if his statement was more existential than that.

He nodded.

Iris twisted her head at him. "Do you actually remember?"

The orc let out a defeated sigh. "It's all really spotty, just some vague memories like the ones about my family. Nothing else."

Iris sighed. She didn't really know much either—what can you really know about a random stranger who dies in the middle of your yard? But part of her really thought she should tell Talon someone had offed him. Possibly that would jog his memory. She twisted her lips, trying to think of a better way of saying it rather than bluntly stating the facts. Something in her gut wanted to avoid it. If she told him, would he want to leave? Of course he couldn't with the binding spell, but she really wanted him to choose to stay. Or what if it changed his personality? The orc spirit Iris had met was completely different from the Talon she knew…vicious, a little rude… the perfect specimen of a bodyguard for a witch aspiring to create an empire, or at least carve a spot for herself in the realm. Iris winced at the thought. Even though she shouldn't, Iris actually liked the current Talon. Plus, what if the truth hurt him? That was the last thing she wanted to do. As it was, she couldn't see how him remembering more of his past than he did would be a positive thing.

"How are you feeling?" Talon asked before Iris formed her thoughts.

"How am *I* feeling?" Iris repeated, and his question only affirmed what she'd been thinking.

Talon shrugged. "Yes."

"Why would you even ask something like that?" Iris brought her hands into her lap and interlaced her fingers, entirely uncomfortable with his question.

"Why wouldn't I? As your bodyguard it seems the more in tune with you I am, the better I can do my job. It's one of the other things I've thought about out here."

He probably wasn't wrong, but even so, Iris poked at the sore spot on her neck. She couldn't quite reconcile Talon. No one really ever asked how she was doing. Maybe her sisters had at one time or another. But not since her father—

"It's bothering you isn't it?" Talon asked, leaning over as if trying to get a better look at Iris.

"You asking me how I'm feeling?" Iris groaned. "Yes. That bothers me."

Talon chuckled and completely ignored Iris's protest. "No, silly. The neck muscle."

Immediately Iris pulled her hand down from the spot, while her mind raced at the fact he'd even noticed her discomfort. "No." An obvious lie.

"Yes it is," Talon insisted. "You've been trying to work out the knot since yesterday." He held out both his hands toward her. "What if I tried?"

Iris's cheeks heated and she bit at her top lip as she turned her attention back to the chickens. The rust-colored one had jumped on top of the henhouse, a green worm dangling out the side of her beak, while the puffy-headed one squawked at Iris from the ground.

If only she spoke chicken.

"No, that's okay," she said. Everything in her made her want to head back into the house. But she didn't want to be there either.

"I'm sorry if I overstepped," Talon said with a genuine tone while bringing both his hands up in apology. "But it can be difficult to concentrate when something like that is so bothersome."

"So now you're schooled about sore muscles too," Iris chuckled nervously to relieve some of the tension while training her interest on a small brown mouse scurrying over to a carrot top in the chicken feed.

The creature made its way around the chickens to the top of the pile, snatched it, and began nibbling on the orange part. Something inside Iris wondered if it was the same mouse she'd brought back to life. Of course, Quince had sworn a random mystery cat had eaten it…and all mice pretty much looked the same.

Talon had turned out to be much more resilient than she thought he might have been…so the mouse could have been too.

"Some ginger tea this morning then," Talon suggested. "Or chamomile to relax."

Both suggestions *were* excellent, and Iris didn't fathom why she hadn't thought of them herself. But as she'd already told Puck that morning, she rarely thought about making life better. Only worse. And apparently that included her own.

Her chest tensed at the thought, and she stood from the hard bench. "I should go." Iris started to turn back to the cottage and then spotted the flower bushes Talon had trimmed. The plants looked neat and as if they were ready for new life. In fact, several of them had fresh white buds just opening. Iris stopped and stared at them. She couldn't help but see herself as those plants, cared for and growing. Suddenly the next breath seemed impossible, and despite herself, Iris longed to stay outside with Talon. To find out what might happen next. "No," she muttered and fought the ridiculous feeling. What was wrong with her?

Forcing her feet to move, she caught a view of the entire yard. There wasn't a weed in sight, and a soft green carpet of grass was starting to grow around the cottage. It had only been a few days since the orc arrived, and the yard was already in bloom…thriving.

"What have you done here?" She kept looking around in near disbelief, and then her gaze landed on Talon. It was like the orc had magic of his own. There was no other explanation. But orcs didn't have magical abilities. Of course, he was a half orc, but he had claimed his father to be human. What was going on?

The space between Talon's thick brows pinched in confusion. "I'm only taking care of the place. I thought you'd like it." He gazed around. "Everything was in complete disarray before. You're a busy woman, and you need someone to share the load."

Iris gulped and planted her hand on her hip. As he was currently, Talon was good. He was kind, thoughtful. There was no denying that. And that realization completely filled Iris with frustration. She aimed to be dark, moody...dangerous. "You understand what I do, right? Who I am." She pointed to the cottage. "Who and what my sisters are?"

He tipped his head. "You're Iris."

"I'm Iris *Weyward*," she said and stamped her foot, but she didn't take her attention off the orc. "Creator of chaos, maker of mischief. I destroy anyone who gets in my way when my magic is working." Iris paused for a second, unsure if she should go on, but she did while shaking her head in annoyance. "I've done things of which you have no idea." One of which was raising Talon from the dead, and he still didn't know. "My sisters and I have incited civil wars!"

(One, to be exact.)

"We have a huge, wicked family tree. Evil is what has been expected of me my entire life. It's my entire identity. My legacy." But something about what she'd said felt more like Iris was desperately trying to convince herself rather than Talon. When she finished, the disobedient, out-of-control tendril of hair was flopped squarely in the middle of her face, and she blew it straight up and out of the way.

But despite her ranting Talon hadn't moved, and he hadn't flinched. "You're Iris. And I'm Talon Gefroy, your bodyguard."

"Did you hear me at all?" Iris demanded. "I'm not *just* Iris—"

"You told me to call you that," Talon said calmly.

She stared at him in disbelief. Of course what he'd stated was entirely true, but it didn't make it any less annoying. Iris groaned out of frustration. Her hands balled at her sides. "Yes! But Talon—"

"I can't remember my past," Talon said. "But we've all done things—"

"I'm trying to protect you," she admitted as the corners of her eyes burned with tears. But there was no way she was ever going to let them loose. "Why won't you listen?" And for one of the few times in her life, she was being completely honest with herself. She *did* want to protect the huge orc in front of her. Staying only put him in danger…from her.

Talon stood from the bench, making the wood crack. He walked to Iris, somehow keeping his steps light.

Iris's heart pounded, but she stood her ground. She was not going to be the one to yield. "My life is too messy and you don't belong here." She hated that she was admitting this, but it was entirely true. In the past year, as much as she'd tried to stay focused and keep her goals at the front of her mind, nothing was how she wanted it to be. Distance from her family hadn't solved their problems as she'd hoped. And continuing at the pace she was currently at, Iris would never achieve more in her life than being the witch outside Fraywell who might sell poisoned apples. She'd never make a name for herself.

A small smile quirked at the corners of Talon's lips. "Unless you fire me, I'm not leaving. I'm in this for the long haul."

Iris's tongue went as dry as if she had just taken a mouthful of stale bread. Would the orc say the same thing if she told him the truth? That she'd reincarnated him and, in the process, broken him…then planned to off the guy as soon as her sisters left? The truth sounded even worse than she'd thought. Panic she barely understood twisted in her mind and chest. At the same time, she wanted Talon both to stay and to leave. But she wasn't going to fire him. She couldn't. Emotion bubbled through her veins.

Instead she took several steps toward the orc and did something she couldn't even explain to herself. Iris threw her arms around Talon and pressed her face into his warm chest. Everything about it felt good. Completely right. But it didn't take long for her to realize what she'd done, and she dropped her arms and took a step back, knowing her cheeks must have been an intense color of pink.

She was almost afraid to look up at him, but something compelled her to anyway.

The orc's features were soft, and he reached to her face and gently pushed the stray hair from over her eye. "When we met I told you that you were beautiful. And I still think that. Nothing I've seen over the past few days has changed my thoughts. I want to stay here…with you." His fingers slipped from the side of her cheek to the sore spot on Iris's neck. "May I?"

Iris gulped and bowed her head.

Talon drew his warm hand across her skin and stopped on the tight muscle. He gently pressed into the spot with his thumb.

Iris shivered at the touch. At first, no matter how gently he worked out the knot, dull pain crept down her shoulder and up into her neck. But she didn't want him to stop.

And as he worked his magic, Iris gazed up to his face and gulped. Talon grasped her waist and lightly touched her.

"May I?" he asked again.

"Yes." She barely got out as the pain in her neck slipped away and Talon pulled her in closer.

He drew his hand from her neck and up into her hair, bending his neck closer to her face. "May I?"

Iris licked her lips, completely unsure what she was getting herself into but never wanting something more. "Yes."

And he kissed her.

Without a doubt, Iris was sure Talon couldn't be in her employment anymore.

Chapter 20

Iris's entire body was on fire from the kiss. From the sweet, tart taste of raspberry breakfast pastries on their lips. From Talon's large, warm hands roaming over her body. From the grazing of his small tusks along the sides of her mouth. It had been too long since she'd had a romantic relationship and *far* too long since it was with anyone she actually liked.

Villainy *was* a very lonely business.

She couldn't remember a time she'd ever felt so much like herself in her entire life…even when her magic was working properly. Iris didn't quite know how, but the orc had done that for her. Something in her life had been missing, and Talon's presence made her feel like everything was going her way even though it equally seemed like everything was falling apart. But for whatever reason, at least in that moment it all felt right. Her hand slipped from Talon's neck to his chest, and all she realized was that she wanted more.

More of him.

"That was—" But she couldn't get the words out after she broke from the kiss, her heart and body aflutter.

"Yes," he said in a low tone. "Yes, it was."

Talon stroked her hair, and the two of them stared deep into each other's eyes as if time had stopped. Nothing would ever be the same again.

After a moment, Iris rose up on her toes to kiss him again, completely wanting to ignore any possibility of conversation about how the kissing would change their relationship. Not to mention the fact that she needed to tell him the truth…all of it, every detail. How she was sorry and wanted to spend her every waking moment making it up to him. Otherwise they could never have anything real, since relationships couldn't withstand such secrets.

But she didn't get that far.

"*Craw, craw.*" The unfortunate sound came the way of the cottage.

Recognizing the sound, Iris broke away from Talon as if she'd been burned. Her attention flicked up to Oberon sitting on the roof, staring their way.

He slowly tipped his head in interest. And before Iris could say a word, the bird spread his wings out fully and took flight toward the front of the cottage.

What did he see? The thought raced through her mind as she rolled through the events of the last few minutes. She wasn't sure if her kissing or doing anything else with her bodyguard would matter to her sisters. It wasn't as if she were a teenager sneaking out to meet a forbidden boy. In fact, Poppy would probably be all for Iris and Talon getting together. Any other time any problems with the situation would have fallen squarely on Iris, since if there was an eventual falling-out between her and Talon, it would be on her to find a bodyguard replacement.

But as it was, Dahlia would blame her for being distracted again…being irresponsible. Blame Iris that they were in danger of not breaking the curse.

And it was true. Iris's mind had been completely scattered from the moment she'd made sure Talon wasn't pushing up daisies. Snails…since the minute she'd gotten out of bed the morning he arrived.

"Um," Iris managed and brought her anxious attention back to Talon. "I need to go deal with that, then we must have a conversation." And before he could say anything, Iris had already raced to the cottage and through the back door.

She made her way past the kitchen and skidded to a stop when she found both her sisters and all three familiars in the living room. Iris's attention immediately drew to the raven perched on the back of the nearest chair, preening his feathers. Had he told them? And how had he gotten inside so quickly, anyway? A small part of her hoped it hadn't been

Oberon on the roof, until she eyed the window pulled open just enough for him to fly through.

Ursula lay on the floor, asleep on her back, belly entirely exposed with her striped tail flicking back and forth, as if she hadn't a care in the world. Poppy stood with a pastry in her hand, held close to her lips, and was about to take her first bite.

She looked Iris up and down. "You look a fright."

With barely a thought, Iris's hands raked through her hair. Without a mirror she couldn't be sure, but her rough hair felt like a frizzy mess. Which it likely was, since she hadn't bothered to brush it after she'd gotten up. But her thought also led her to remembering Talon had called her beautiful again and the fact that her spell to bring him back from the dead might have truly affected his ability to see reality. Despite all that she managed to say the obvious: "I've been outside…with the chickens." Iris dropped her gaze to Quince, who sat on the floor with half a pastry in his paws, happily munching away.

He'd have given her a clue if she was about to be ambushed, right?

"Hey." The hedgehog raised a paw as a salutation and then resumed eating, giving zero sign if Oberon had said anything about Iris's escapade in the backyard.

"Of course you have." Dahlia, dressed in her typical black garb and ready for the day, strolled over to the dining table and sat. She lifted a teapot high and poured the liquid inside into her waiting cup, the steam rising from the top forming wisps that reminded Iris of tiny ghosts. "But I'm not entirely sure why you'd think it was something to announce to us all." Her sister took a sip of her tea and arched her brow.

Iris's insides tensed at Dahlia's too-calm demeanor. Did she know something? She always seemed to know *something*.

"What's the plan today?" Iris tried to change the subject but scrutinized Oberon, who still sat on the back of the chair, poking the feathers under his wing with his beak. She also really wanted to look back at the kitchen. Where was Talon? Hadn't he followed her in?

"If it were up to me," Poppy said, "we'd be eating these pastries all day." She licked her lips and took another bite of her breakfast. Several toasted flakes floated to the ground, and a bit of jam dribbled down the side of her mouth.

"Ohhh…excellent idea," Quince piped in and finished off his last bite. While still chewing, he rolled onto his back and patted his round tummy, which looked like someone had blown it up like a giant soap bubble.

If it were up to me, Iris thought, *we'd stop stalling and attempt a spell.* But she also knew full well she'd done things that had contributed to the holdup, so saying that out loud was fruitless and would only serve to make her older sister shoot her a condescending glare.

Dahlia stood, the fabric of her dress flaring out as if a small gust of wind had suddenly blown inside the cottage. She took another sip of her tea and said, "Then it's a good thing none of you are in charge. I think we have a few possibilities regarding the culprit… My money is on Diana, since she never really liked us. The spell choice is a little iffy, but we can at least run some trials."

Finally, Iris thought. "Why didn't you say so sooner?"

"I needed a bit more information." Dahlia motioned to her notes. "I didn't want to be wrong. Plus, there's something else I need to deal with."

Poppy let out a groan. "Anything to take a break from all this studying."

But as soon as she spoke, the back door opened, and Talon finally came into the kitchen. He peeked around the corner, and, unable to help herself, Iris's attention zipped to the orc, who gave her a small grin.

Iris fought a similar expression as her neck and body heated up again. She quickly returned her attention to Dahlia and rubbed her hand over her cheek and neck, trying to hide any color that might have appeared there without her permission.

Her older sister narrowed her eyes at Talon and then trained them on Iris. "We need to talk." The declaration came out low and gravelly.

Iris froze. There it was. Dahlia knew something...or at minimum she thought she did. Of course, Iris had heard that statement before from her sister too many times over the years when Dahlia had gone into mothering mode. And she had done that since the day Iris was born. "Okay?" She looked over to Poppy, somehow hoping for backup.

As half expected, her younger sister only waved and didn't look up from the few bites she had left of her pastry.

"What do you want to talk about?" Iris said while her

hands tingled and she did everything in her power not to look over at Talon again. She was pretty sure he might be the only one in the room to actually support her, since Quince was already asleep on the floor after his big breakfast. He'd basically sold her out over a pastry.

"Not in here," Dahlia said and placed her tea back on the table.

"Where then?" Iris asked, looking around the small space. The only other place to go was one of the bedrooms.

But her sister only breezed past her and gestured to the front door. "We're going for a walk. I need some fresh air."

Iris gazed down at herself, realizing she hadn't even gotten dressed yet, but she knew her sister wasn't going to wait for her to do that. The tingling of embarrassment came over her with the remembrance that everything that had transpired that morning with both Puck and Talon had come to be while she had been barefoot in her robe. So much for her witchy reputation. That said, she steeled herself for whatever Dahlia had to say and slipped on an old pair of boots before she followed her sister out the door.

Once Iris got outside, Dahlia was already on the path and going in the opposite direction of Fraywell. Iris had to jog to catch up with her.

"What are you doing?" Dahlia asked once Iris stepped beside her. Her tone was infused with a low level of anger but, if Iris wasn't mistaken, also a twinge of worry hung at the edges. If asked, though, Dahlia would never admit such a thing.

"Taking a walk with you," Iris said, regretting it immediately, since she was quite aware that wasn't what Dahlia was asking.

Dahlia halted and spun on her pointed heel toward her sister. She crossed her arms over her chest and blew out a deliberate breath before she said, "Something has changed with you. Both Poppy and I can feel it."

"You've been talking about me?" Iris asked, her nervousness doubling.

"Of course we've been talking about you, Sister." Dahlia scoffed as if her answer was completely obvious. "You've never been the most focused of the three of us…"

Iris's ego bruised slightly with those last words, particularly since she believed her focus had improved in the past year, but neither of her sisters had been there to see. She'd made to-do lists, gained a repeat clientele. And Poppy wasn't exactly the queen of concentration.

Dahlia continued, "But whatever is going on with you has to do with more than this curse." She swept her hand through the air and formed it like a claw while misty blue tendrils crept over her skin, then vanished. A look of frustration came over Dahlia's face, and she shook her hand as if to throw the barely there magic away.

Something in that moment inexplicably made Iris want to reach out to her sister and comfort her. Dahlia was hurting, frustrated. But Iris knew better.

And then Dahlia came right out with it. "Why haven't you told us more about Talon?"

Nerves burned in Iris's chest from the question, and she tightened the top of her robe against herself to cover any evidence of agitation. "I'm not sure what you mean?"

Her sister tipped her head in question. "Then I'll be as clear as I can. How long has the orc been in your employment, and where is he from?"

Iris's mind worked to put together the timeline, but she quickly realized how it sounded and didn't say a word. She didn't quite believe it herself.

Dahlia's nostrils flared. "Oberon went into Fraywell, and the people there were talking about him. How he only showed up days ago and they'd never seen him before. Is this true?"

Iris nodded. It wouldn't do any good to lie to her sister. She was never very good at it. "He came the same day you arrived," she admitted.

Dahlia squinted in confusion. "And you hired him on the spot?"

Iris came out with it. "He was dead. He died in my yard. Someone tried to…" She stopped, gazed around, then ran her index finger across her neck.

"Who?" Dahlia's irises became like two moons, and her voice rose nearly an octave. She started walking again, crossing her arms tightly over her chest.

Iris followed her, slightly relieved her questions didn't involve the kiss. Oberon may not have said anything after all. "I don't know. I needed to hire a new bodyguard… It was on my list of things to do. He arrived and seemed like the perfect candidate. I conjured his spirit to make sure he was interested. It wasn't a big deal. I cast the spell, did a binding."

Dahlia kept moving but raised a brow and pointed back at the house. "That orc back there in your kitchen making muffins or snails-knows-what was the perfect candidate for your bodyguard?"

All things considered, it sounded ridiculous; Iris was fully aware of that. "At the time I thought so. He was…different."

"Different how?" Dahlia asked.

Iris wasn't quite sure what she might be getting at. "What one would expect from a mercenary…vicious? I performed the spell, and he woke up," Iris said. "And something was wrong. He couldn't really remember his past, only bits and pieces…and he was like he is now."

With a scoff, Dahlia halted again. "And you didn't simply do away with him immediately?"

"I know, I know," Iris said, her gut tightening at the line of questioning. It wasn't as if Dahlia had actually gotten rid of anyone herself. At least as far as Iris knew, since they hadn't spoken in a year. "I considered it and decided to give it a week…but he is improving. He's not what I expected at all but seems to be working out…sort of."

Dahlia shook her head. "Pretty sure he was a victim of the curse too."

Iris couldn't disagree.

"You shouldn't get too attached," Dahlia said. "We have to protect ourselves in these situations. And you need to be at your best if we even have a chance at breaking this curse."

Iris's breath picked up slightly. She was already attached to Talon.

Chapter 21

Iris's mind whirled with the idea that she should tell Dahlia more of what was going on...the kiss with Talon...the fact that she had felt strangely nice lately... all the things that had happened to her from the day her sisters had arrived. She longed to put their differences behind them and have Dahlia and Poppy back in her life for more than a few annoying days while trying to break a mystery curse.

As her older sister waited for a response, Iris opened her mouth to do just that—or at least some version of it—but didn't get the chance to say a word.

"Yoo-hoo!" a woman's voice called out, and Iris winced at the realization of who was following them.

Both witches whipped around to find Kate behind them, raising her hand in the air like she was trying to get their attention in a crowded area instead of on an isolated path. The woman's flowy pink dress puffed out slightly behind her when she picked up the pace to catch up with them.

Without even meaning to, Iris let out an annoyed sigh. Kate was pretty much the last person she wanted to see.

Well…Puck was a close second.

Next to her, Dahlia's lips turned down into a solid scowl at the woman approaching them, which, in reality, wasn't too far off from her normal look. And the expression didn't seem to ward the neighbor off anyway.

"I'm so glad I caught you," Kate said, slightly out of breath and looking straight at Iris. Then she turned her attention to Dahlia. "Oh, who is this?" Without hesitation, she stuck out her hand as a waiting offering.

The woman appeared completely incapable of reading body language.

Iris stiffened in anticipation of what her sister might say or do.

Not surprisingly, Dahlia gazed only halfway down to Kate's hand as if she'd been offered a rotten tomato. She already had her hand raised to her side and her fingers looked like claws, but she made no moves to reciprocate the gesture.

The three stood there for what seemed to Iris like an age before she said, "My sisters are in town." Why Iris said something even that cordial was beyond her.

A low growl vibrated in Dahlia's throat as if to warn her off, but still Kate only stood there with a relaxed grin stretching across her lips as if the three of them were having a pleasant conversation.

Iris's fist balled, then released. She finally said something close to what she wanted to say. "What do you want, Kate?" There was no reason for this kind of neighborly nonsense.

"I was hoping you could send…what's his name… Talon…over to do me a favor," Kate said while playing with a tendril of her grayish-blond hair.

Sudden and intense jealousy gripped Iris's entire body as her eyes dropped briefly down to the woman's low-cut shirt. There was absolutely no way she would ever send Talon over to Kate's cottage to do anything. "Whatever it is, *I* can do it." She wanted to slap her palm to her mouth in disbelief she'd even said such a thing.

"Oh." Kate pulled her head back in surprise, then waffled her attention between the two sisters again. "Are you sure?"

"I'm sure. I'll be there in a minute," Iris said curtly. "But I need to finish something up here." She twisted to a blank-faced Dahlia, who only nodded once.

Kate's forehead creased briefly and then her expression morphed into a friendly smile that might have been genuine, but Iris declined to dwell on it too much. "If you insist." The woman turned and hurried back down the path to her cottage.

"I hope you're planning on taking care of that *problem* while you're over there." Dahlia's stare never left Kate. "If my magic were working, I'd have dumped a rain cloud on her right now. That woman is trouble. I can tell."

Iris sighed, fully agreeing with Dahlia's sentiment and equally glad she at least had intentions of backing up her younger sister. "Even you understand the complexity of ridding yourself of annoying neighbors if you don't want the villagers running us witches out of town with fire and pitchforks. Particularly if we're in the middle of magic troubles."

Her sister's scowl softened and turned to the slightest expression of mirth that Iris hadn't seen in a long time. "Oh, yes. I'm aware." She patted Iris on the shoulder. "Don't be long. We really need to solve this curse today. And we need to talk more about Talon."

Iris nodded, but her belly pinched. Before heading to Kate's, she watched her sister travel down the path back to the cottage. Something about the way Dahlia held her head made Iris infinitely aware that her older sister was lonely too and didn't want to admit it. But she quickly shook off the thought and emotions that came with it and marched through the open gate to her neighbor's home.

After passing the garden, overflowing with vegetables, herbs, and fruits, Iris arrived at Kate's door. A small yellow heart, no bigger than Iris's hand, was carved and painted into the center. A groan left her mouth at the cheery sight. She briefly thought about knocking…but since when did Iris have neighborly manners? At least she wasn't planning Kate's immediate demise. That was neighborly enough.

Instead of knocking, she reached for the knob, put on

a respectable lip-curling snarl, and flung the door wide. "What is it you want?" Of course Iris made sure to make her tone as unpleasant as possible to encourage Kate to never speak to her or Talon again.

Before another word came from her mouth, she paused and could do nothing but gaze around at the place. As expected, it was the complete opposite of Iris's sparse decor. While there was a living area with a fireplace and hearth, Kate's fireplace was draped with foliage, probably from the nearby Forest of Arden. Iris had been out there to forage a time or two for ingredients. Several calm, pastoral paintings featuring fluffy sheep hung on the walls, and the blue chair next to a matching couch was dotted with multiple frilly pillows. The scent of lavender caught Iris's nose as she took another step into the room. The place had a complete atmosphere of calm she hadn't expected (what she'd expected she wasn't sure, but it wasn't that), and it immediately transferred to her body. Her shoulders dropped for a second.

But the peace didn't last long.

Kate stood in the kitchen already preparing a cup of tea, with a second cup waiting next to it. "No need to worry about that. But you seem stressed," she said in a soft, mesmerizing tone.

Iris recoiled from the declaration and left the door open behind her…just in case (in case what…she didn't really know, although the throw pillows really did look a tad dangerous). "I'm not stressed."

It was a complete lie and she knew it, but she didn't need

Kate privy to her business. Her hand reached immediately to the knot at the base of her neck.

"Hmmm." Kate finished pouring the tea into the first cup, then started on the second. When it was full she picked both up, walked to Iris, and handed one to her.

Iris didn't know why she took it, but she did. The scent wafted up into her nose. Chamomile mixed with a hint of lavender. It wasn't her favorite blend, but being a witch, she'd used the power of the herbs for calming the senses.

She wasn't even sure she wanted to be calm. Iris's brow furrowed as she stared down at the still swirling tea. *Maybe it's poison!* The thought kept her frozen in the entryway while Kate took her own cup and sat on the waiting blue chair, sinking deep into the soft cushion.

The woman gestured to the couch. "Have a seat."

Iris gritted her teeth. She didn't want to sit down, but she took her possibly poisoned tea and walked to the couch anyway. "Why am I here? What is it you needed me to do?" she asked before nearly involuntarily sitting down on the plush seating.

Somehow, the furniture was probably the most comfortable thing she'd ever sat on. After settling against a floral print pillow with lace edging, she completely blew off the notion that the tea was poisoned and took a sip. Strangely, the flavor was comforting on her tongue, and the temperature was just right.

"Why *are* you here?" Kate settled back into her chair, and somehow the question rang with existentialism.

Iris blinked twice, not fully believing she was considering continuing to sit there, drinking tea and talking with Kate, of all people. "You asked me to do something for you."

Kate shook her head and grinned. "I actually needed *Talon's* help with something. You're the one who volunteered to take his place. But then, all my clients come here for a reason, so I have to ask. Why *are* you here?"

"Clients?" Iris took another sip of tea and avoided the question. "I'm *not* a client." Her legs itched to get up to avoid what felt like an accusation, but she was suddenly compelled to ask, "So all those people who come here are clients?"

"Mm-hmm." Kate sipped her tea and looked up with smiling eyes. "Everyone who comes here has something on their mind. They talk and I listen." She shrugged. "Sometimes I offer advice, sometimes not."

Iris gazed around in disbelief. "You mean to tell me that everyone who comes here sits on this couch…to tell you their problems?"

"Sometimes they stand or sit on the floor. And it's not always problems." Kate said. "But yes. When it comes down to it, that's exactly what happens."

"I thought—" Iris started.

"Of course," Kate said, holding her cup with both hands on her lap. "And would it matter if what you thought was true?"

Iris bit at the inside of her mouth as the tea and guilt sloshed in her middle. She'd judged Kate for no reason…

and no, whatever she'd thought about her before shouldn't have mattered. Not wanting to deal with her annoyance, she pushed it aside. "People come here to talk to you? And you get paid for it?"

"That's what I said," Kate answered.

Iris eyed the open door, still itching to leave yet not doing it. "There's no sign out front."

"Not everyone needs a sign to find the place." Kate placed her tea aside before looking back at Iris. "You found your way inside today."

Confused, Iris gazed down at her tea. The leaves floated around inside the cup and she wondered what the reading might be once she finished, but she'd never find out, since she didn't plan to drink it all down. Something came into her mind she'd never considered. Before she asked the question, Iris scanned the room again. Kate was different from what Iris had expected…and Iris felt different too. What if it *was* the tea? But from the taste she was almost certain there was nothing enchanted about it…or poisonous. "Are you a witch?"

Kate chuckled and lowered her shoulders. "You aren't the first to ask. But no…not in the way you are a witch. Or your sisters."

Although Iris didn't really know what that meant, she accepted her neighbor's answer. Very unlike herself…but that seemed to be a life theme as of late.

"I assume the redhead is your other sister?" Kate asked. "You all have the same walk…the same tip of the head."

Iris glared at her neighbor, and a buzzing annoyance

returned to her chest at the thought of the woman always spying on her from the front window. But the feeling was tempered by the idea that maybe Kate had seen loneliness in them too. "Yes," she admitted.

"Are they in town for any reason in particular?" Kate asked.

There was no way Iris was talking to Kate about the curse, because that was not her business. "Just visiting." She did her best not to allow any emotion to seep into her words.

"Family can be difficult," she said, placing her elbow onto the chair arm. "It's a common theme I hear from my clients."

Am I one of Kate's clients now? Iris thought, fairly sure she'd never given consent to such a thing. She took a sip of her tea, but it had gone cold already. "Tell me about it." The words slipped out of Iris's mouth without her permission. She glanced down at the somehow already lukewarm tea, and to make sure it wasn't somehow influencing her, she quickly put it aside on the table flanking the couch.

Kate chuckled and leaned her chin onto her palm. "I think that's what you're here for."

Iris twisted her lips and stared intently at her neighbor. Her mind going back and forth, she grabbed a throw pillow, placed it on her lap, and held it there. "I've always had one goal." She stopped there, since it wasn't entirely safe to admit to someone she barely knew the specifics of her intentions. Iris and her sisters had looked up to their father. They all wanted to be just like him…striking fear around the realm. He was everything to them after their mother had passed. Iris needed to make him proud. "But in the last few days something has changed. My mind has been in a different place."

"Hmm," Kate said, without offering any input.

"I…*hired* Talon and then my sisters arrived," Kate said. "The three of us have a problem to solve."

"It's a difficult problem?" Kate asked.

"Yes…and we've been using my father's books to try to figure out a solution," Iris admitted, pulling the pillow in closer to her chest.

Kate leaned closer. "Your father? Are you close?"

In an instant Iris's mouth went dry.

"I didn't mean to overstep." Kate must have noticed the shift in Iris's demeanor, because she leaned back in the chair as if to give her more space.

Silence danced in the room before finally Iris spoke. "My father…he…we're estranged." The words felt almost good coming from her mouth. Neither she nor her sisters spoke of him much since he'd *changed*.

"Is he like you and your sisters? Nothing wrong with that." Kate asked.

Iris gulped. All their lives he'd taught them everything he knew about spreading depravity. Then one day he'd woken up and changed his mind. "A witch? Yes." But the reality was her father had gone from being a powerful, evil witch…to one who did good. And Iris still couldn't reconcile that… It was one of the reasons she'd barely looked at his books before the last few days. She refused to become like him and give up everything she'd worked for her entire life.

"And did using his books to solve this problem bring up...emotions you don't like?" Kate asked.

Iris drew the pillow even closer to herself with both hands. Her father had turned good, but she'd run from him. Left the house she grew up in...but Talon was good too, and now *she'd* been doing good things as well. Her mind churned with the thoughts. What did it all mean?

Suddenly Iris was filled with the painful urge to admit to Kate how she was keeping a secret from Talon and knew it was entirely wrong of her to do so, but she had no idea how to tell him or how to fix the problem. She also wanted to say that she had no idea what her place in the realm was and that she was done chasing goals that weren't hers anymore.

Kate's eyes crinkled at the corners. "You don't need to say. It's just something to consider."

After glancing over at her tea, Iris said, her voice quivering, "I think I should go now."

"You're free to leave," Kate said.

With that permission, Iris pushed the pillow off and was on her feet, emotion like a storm whipping her heart.

Before Iris opened the door to escape Kate said, "Keep in mind, sometimes solutions are closer than you think if you only take a step back to look."

Unable to contain her emotions, Iris burst out the door and slammed it behind her. What did Kate actually know about her, anyway?

Nothing. And, terrifyingly, everything.

Chapter 22

Feeling like the wind had been knocked out of her, Iris made her way down the path and stopped at the gate. She gripped on to the rough post as if it were the only thing in the realm that could hold her up in the moment. As she tried to sort her thoughts, the spicy scent of the lavender and herbs growing in Kate's garden hit her senses and made her head spin.

"This *has* to be a dream," Iris uttered out loud and ran her hand over her flushed face. Everything had been so off the last few days, and suddenly none of it felt real…the curse, her sisters, tea with Kate, all the pancakes Quince seemed to be able to eat, Talon…the fact she'd been sort of nice to Puck.

"I was nice to Puck?" The recent memory pricked at her brain. She shuddered, and pain throbbed in her neck. Iris pushed her thumb to the bothersome spot and hunched her shoulders. "What in the snails is wrong with me?"

But it wasn't a dream, as much as that might have seemed logical. Or preferred.

Against her will Kate's words floated through her mind. *Sometimes solutions are closer than you think if you only take a step back to look.*

Ugh. What *did* that woman know about her? And if she did have some sort of magical answer, why'd she have to be so damn cryptic about it?

The last thing Iris really needed in her life was to be more confused and annoyed by Kate. But the real problem was, at that moment Iris was more annoyed at herself.

A growl rumbled at the back of her throat. How could Iris just now be recognizing that her perception of Kate might be wrong after having lived across from the woman for a year? That her perception of *everyone* in Fraywell might be wrong.

She might have been wrong about herself.

The concepts burned at the back of her mind. Thinking such a thing bristled against everything she'd thought was true her entire life. What if she was becoming her father? Good? Was it catching? Iris clawed at the fence post in frustration, chipping away at several wood fragments and sending them flying into the air.

"Ouch!" she said, pulling her hand back as a large splinter

embedded itself in her thumb. Immediately she jammed it to her lips and worked the annoyance out with her teeth. She winced as the earthy taste of the wood and dirt from the splitter invaded her mouth, but she kept at the task, determined. When she finally succeeded, she spat the piece of the wood to the ground.

Examining her thumb, Iris considered how she'd always known what she wanted in life…known who she was. And now she didn't anymore? Was she starting to see the people around her as relatable? *Ugh.* She eyed her shabby cottage, knowing her sisters were waiting for her inside. They definitely were not relatable, since if anyone ever got too close they both had habits like turning people into newts, to name one.

But Talon was in there too.

Iris blew out a breath and held it inside her cheeks for a second before she blew it out.

Was it weak to want to go to him? She didn't know anymore, but without her permission, her chin quivered.

Desperate to make herself feel better and normal, she held out her hands in front of her and closed her eyes. She ground her feet into the dirt to draw the elemental magic waiting there into her body. Tingling traveled from her feet into her legs and upward. She willed it into her palms, opened her eyes, and turned her palms upward. Hope danced in her belly as an orange glimmer faded in and out over her skin.

Yet as quickly as it came, the flickering vanished and Iris

blew out a frustrated breath. What was it going to take to break the curse? She cast the thoughts aside and forced herself across the road to her cottage.

Before she opened the door, Iris took in another big breath and held it for a second. After finally releasing it, she twisted the handle and entered. A waft of spicy baked goods hit her nose the second she walked through the door.

"What in the snails took you so long?" Poppy meandered from the kitchen with a sticky raspberry pastry in her hand.

But Iris's attention drew to Talon standing in the kitchen and saying something to Quince that she couldn't hear. The hedgehog chuckled, and Iris's mouth went dry. Were they talking about her? Her thoughts flipped to what her sister had said earlier. "I couldn't have been gone more than ten minutes."

Dahlia lowered her book and raised her attention to the clock on the wall. "I left you over an hour ago."

An hour? Iris scoffed, utterly confused. "I was not at Kate's for an hour."

While taking a large bite of the pastry, Poppy leaned her free hand against a dining room chair.

"Over an hour," Dahlia retorted.

What had happened at Kate's ran through Iris's mind, and she balked at the thought she'd been there more than a few minutes. But the tea had gone cold… How had the tea gone so cold? Whatever the truth was, she shook it off. She needed to keep her mind clear even if everything was so entirely befuddling.

"None of that matters," she announced and made her way to her bedroom to change.

"Escaping again?" Dahlia asked from down the hall.

Not answering, Iris scoffed and hurried into her room. There she quickly threw on some of the clean clothes Talon had stocked her drawer with. She tucked the white cotton blouse into her full tan skirt and took a brief look at herself in the mirror. Her hair was indeed frizzy, but that was a problem for another time, so she hurried a brush through and secured it with twine into a ponytail. When it was done, she marched back to her sisters.

Poppy finished up her last bite of pastry while Dahlia was back to making notes from a book called *The Liar's Handbook*. Iris narrowed her eyes at them.

"Sitting around like this is never going to solve this issue." She gestured to the door. "Someone who's out to get us could be on the way, and we're not doing anything about it."

Dahlia lowered her book again. "And how have you been working to solve the problem?"

Iris scoffed. She wanted to tell them, *By wanting to do a clarification spell again…by doing anything more than you are doing*. But it was true… She wasn't doing any better than they were. And maybe she was doing worse.

Knock, knock. The sound came from the front door.

Iris flung around at the sound and balled her hands into fists.

"Who is that now?" Dahlia rumpled her eyebrows and

shut the book in front of her. "That nosy neighbor of yours? With all these interruptions, I'm not sure how we're ever going to get anything done." She glared at Poppy, who'd finished her brunch and was working on her embroidery again.

"What?" Poppy said innocently. "This helps me process."

Iris bit her lip and stared down at her feet. She really hoped it wasn't Kate.

Dahlia tsked and shook her head. "It would be great if you'd *process* a little faster."

Poppy wrinkled her nose at Dahlia, then turned to Iris. "Once we get our magic back"—she stopped stitching and held her needle in midair with the thread hanging loosely below it—"I might cast a little hex on your neighbor." She leaned in and lowered her voice. "No one has to know."

It wasn't the worst idea, since Iris probably couldn't handle being roped into one of Kate's little chatting sessions in her house again. Even so, she waved her little sister off. "Let me handle my own business. But thanks for the support."

"Suit yourself!" Poppy yawned and returned to her embroidery.

Knock, knock came again.

What if it was Puck again or someone else from Fraywell? A chill ran down Iris's spine as the thought she might suddenly have a steady stream of villagers knocking on her door for social visits made an unwanted appearance in her mind.

"Snails, I'm coming!" Hurrying, Iris made her way over to the door and unlocked it. To be safe, *and* completely unwelcoming to whoever was on the other side, she only cracked the door open, fully expecting Kate. "What do you wa—" she started, but the words entirely fell away when before her stood a milky-pale ogre with his arm in a sling and a fairly large knife affixed to his belt. She quickly drew her attention behind her and back to Talon in the kitchen. He'd just pulled out a tray of the cookies she'd smelled earlier from the oven, and Quince held out his little paws asking for one.

Talon threw out his hand and shooed the hedgehog away. "It's still hot."

Quince groaned and deflated.

"Who is it?" Poppy called.

Iris winced as awkwardness and confusion at the sight of Jamy, her old bodyguard, raced through her entire body. "No one," she managed and hurried outside to speak to him, fully knowing that her declaration likely made the *no one* sound like a lie.

"What are you doing here?" Alarm sounded at the edges of Iris's question. Jamy showing up threw her brain into a tizzy. She didn't want Talon to see the ogre.

Ugh. Nothing felt real anymore.

"No one, huh?" the ogre said in his deep voice along with a chuckle. "I thought we knew each other better than that."

Iris shook her head, trying to clear away all the fuzz in her brain. "Jamy, you vanished…left me completely without protection." She planted herself, suddenly realizing she wasn't the one who needed to be on the defensive. Jamy's disappearance wasn't her fault. Instantly she straightened and squared her shoulders. "I had to move on." But really she wanted to ask him how his arm had gotten hurt.

The ogre twisted his lips and wrinkled his forehead. "Of course. I thought you might like an explanation," Jamy said, stuffing his large, meaty hand into his pants pocket.

"An explanation?" Iris waved him away from the house but eyed his sling again. What had happened to him? A tiny sliver of herself felt like she should care since they'd been working together for so long before he'd left. But she pushed that part of her aside and said, "I let you go on a holiday with your family, and you never came back. Seems pretty self-explanatory to me. You're lucky I didn't cast some sort of horrific spell on you." But she couldn't help eyeing his face where there were several fresh scars. One directly over his left brow and another diagonal on his right cheek. "You left me with a real problem."

The ogre furrowed his brow. "I know. And that's why I'm here. I do owe you an explanation."

Iris crossed her arms over her chest, not sure if she wanted to hear whatever it was Jamy had to say. She'd moved on. And yet, she did appreciate his commitment.

The ogre took in a deep, settling breath. "As I told you, before I left," Jamy said, "I hadn't had any sort of holiday in quite some time. And the wife and kid were having a great time by the seaside…sandcastles and all that."

"This is your explanation?" Iris muttered dryly. "It's not exactly making the situation better."

Jamy gestured to his injured arm. "I'm getting there. Just thought you might like the whole picture."

"Fine." Iris waved him off, her mind on Talon and her sisters inside. "But make it snappy."

The ogre cleared his throat and continued. "'Bout a week in, something happened."

"And that is?" Iris asked, looking around. She half suspected Dahlia might be at the window looking out at what was going on.

"Don't worry. I'm almost there," Jamy said with a gulp. "You are well aware I had a past when you hired me."

"Yes," Iris said. "That was always part of the appeal."

Jamy shrugged. "Of course. But it seemed to have caught up with me."

"I suppose that explains that arm?" Iris gestured to the sling. At the same time she also could have sworn she'd seen Kate's curtain pull back.

"Um. Yes," he said, raised his arm, then winced. "Some old debts and grievances came back to haunt me, to say the least. But now that I'm on the mend I wanted to make you aware I didn't leave you without a bodyguard on purpose."

At that point Iris should have sent him on his way, turned around, and gone back to working on breaking the spell with her sisters. Instead she was compelled to ask, "So what exactly happened?"

"It's kind of a long story," he said while shifting his feet in the dirt outside her front door. "But if you have the time…"

She didn't. What she really wanted to do was find Talon so they could talk...so she could tell him the truth. "Sure."

Jamy wrung his hands. "Okay then. As planned, the family and I were headed home, and it should have put me back in Fraywell a couple of days ago...just as we'd discussed. But along the way, I caught wind of a mercenary looking for someone of my description."

"A mercenary?" Iris wrinkled her nose as something tickled the back of her mind.

"Yeah," Jamy said. "And to be sure the wife and kid traveled safely back to Springburn—you know, her family is all there—I had to throw the guy off my scent."

"Of course." Iris's mouth went dry and she desperately wanted him to get out whatever he was going to say. It couldn't have been worse than the places her mind was going.

But Jamy only got as far as opening his mouth to speak when Talon rounded the corner of the cottage with a chicken in hand.

"Iris," he said. "The chickens—"

As the words exited the orc's mouth, Jamy whirled around to face him and released a growl that shook the cottage roof.

"You!" Jamy roared and reached for the large knife on his hip.

Chapter 23

"You?" Talon's pupils enlarged with recognition and horror. He dropped the rust-colored chicken, who shrieked and immediately scurried around to the back of the house squawking all the way. "Run, Iris!" were the next words that came out of Talon's mouth. Then he dropped into a fighting stance and let out a counter-roar that shook the roofline. (Undeniably the most impressive one yet.)

Utterly confused at what was going on, Iris stood frozen instead of obeying Talon. All she knew was that both her bodyguards were in front of her, and they had already met each other. She hadn't even wanted them to see each other, and apparently the situation was much worse than she ever thought it might be.

DEATH MEETS CUTE

But Iris didn't have to stand there long. It was as if time had slowed as Jamy lunged toward Talon, his knife ready to strike.

Despite all that chaos, somehow Iris managed to shift out of freeze mode and put to use some of those fighting skills she'd worked so hard to teach Quince. Barely even realizing what she was doing, she leaped into action and dashed between the orc and the ogre, one hand thrust to Talon's muscular chest and the other out at Jamy.

"Get back," she screamed at the snarling ogre, as the intense need to protect Talon coursed through her body.

Tingling magic flowed through her body as she channeled it from Talon. Suddenly an iridescent reddish force blew Jamy to the ground and onto his back with a thud. As quickly as it had come, the magic was gone and the knife went flying and wedged itself into the dirt with a *plunk*.

Jamy clutched his arm and groaned while Iris swung her attention back and forth between the two.

Stunned at what had happened, Iris felt her chest heave for a breath that didn't quite want to come. Her mind reeled. What just happened? How did she do that? Iris tried to conjure it again, but nothing.

The only magic she'd ever had was the ability to create heat. What had come from her just then was different... some kind of energy. But it was gone. Even so, she didn't need to let Jamy know that in case he tried to attack Talon again. So she kept her hand out anyway.

The ogre whined as the cottage door opened and Poppy's face appeared.

"What's going on out here?" she said, her voice full of alarm.

Had Poppy seen what Iris could do?

Heart pounding, Iris twisted to her sister. "Nothing! Only a misunderstanding."

"Misunderstanding?" Jamy sneered from his place on the ground. "Is that what you call this?"

"Yes!" Iris insisted and gestured her sister back into the cottage. "I've got this." But it wasn't just a lie to Poppy. Iris wasn't sure she'd "got" anything.

Poppy raised her brows high as she scanned over the motley group. But shortly after, the witch shrugged. "Carry on then." Then she walked inside, closing the door behind her.

Iris could only hope Dahlia wouldn't be close behind, or at least that she would be equally casual about the obviously concerning situation.

"Are you okay?" Talon asked Jamy as soon as the door closed, his voice full of worry. He tried to move toward the ogre, but Iris stuck out her hand and stopped him.

"You tried to murder me, you lily-livered stewed prune!" Jamy growled and pushed himself up with his good hand. He glared at Iris. "And what was that?" The ogre placed his hand on his chest. "You trying to kill me too?"

Talon stepped back and blinked several times as if he remembered something. "I *did* try to kill you. Just outside Fraywell a few days ago." He moved his questioning gaze to Iris. "Did you know this?"

Iris fervently shook her head. It was the truth. But even if she had...would she have told him? Guilt and regret for not telling Talon rounded in her chest.

The orc gulped, and his brow wrinkled as if trying to remember something. "I think you succeeded."

A jolt zipped its way through Iris's chest. Were Talon's memories returning?

"Good." Jamy spat out the word. "I got a pretty good stab in before I was able to lose you," he said, finally standing. When he was upright he looked Talon up and down. "Why didn't you stay that way?"

Talon patted his torso and then reached around to the spot where Jamy had landed a death blow on his back. He spun his concern back to Iris. "You brought me back to life...for a job." The orc squinted while the lines on his forehead creased.

"Yes?" Iris lowered her hand and took a hesitant step back, still somewhat concerned that Dahlia was on her way out and fairly confident that the orc's memories were indeed coming back. "But I interviewed you before I did it." She didn't mention the interview was entirely Quince's idea. "You agreed to the terms."

"You didn't tell the guy he'd been dead?" Jamy brushed himself off. "Seems like a pretty important thing. What? Were you just going to off this poor sap if the position didn't work out?" He let out a low chuckle.

Her eyes trained on her old bodyguard, though words remained stuck in the back of her throat. Finally Iris blurted, "You *did* kill him!" But she knew she deserved the judgment.

"Were you going to kill me?" Talon asked, hurt peppering his question.

His question made the realm feel like it was going to collapse onto Iris. "Um." That was all she could get out, and in that moment as her heart contracted, Iris wanted to entirely disappear. This wasn't how the apology was supposed to come out. Iris had wanted to break it to Talon slowly…to be able to apologize profusely. Instead she was messing everything up, since she had no idea how to be a good person.

"Iris?" Talon's voice was soft.

"I wanted to tell you. I was just about to." Iris attempted to defend herself but stopped when she saw the forlorn, hurt look playing on Talon's features. "I wasn't even sure I'd be able to do it anyway."

At once, Iris regretted the clumsy explanation.

Confirming it was a terrible thing to say, Talon winced.

"Well," Jamy said, shaking his head. "Unless you plan to get rid of me too, I think I'm going to go. Seems like you two got bigger things to work out."

Iris whirled on the ogre and shot out her hand, hoping to do just that…or at least blow him on his ass. But nothing happened. Instead she ended up looking absurd with a scowl pulling down her face, all while contemplating how better to defend why she'd lied. But instead of anything helpful, old self-preservation methods reared their heads. "I'm a terrible person! You were both aware of that. Why would you expect anything less?" Horror filled her entire being and tingled in her limbs as she spoke. The words sounded even worse than the last ones, and she wished she had the ability to scoop them up and put them back into her mouth, where they could stay in secret.

But of course...that was impossible.

Jamy glanced at Talon and tipped his chin. "We're even. Looks like you have bigger troubles than me." With that he turned and made his way back to the road in front of Iris's cottage. He didn't look back.

Iris wanted nothing more than to disappear too, and for what seemed like an age the two of them stood there...not speaking...not moving.

At one point, Iris even hoped Kate might come out of her cottage or a chicken would round the corner. Either would have been a welcome distraction.

But none of that happened, and Talon spoke first.

"So first you didn't tell me the slightly important detail that I was dead. So you were aware I'd probably at least tried to take *someone* else out...who then turned out to be your old bodyguard." Talon's chest heaved for breath.

"I didn't know it was Jamy," Iris said. She really did feel bad for Jamy though... The ogre had only been on his way to tell Iris what had happened to him, and she nearly got him killed (again) for the favor. "At least it didn't end up being *me* you'd been sent to do away with." Iris gritted her teeth at her inability to say anything right.

The situation was *not* improving.

In fact, she was doing a horrific job.

"You *thought* that?" Talon's voice raised in pitch while his eyes widened like saucers. He spun on his heel and marched around to the back of the cottage.

Iris followed, hot on his tail. "Dahlia mentioned it might have been a possibility." She was well aware Dahlia had not said that *exact* thing, although she had questioned Talon's reasons for being there. "But she's always been a tad dramatic."

Talon eyed her with a searching distrust Iris hadn't seen before, and the look hollowed her.

"Maybe *I'm* dramatic," Iris admitted, spitting the bitter words out as quickly as possible.

Talon scoffed in disbelief. "You don't say?" He paused for a second. "And you were just going to off me if *things didn't work out*?"

What he said was *completely* true, but Iris no longer wanted it to be. She wished she had the type of magic to go back and change it all and do it right from the start. But as far as she knew, it didn't exist. "I decided not to," Iris managed under her breath.

She wanted nothing more than to get away. Far, far away.

Talon turned slightly away from Iris, then bared his teeth and let out an extremely respectable roar. "You should have told me! I really thought I could trust you, Iris."

The first thought that came into Iris's mind was to compliment him on the roar and the growl he'd used to warn off Jamy… He'd really improved the skill. But it was best to hold back on telling him any such thing at that moment. Instead she fought against the churning in her belly and squared her shoulders. "There wasn't ever a good time to tell you." The words came out pretty desperate...and hollow all the same.

"The fact I've been a mercenary was a pretty important thing!" Talon insisted and curled his arms in front of him, as if he was protecting himself.

(Yep. All his memories were back.)

Iris gulped.

The orc gazed down at his hands like he was studying them. "You let me think my life was all sunshine and cupcakes, but really these hands have done things I'm pretty ashamed of." He shook his head in disbelief. "I really need to go apologize to Jamy."

Iris wanted to scream. *The ogre actually killed you!* But none of that would do any good at that point. Talon wasn't mad at Jamy... He was angry at her. And of course, Iris had done plenty of things in her life that weren't exactly on the up and up, but she doubted mentioning the fact to Talon was going to make things any better for him.

"Who am I, anyway?" Talon groaned.

"What about the other stuff you told me? Are those memories real?" Iris asked, remembering what Talon had said about his family...that his orc mother had taught him to cook and bake. He had happy memories with them. At that point, a twinge of jealousy hit Iris, and she wished she had more of those types of memories with her sisters.

Talon growled in frustration. "Yes. But now it's all poisoned." His tone was peppered with disappointment, and he turned completely away from Iris. "Everything is poisoned."

Distaste played at the back of Iris's mouth. "Then what if I was right about not telling you?" Iris made a move toward him, then stopped when he edged from her as if she were the one who was poisoned. That said, Iris didn't give up. "Look at how you're suffering." Keeping the little she did know about him to herself had mostly served her. She'd grown to like who he was, even though she shouldn't. In all honesty, she'd been afraid his old personality wouldn't have liked her so much either. But now *everything* was falling apart, and she'd never find out. She'd gone and hurt the one person that she wanted to protect.

Talon ran his hand through his short hair multiple times. "I don't even know what to think anymore." He gazed around the yard and focused on the barn. "But I have to leave."

Iris's heart nearly jumped into her throat. Talon couldn't *leave*. "Why?" Her voice sounded panicked, and she reached out to his arm, but he pulled away from her grasp. The loss of his touch as he withdrew immediately rippled through Iris's entire being.

The wind picked up, drawing gray clouds closer, and that day they were not a comfort. Behind her, the open barn door slammed shut, and Iris winced from the thud.

"Because I need to think," Talon said and turned his attention completely back to her. "To sort out what my life is about. I thought I understood what I was getting into here, and it turns out I didn't. And I'm not even the person I thought I was. I'm not safe."

Her breath short, panic raced through Iris's mind, as suddenly everything she thought she had seemed like it was slipping away. She brought her hands forward and planted her feet into the grass underneath her, taking another chance at drawing the magic living in the strands into her body. A barely there shimmer flickered over her palms. "If I could just get my magic working again, I'd try to cast a spell to make you forget again." She whipped her head around. "Quince could help me amplify it."

Talon's mouth fell agape. "Forget? What are you talking about, Iris? It's not that easy."

The magic vanished from Iris's palms and the energy drew back into the earth, thrusting her into a heap on the ground. "Then you'd stay. And we'd be happy!" The words came out of her mouth as desperate, and Iris knew it.

The orc drew his hands together, and his features drooped in sadness. "There is nothing more I want than to be happy. But this happiness we have here? Is it real? Happiness can't be based on a lie."

His words felt like a punch to her gut, and Iris threw her hands over her middle to protect herself. But she had no words to make what he'd said go away, since his statement was entirely true. Salty tears burned at the corners of her eyes, and in one of the few times in her life, she allowed them to fall.

Iris hadn't been honest. Not with herself...not with Talon...not with anyone. Instead, she'd hoped it wouldn't matter. That it wouldn't affect her.

But it did.

It affected everything.

Iris gulped and wiped the streaming tears off her face and stood. After a moment, she tipped up her chin and gazed at Talon.

A trail of his own tears shimmered over his green skin.

"You *should* go," Iris admitted. "You don't deserve to be hurt anymore."

Pain flickered in Talon's expression, but he nodded. "Goodbye, Iris Weyward."

Iris had to choke back her emotion at hearing him say her full name. "Goodbye, Talon."

Without another word between the two, the orc turned.

Then Iris stood in the beautiful yard he'd created, the wind blowing and the chickens clucking beside her as Talon Gefroy trudged away, leaving her behind.

Chapter 24

As soon as he was out of sight, Iris drooped forward. She drew her frustrated hands into her hair and sobbed into her skirt for what seemed like an age. Admittedly, she was terrible at both being evil…and good all at the same time.

Finally she stood and did her best attempt at composing herself. She straightened her skirt and blouse, but they were stained with tears and full of wrinkles. Iris gazed around the yard and homed in on the wooden bench in front of the henhouse where she and Talon had sat. The place they'd shared their first and sadly what might have been their only kiss.

Not that a henhouse was all that romantic.

But it was to her.

Iris let out a sigh of defeat and walked to the bench. As she slowly lowered herself onto the wooden seat, cool air filled her lungs and the churning mess inside her stilled.

Her life was not the same as it had been before the week had begun. And she wasn't sure if it ever would be again. Reality was, Iris didn't even know who she was anymore.

One of the chickens—the white puffy-headed one; Iris had no clue if she was Viola, Valentina, or Valeria—came strutting on over to her, pecking at the ground along the way.

The bird held her head high and looked as if she didn't have a care in the world. Iris shook her own head. How could a ridiculous-looking creature like that have so much more confidence than *Iris Weyward*?

One of the three Weyward sisters…makers of mischief, harbingers of doom.

The bird hopped up onto the bench next to Iris and stood there, staring. In any other lifetime Iris would have shooed her away and threatened to turn her into a stew, but instead she reached out and touched the chicken's puffy head. It was soft, even silky under her fingers.

She'd never really known.

As quickly as the chicken had come, either Viola, Valentina, or Valeria hopped down and resumed pecking at the ground.

"What *else* am I missing out on?" Iris muttered to herself as thoughts of the last few days rolled through her mind.

She was missing out on a relationship with her sisters… that she knew. And *that* relationship could possibly still be salvaged.

Iris gulped as the breeze blew through her hair. She was unwilling to shut out her sisters, because they *were* actually important to her. Sure, they were very different people, but long ago they'd always been there for each other. What had happened to them?

Her hands balled into fists. First Iris needed to accept who she was. Recognizing only the shadowy side of herself, she had denied who she actually was, and she would no longer allow it.

Then suddenly a thought rolled into her mind. What if depressing the wholeness of herself was destroying her… destroying the magic inside her? Destroying the magic between Iris and her sisters?

Heat pricked at her palms, and slowly she allowed her fingers to open. Brilliant magic reverberated over her skin while she watched it in awe, slowly realizing the answer.

She'd had to let Talon go…but she didn't need to lose her sisters.

And they didn't need to lose their magic.

Heart pounding, Iris burst through the door, and the *thwap* reverberated throughout the open space, shaking the cottage walls.

"What's gotten in your bonnet?" Poppy complained while munching one of the fancy sugar cookies Talon had gotten at the market.

Ignoring her sister for the moment (and definitely not wanting to tell her the baked goods would come to a stop, since Iris had no idea how to make them), Iris immediately dashed to the kitchen. She bent down and opened the lower cupboard. It was dark inside, but she reached her arm in and riffled around in the back until she found what she was looking for: a basket to hold all the ingredients. Then she raced to another cupboard and started pulling jars from the shelves where everything had been neatly organized by Talon.

"Rue, sea holly, eglantine," she muttered to herself as her hands shook. Doubt about what she was going to do played at the back of her mind, but she was positive it was the curse trying to get her to stop, and Iris wasn't going to let it get the best of her.

"What in the snails has gotten into you, Iris?" Dahlia rounded the kitchen corner and stopped at the edge of the wooden counter.

Trying to maintain her focus, Iris continued filling her basket. The spell took a lot of ingredients, and it needed to be exact.

"Iris!" Dahlia demanded her attention.

"I hear you, sister, but I need you to trust me." Iris stopped and looked at her older sister directly. "Just give me a minute and I'll explain it all."

Poppy appeared behind Dahlia, half a cookie in hand, and scanned the kitchen. "What's going on? Did Talon leave? Please tell me Talon didn't leave."

"Yes. He's gone." Iris's heart raced at the mention of Talon, and she wished he hadn't left. But the orc needed space, and Iris hadn't been honest with him. That was completely her fault. And if she were in his place, she would have left too.

Even if she was diabolical, lying to the people she cared about was never a good thing. If Iris had learned anything from her short time with Talon, it was that the people you loved were precious, and she wasn't about to let the rift continue with her sisters.

She may have lost him…but she was not going to lose her family.

"But who's going to make lunch?" Poppy asked, an obvious alarm in her voice as she gazed up at Dahlia.

"Why are you looking at me?" Dahlia sneered. "You have two hands. Make yourself a sandwich."

With the basket nearly full, Iris breezed past her sisters, but not before she'd pushed the load into Poppy's hands.

"What am I supposed to do with this?" Poppy said, riffling through the basket contents and holding up a jar of wild thyme. "Is it for lunch?"

Iris gritted her teeth at her sister's silliness and spoke as slowly as possible without her voice shaking. "No. It's not for lunch—just hold it for now. I need you to trust me instead of asking so many questions," she said on her way to grab *A Midsummer's Guide to Enchantment* from the bottom of a stack of books. But of course, Quince lay sprawled out on the top book fast asleep. Not even the door slamming had woken him.

"What are we trusting her about?" Poppy whispered to Dahlia.

"How am I supposed to know?" Dahlia said, and though Iris couldn't see, she was pretty sure her oldest sister had rolled her eyes, since that's what she always did when she found her younger sisters ridiculous.

Not wanting to just dump Quince off the books, Iris gave her familiar a quick poke. "You need to wake up. We have work to do."

But he didn't. Instead the hedgehog rolled over and the front half of his body flopped over the stack of books. He let out a snort.

"Oh, snails, you useless beast," Iris shouted, her patience completely gone. "Quince! Get it together for once!"

Oberon, perched on the back of the living room chair, flung out his wings upon Iris's outburst. "Wake up, you spiny hedge-pig!"

With that, Quince's eyes shot open. "What? What?" But then he became aware of his precarious position, gasped, and tumbled completely off the stack onto the table, landing splayed out on his belly. "Ugh," he managed. "What's going on? Did someone else die?"

Iris shook her head at her familiar and let out a long, entirely exasperated sigh. "No one died. Now get in my pocket," she said, even though hesitation over doing any of what she was considering crept into her mind again. "Damn curse," she muttered and staved off the emotion.

The hedgehog gazed around the room, then up at Iris

with a stunned look on his face. "I was having the best dream. Talon made these yummy—"

Her heart winced again.

"You can tell me about that later! Get in my pocket now before I turn you into a cat!" Iris demanded. Knowing the threat would get him moving and she could apologize later, she held open her skirt pocket for Quince to crawl into.

"A cat?" Quince sneered while his expression turned from dopey to entirely offended.

Ursula lifted her head over the living room chair arm. "You wouldn't dare," she growled and laid her ears flat against her head.

"Yes!" Iris gritted her teeth at her familiar. "I've always wanted one."

"Really?" Ursula yawned, then stood and stretched. "I mean, I understand why."

"Okay, okay." Quince pushed himself to stand and waddled to the edge of the table. From there he jumped into Iris's open pocket. Safely inside, he wriggled around and popped his head out to see what was going on. "You don't have to be so pushy."

Iris wrinkled her brow and flared her nostrils. "It seems like it is a prerequisite." With that, she finally grabbed the book she wanted from the bottom of the stack, making the others tumble onto the floor with a tremendous thud. Now wasn't the time to deal with those, though, and she left them where they landed.

Instead Iris turned back to her sisters. Their eyes traveled over her entire body as if her senses had flown out the newly cleaned window.

Maybe they had, but Iris didn't care anymore. Fixing what had gone wrong was more important.

"Would you *please* tell us what's going on, Sister?" Dahlia stood with her arms crossed impatiently while Ursula sauntered her way, tail held high.

Out of nowhere, the cat took a ferocious swipe at Quince, who was hanging from Iris's pocket. But that time the hedgehog hissed back at her, baring his small, sharp teeth. Ursula picked up the pace and rounded Dahlia's leg.

"Stop it, you two," Iris said, but she knew she'd been the one to start it by threatening to turn Quince into a cat. She cleared her throat and did her best to ignore the nervousness buzzing in her fingers. "I know this is going to sound absurd, but we are getting nowhere with this curse. I have an idea, and I need you to listen."

Dahlia's eyes narrowed, and she opened her mouth to speak about what Iris knew was likely an objection.

"Let. Me. Talk," Iris demanded and held out her free hand, where a tiny but definite glimmer of orange magic appeared.

Her sister snapped her mouth shut.

"I don't think Jupiter or Diana or Sycorax caused our curse," Iris got out, suddenly unsure of herself but keeping her composure.

"Was it Hecate?" Poppy piped in and drew up her finger. "I kept thinking about Hecate and that guy who escaped us... Fleance might be responsible." She pursed her lips. "We did off his father and all."

Dahlia scoffed and wrinkled her nose at Poppy. "And you didn't think to mention that days ago?"

"Stop it! I can't take this anymore," Iris yelled, doing everything in her power to stand up to both the curse and her sisters. "*We* caused this curse, not anybody else... *We* are responsible for slowly ruining our magic."

A moment of silence hung between them. Even Ursula stopped mid-curl around Dahlia's leg. But soon enough Oberon gave out another squawk from his place on the back of the high-backed chair.

"You can't be serious." Dahlia, of course, was the first to dissent while she snaked her arms over her chest in obvious disbelief.

Poppy shook her head at double speed. "I agree. That's completely ridiculous. Why the snails would we do that to ourselves?"

But Iris held her ground. "Hear me out. I don't disagree with what you're saying. It does sound ridiculous, and I've been fighting the idea since I melted the cheese when Talon and I went on that picnic."

"Cheese? What cheese?" Dalia narrowed her eyes into slits.

Snails. Iris had never even told them about the cheese, but hearing her sister ask made the incident sound so much more ridiculous than it had been when it happened.

Iris hissed at Dahlia, partially to assuage her own

discomfort and also to make her older sister stop talking. Both worked. "Yes! The *cheese*!" If nothing else at that point, Iris was going to own her nonsense, if that's what it took to make things right again. She quickly blurted out the whole cheese story and ended it with, "The answer has been staring me in the face for days, and I avoided seeing it."

"So the answer is cheese?" Poppy dug through the basket she was still holding. "I don't see any in here."

"Ugh!" Iris threw her hand into the air and tipped her chin up to the ceiling in frustration.

"I don't think it's in there, Sister." Dahlia snagged Ursula from the floor, making the cat let out a high-pitched whine. "But fine, Iris. If it's the only way to get you to settle down," she said while stroking her cat's striped head. "Please fill us in."

The emotionless expression on her older sister's face was complete confirmation she had no interest in actually listening to Iris. But it was opportunity enough. Taking her chance, Iris flipped open her book, found the page she wanted, and stuck her thumb in, holding her place so she could find it again later. Then she trained her attention back on her sisters. "I think it started at Hillock."

Poppy's face screwed up with confusion. "Hillock? But our magic was fine until a few weeks ago. We haven't been to Hillock for—"

"Just over a year," Iris finished. "Meaning, we started feeling the effects on the one-year anniversary of the day we stopped speaking to each other."

"Ohhh…I think it was a full moon that day too," Poppy chimed in and wrinkled her nose as if in deep thought.

"Don't encourage her," Dahlia muttered while shaking her head. "And you are the one who left first, Iris."

Iris gulped. She had been the one who'd started it all. And she would be the witch to end it. "I did," she said, keeping her voice from shaking. "And I apologize for walking out on you both." Not really wanting to give Dahlia the time to gloat, she eyed Poppy. "And the moon *was* full." Iris had tracked it in her notebook.

"This is absurd," Dahlia said and plunked Ursula back onto the floor, where the cat let out a whine. "You're wasting time, Iris."

"I have heard that the moon is made of cheese," Poppy announced. "But I'm sure that's not true."

Frustration brewed in Iris's chest, but instead of yelling at or scolding her sisters, which she fully well knew would do no good, she calmly blew out a long, very deliberate breath before speaking. "Our magic can be amplified, right? Our familiars help us do it all the time." As she said the words, Quince kicked his back legs inside Iris's pocket.

"Of course. Everyone knows that," Dahlia said with a twinge of a sneer in her tone.

Iris gulped and reminded herself that the worst of this situation was due to the curse. Yes…her sisters were difficult, but not *that* difficult. "What if more…*things* amplify it… or strip it away?" She truly didn't want to admit what those *things* might be to herself…let alone to her sisters. "I think the curse is even causing us to have a harder time working together. None of us are as focused as we usually are."

Recognition passed over Dahlia's face, and she slipped her arms across her middle begrudgingly. "I'm listening."

"Me too," Poppy piped up, probably still hoping cheese was somehow involved.

The next words Iris had to speak played at the forefront of her mind, and her body burned like fire. What she was about to say was not likely to be well received by her sisters. Her thumb rubbed at the book page she'd stuck it into, and Iris forced it open to reveal the spell. "What if Dad was right?" The words spilled out like milk from a pitcher, and she was unable to take them back.

Both of her sisters' eyes became like saucers, and hisses sounded all around from both the women as well as Ursula, whose tail looked like a Callistemon in full bloom.

"I know, I know!" Iris flung her hands in the air.

"What have you been keeping from me?" Quince demanded from her pocket.

Poppy launched herself at Iris and latched her arms around her neck. "Don't you leave us too!" she sobbed.

"I'm not leaving anyone," Iris insisted. "I just think we need to consider looking at this situation differently."

"You're still sounding a lot like Dad." Dahlia stayed planted in her spot with Ursula peeking out from behind her black robe. "Better explain yourself quickly."

"When Dad made his announcement," Iris started, "it shocked everyone. And while it should have brought the three of us together, it made everything worse. It broke something. We tried to put it all behind us, and even though we were able to complete the Hillock project, we couldn't get along. The sisterly bond we shared was strained...like it still is. Our argument was the final straw that slowly made our magic become less effective. You didn't get a shock from the clarification spell because it was another witch... It was because you did it without me." Her head grew light, knowing she wasn't explaining it very well.

"So this is Dad's fault?" Dahlia scoffed. "Of course it is."

"No. It's *our* fault," Iris insisted. "And we have to heal the rift, or it's only going to get worse." She peeled herself from Poppy's tight grasp and stepped to the side. "How about I show you?" She presented her hand and focused on the skin of her open palm while inhaling deeply into her diaphragm. Instead of pushing away the thoughts of Kate, Puck, Lysander, Herman, and the other villagers—who were in fact terribly annoying; there was no argument in that—she embraced the emotions she'd had when she'd done something even halfway kind for them (even if it was by accident). How they'd returned kindness. Memories of the drink Herman had offered her, the way Kate had willingly listened to her when Iris had apparently needed it, Puck's gratitude for her help with singing and that they'd slightly threatened her (Iris found that begrudgingly admirable).

And then, of course, there was Talon.

At that thought Iris breathed out the air from her lungs and gazed down at her palm, where powerful magic tingled over the skin. The warm sparkles danced up into the air like scarlet fireflies in the night. Her attention flitted to her sisters, whose mouths fell agape. As Iris's thoughts dissipated, the magic faded, so she closed her hand to snuff out the rest.

"That's it?" Poppy asked. "So you're healed now?" She tried conjuring a flame on the tips of her fingers, but only a weak trail of smoke drifted off her.

"No. The curse isn't gone when I do that," Iris admitted. "But it made me realize what the problem was."

"And…?" Dahlia prodded.

"I can't hold the magic for long, but as much as I hate to admit it," Iris said, taking in a deep breath before she uttered the next words, "Fraywell and the people in it are working as an amplifier for me. Specifically kindness…maybe even love." The admission came out like a rushing river.

Poppy gasped and threw her palm to her mouth in horror.

Dahlia closed her lips, twisting them for a second before she spoke. "So are you telling us you inherited Dad's new propensity for…kindness?" The last word came out as if she'd eaten an unripe grapefruit. "What does this have to do with the curse on all of us?"

"Don't tell me we all have to be *good* to get rid of it!" Poppy exclaimed and blinked several times. She held out her elbow, and Oberon flapped his wings from the chair, then flew over and landed on her arm and nuzzled into her hair.

Iris glanced down at Quince, still peering out of her

pocket. He gripped the edge of the fabric with his tiny paws as if he might dart back inside at any second if necessary. "I don't know anything."

Iris's familiar was terrible moral support. But at that point in her life, she expected nothing less…she didn't really deserve it. Going forward, changes would be necessary on her part.

"Please don't tell us that." Dahlia had tipped her chin down and regarded Iris from under her lashes.

"I can't say that some amount of kindness might work as an amplifier for you either," Iris said. "But I'm pretty sure the curse is caused by our refusal to work together. Since you arrived…at least for you two, the magic loss has worsened. I suspect Talon and Fraywell are the only reasons it hasn't for me."

Dahlia opened her mouth to speak, but Iris whipped her hand out, red magic sparkling over it briefly to stop her. "We need to cast this spell." She grasped the book and flipped it open to the right page, then held it out to them again.

"That is a child's spell." Dahlia scoffed as if it were beneath her.

"But it's the first one we did together," Poppy squealed and reached for the spell book while trying to balance Oberon, who'd moved to her shoulder. "It was Mom's book."

Iris winced slightly at the mention of their mother. "Maybe she's trying to tell us something." Reluctantly, she handed the book over to Poppy. "I think it will solidify what we promised each other so long ago."

Her younger sister smiled and grazed her fingers over the page as if enjoying a lost memory.

"It's not going to work," Dahlia muttered, her voice gravelly.

"You should give it a try," Ursula said from the floor. "Nothing has been the same since Hillock, and you know it."

Dahlia's jaw tightened. "I guess we don't have anything to lose."

Chapter 25

Not long after, the three sisters stood around a cauldron they'd dragged from the barn, fire licking at the metal sides and boiling water inside the drum steaming out the top.

"This is going to work," Iris said, her heart pounding. "I know it." But there was a tiny part of her that wasn't sure. In all honesty the solution seemed too simple.

Quince hung out of her pocket, and Iris gave him a nervous pat on the head.

"I hope so," Dahlia groaned. "I'm tired of sharing a bed with this one." She tipped her head to Poppy and whispered, "She's terrible at sharing the covers."

Poppy didn't react. Instead she said, "I forgot the spoon."

After looking around, she placed the basket of ingredients onto the ground. Oberon flew off her shoulder as she turned on her heel to head back to the cottage.

"I've got it." Ursula dropped a large wooden spoon on the ground from her mouth. "Can we get this moving?" she yowled. "I have better things to do."

Dahlia scooped her cat from the ground and gave her a little scratch under the chin. "Don't we all?"

"Oh, sorry," Poppy said and hugged herself. "I'm just so nervous."

Iris, nervous too but not wanting to admit that, grabbed the basket and helped Quince onto her shoulder. "Are we ready?" She looked around at her sisters while Oberon and Ursula took their places.

Poppy bobbed her head vigorously and picked up the spoon.

Dahlia only shrugged. "It's worth a shot."

A small smile stretched over Iris's lips, and she invited her sisters around the cauldron. They eyed each other, and Iris began adding the ingredients one by one.

A little rue, a good dose of midnight weeds, a frond of fennel. She was careful to follow the recipe exactly.

With all the ingredients inside and Oberon perched on her shoulder, Poppy stirred the mixture. The steam wafted up into all their faces and created a cloud around them.

Iris's head became light from the smoke mixed with the sharp scent of the herbs, which burned the back of her sinuses.

"This better work," Quince whispered into Iris's ear.

"It will." Iris was sure of it, and she reached out to take both her sisters' hands.

Glimmering magic wove in among them, and Poppy gasped.

"Now the spell," Iris whispered. "You remember it."

The sisters gazed at each other and began to speak in unison the words they'd spoken so many years before:

"Sisters, sisters, come one come all,
Troubles, troubles not one befall.
Bonds of steel and spider silk,
Clung together as one ilk.
Nothing more and nothing less,
Never ever acquiesce."

As the words came from their mouths, warmth spread out from Iris and radiated over her, Dahlia, and Poppy. With their hands interlocked around the cauldron and the bubbling contents inside, the sisters' magic grew until it shot into the sky over them like lightning, creating a near vortex swirling above.

The energy surged inside of Iris and traveled over every inch of her body. She had never felt so powerful in her entire life. It felt like in that moment, she really had the ability to rule over the realm.

But instead, Iris fought to draw the magic back into herself and out through her sisters. It was the same magic she'd used while protecting Talon from Jamy.

Memories of their childhood came to her: running in the field next to their home, playing "turn each other into newts," laughing, falling down into the grass and watching clouds roll in, holding hands with them just like they were in the present.

Warmth filled her chest as they studied each other, and slowly the magic surrounding their circle vanished.

Without a word, they unlaced their hands and held them out over the center of the cauldron. In unison, blue, orange, and red magic swirled over their palms. Dahlia's danced with iridescent water drops, while a good-sized flame ignited in Poppy's palm. Heat glimmered over Iris's palm, and seeing it was like welcoming an old friend.

"Pretty," Quince said and scaled down Iris's blouse and to the ground. "I'm headed for a snack."

Iris paid him no mind. Instead her lips twisted into a smile as she focused on the magic. "We did it," she whispered.

"*You* did it," Dahlia uttered.

Both Iris's and Poppy's pupils enlarged with shock at their sister's admission.

"What?" She wrinkled her nose while Ursula walked away to stalk the chickens. "I can admit that."

All sorts of thoughts whipped through Iris's brain to shoot back at her sister, but honestly? She loved Dahlia and decided it was best to lean into it. Iris only raised her brow and said, "Thank you."

"Group hug!" Poppy yelled, and immediately Oberon flew off her shoulder to the roofline, where he flapped his wings several times before settling them against his body.

Dahlia flung her hand out to stop her sister just as Ursula pounced at a chicken. Luckily, it skillfully avoided the attack. "Oh, I don't think that's nec—"

But Poppy was a force too strong, since she already had her sisters in her arms, basically squeezing the life out of them.

In the end Iris kind of liked the warm embrace. And since Dahlia didn't immediately pull away, she might have liked it too. At least a little.

"Okay, okay," Dahlia finally said, dramatically gasping for breath and twisting away from them. She gazed around the yard as if she was looking for something and then back at her sisters. "We need to get back to normal."

Normal? Iris didn't even know what normal was anymore. Would she start taking potion orders again? She wasn't quite sure how she was going to go back to despising Kate…when in reality she probably should make an appointment with her…to talk. Iris had a lot of issues that she still needed to work out. She shook away the absurd thought. That was a problem for later. "I guess we should clean up," Iris managed, her attention moving to the cauldron and the stray ingredients strewn all over the ground.

"Not yet," Poppy insisted. "Something happened back there with your magic."

"You noticed too?" Despite what Iris had felt, she couldn't quite believe it had really happened twice.

A wide smile stretched over Poppy's lips as she brought fire into her palm. "I think everyone did."

Iris flicked her attention to Dahlia, who stood with her

arms crossed over her chest. "I don't know what you're waiting for."

Before she could stop herself, Iris threw her arms out in front of herself. With barely a thought, a force that was nearly transparent, save for a touch of red iridescence, emitted from her. The energy drove both her sisters back and nearly off their feet. Iris hardly believed what had just happened as her head spun like a top.

Her younger sister gasped, then let out a giggle. "Whoa… when you said Talon was amplifying your power, you really meant it."

The mention of Talon brought the spinning to an immediate stop.

Dahlia gazed around again. "Wait. Did Talon really leave?" she asked, her tone surprisingly sincere.

"He did," Iris admitted, and suddenly she ached with emptiness. She nearly forgot about what she'd just done. Normal wasn't going to be normal without him. "I lied to him."

Her older sister tapped her lip in thought before she spoke. "I saw you really liked him."

Iris hung her head. "I did. He changed me for the better."

"He definitely changed your cottage for the better." Poppy gazed around at the yard.

Dahlia raised a brow. "Is that what you really want from life, Iris? To be better?" Her tone was slightly judgy, but Iris would have expected nothing less. The soft feelings they'd regained from the spell couldn't last forever.

Her first instinct was to blow off the question. Make her

answer sound like her enjoyment of Talon was about cupcakes or clean laundry. But she thought better of it. If there was any time to be honest with her sisters, it was then. "I think I do. I'm not sure what that means yet. But yes. I guess I'm going to have to figure it out on my own."

"How'd you release him from the binding spell?" Poppy asked and played with a curl dangling over her shoulder.

Iris's breath hitched. "The binding spell?"

"Yeah," Poppy said. "Dahlia mentioned after you did the whole raising-from-the-dead thing, you bound him so he couldn't just take off."

"Ugh," Iris groaned. She hadn't even remembered that before he'd left. "It means he won't be able to leave Fraywell."

"Then go release him," Dahlia said like it was no big deal.

But it was a big deal.

"He's going to think I lied to him again," Iris said, guilt clamping down on her again.

"And?" Dahlia said.

Iris shook her head in disbelief. "Haven't you been listening to what I've been saying? I don't want to lie to him. I love him!" She slapped her palm to her mouth in disbelief at her admission to both her sisters…and herself.

"You love him?" Poppy asked, looking up in thought. "I mean…maybe you loved the cookies."

Dahlia groaned at her youngest sister. "Enough with the cookies, Poppy."

"What?" Poppy said. "They were delicious. Are there any left inside?"

She was probably trying to get out of cleaning up.

"Poppy!" Iris yelled in frustration, since things were already back to normal. Tears rolled down her cheeks for two reasons. One, she truly didn't want Talon to think she'd kept it from him on purpose, and two, because if she broke the binding spell, Talon would really leave Fraywell. She'd probably never see him again.

Dahlia took Iris by the shoulders and stared her in the eyes. "No matter what happens, you have to take care of this. If you do love Talon, you'll need to put your pride aside and do what's best for him. And if you need us to go with you…we'll go."

"We will?" Poppy asked and looked at her sisters. "Oh yes! We will!"

There was always a chance those soft affections really hadn't disappeared.

Iris gazed up at their faces and knew that what Dahlia was saying applied to herself as well. She loved her sisters, and she'd do almost anything for them…even if she rarely said as much.

"Let's go then," Iris agreed, and the three of them wasted no time setting off toward town.

Chapter 26

After a sprint into Fraywell, Iris's pulse raced, but she quickly realized she had no idea where Talon actually was. Her best bet was the inn.

She ran up the steps and threw her hand out, forcing energy forward at The Boar's Head front door. Not realizing her magic would be so strong already, she startled when the door flung open so hard that it slammed into the wall behind it.

"Whoa," Quince said from Iris's skirt pocket.

She winced at her newfound powers, but didn't stop. Iris kept moving while her sisters ran in behind her, followed by both their familiars.

No one was missing out on the excitement.

"How can I get some of that?" Poppy exclaimed, her voice high and excited.

"You want to start caring about other people too?" Dahlia asked.

"No!" Poppy insisted and waved her hands vehemently. "Why would I want to do that?" She swiftly lit a fire in her palm, as if to comfort herself that her powers were enough.

Behind them, Oberon swept through the opening and landed on a wall sconce. "Craw, craaaw." He let out the call like some sort of announcement of the witches' arrival, as if the fire and door slamming weren't enough.

But Iris did her best to ignore them. First of all, she didn't really care what her sisters thought about her choices. As she always had, Iris reveled in her independence. Still, she was glad for the support of their presence. Second, she was much more focused on the packed foyer, and the tavern to her left, since everyone near the door, nearly in unison, had turned their attention to Iris.

"Where's Herman?" Iris announced to a woman closest to her with a beer stein in hand. If anyone in town knew where Talon was, it was Herman or Lysander.

The woman looked at her companion as if he might have the answer.

"Herman!" Quince yelled from Iris's pocket. "We need to find him!"

"I don't know," the woman said and shrank back as if she was unsure what Iris might do to her.

Iris clenched her jaw in annoyance but decided to

overlook it. At least someone was still afraid of her, and that was something.

"Pretty sure he's in the back," the woman's companion said and pointed to the door behind the registration desk, staffed by a small minotaur wearing a smart blue jacket. Iris had never seen the guy before, but his name tag read Veneth.

Wasting no time, Iris motioned to her sisters to follow her.

After pushing her way through the people, Iris got almost to the entrance when the minotaur twisted toward her. "Hey, you can't go in there," he announced with his barely there authority.

Before Iris got a word out, Poppy ignited fire in her hand and thrust it out to the minotaur. "Look, Veneth, she's going back there whether or not you want her to."

A tiny amount of guilt whipped through Iris's middle, tempered with pride that she and her sisters were working together again. Iris grabbed Poppy's forearm and pulled it down. "We're not looking to set the Boar on fire," she said. But then she set her gaze on Veneth. "We *are* going to find Herman, though. It's important."

Veneth threw up his hands in surrender, then gestured to the door. "Fine, fine. Be my guest."

With that, Iris threw open the door and dashed into the hall. Savory aromas of the cook likely preparing lunch for the tavern customers hit her nose, and she turned left to follow them. Ahead was a door labeled *Kitchen*, and she burst through it with her sisters still behind her.

"Herman!" Iris yelled, scanning the room. Several people

were chopping vegetables, making bread, and plating food. The kitchen smelled amazing, like savory roasting meats and fresh produce.

Beyond them the paunchy man stood next to Lysander, their backs to Iris. Upon her announcement, the innkeepers whirled around to face her.

"What are you doing here?" Lysander asked, holding a knife in one hand and a jar of mayonnaise in the other.

"Looking for Talon," Iris admitted, sweat dripping down the side of her face.

Herman wiped his hands on his apron and tipped his head to look at the rest of the Weyward sisters behind Iris. "He's not here."

Iris's heart skipped, unsure what that meant. Not at the inn? Not in Fraywell?

"What Hermy means," Lysander said, obviously tuned in to Iris's desperation, "is we sent him out to the market. It's been a busy day already. I'm sure you can find him there." Lysander gave her a warm smile.

The fact Talon hadn't left meant the binding spell still held. "Thank you," was all Iris got out before she turned to her sisters. "I need to talk to him by myself." She gulped. "Thank you for coming with me."

Dahlia surveyed the kitchen. "We might get something to eat and wait for you."

"I am starving," Poppy said with a shrug.

Iris gave her sisters a quick squeeze on the arms, but Dahlia stopped her before she dashed from the kitchen.

"Are you sure you don't need us?" she asked, with just an ounce of kindness in her violet eyes.

Iris blew out a quick breath. "I'll always need you. But this I have to do by myself."

Dahlia bowed her head, and Iris dashed out into the inn's foyer, then outside.

The streets were packed as Iris left her sisters behind and cut through the streets to the market. Sweat poured down the sides of her face and back. Everything seemed so silly…telling Talon how she felt should have been no big deal.

But it was. It was the last act of love Iris would be able to do for Talon before he left.

"Hurry, hurry," Quince yelled from her pocket. They ran through the maze of stalls, as if her familiar understood her need.

"What do you think I'm doing?" Iris asked her familiar as he clung to her skirt for dear life.

Scents of sugar and spice-roasted nuts, malty ale, and roasting meats buzzed at the back of her nose and slightly distracted her focus as she searched for the tall orc. He stood a head over the most average of folks, so he shouldn't have been too hard to spot, but she didn't see him.

Iris's legs burned, and she was more than aware that people were looking at her and she probably looked ridiculous. But she didn't care. She didn't care if she was completely out of control and everyone saw…only Talon mattered.

Finally she spotted his big green frame, a wicker basket

draped over his arm as he stood at the flower vendor. Warmth flooded her entire body.

Iris slowed down and then stopped, just watching him examining an enormous bunch of daisies. She quickly chewed off her jagged thumbnail.

"What are you waiting for?" Quince asked.

Iris didn't answer right away; instead she kept her attention on the orc. Her mouth was as dry as week-old bread.

As she watched, Talon held up the bunch of flowers and smiled, but his expression didn't extend to his eyes. The sight pained Iris, and she blew out a quick breath and started walking again.

Before she got there, Talon returned the flowers to the display and turned, stopping Iris in her tracks while everything else fell away but him.

"You're not going to get them?" she asked.

Talon furrowed his brow but kept his attention on her. "I have no one to give them to. They won't make it on the journey back home."

"To your family?" Iris asked, biting her lip.

The orc nodded.

"When do you plan to leave?" Iris asked, knowing full well the spell she'd cast was likely holding him in Fraywell.

Confusion passed over Talon's features. "I'd planned to go today, but then Jamy and I had a drink and sorted everything out. He even apologized for calling me a stewed prune after I told him I was sorry for trying to kill him." He gazed up at the sky. "And now it's getting late…"

He went on with several more excuses while Iris's stomach tightened more and more until she could no longer hold in the guilt.

"You won't get far if I don't release you from the binding spell," Iris whispered and eyed him shyly.

Talon narrowed his eyes in confusion. "What are you talking about?"

The truth playing at the tip of her tongue, Iris took in a deep breath. "It was part of the spell I did to bring you back to life. It wouldn't have mattered who you were. I had to cast a spell that would keep you from actually leaving…" Iris paused for a moment, wincing before she finished the sentence. "Your job." But the situation had actually turned out to be no longer about a job… It was personal. She couldn't stand the thought of Talon leaving *her*.

But it was the only choice. Her feelings didn't matter… this was only about him.

"Unless I release you," Iris admitted, "you won't be able to leave. You won't be able to leave Fraywell and go back to your family."

"And you didn't tell me that either?" Talon's tone didn't ring with accusation, but the question still clenched at Iris's chest.

"I didn't remember," she said. "That's the truth. And it's why I'm here now. To fix my mistake." Iris gulped. "I'm so sorry for everything I did. It sounds trite, but I care about you, and I should have told you the truth sooner." She shrugged. "Of course, there's no way to make the past right again, but letting you go is the least I can do."

Talon's nose wrinkled slightly.

Did he believe her? Iris had no idea.

"Please give me your hand," Iris said, her voice shaking. She tentatively held out her own with the hope he was still willing to even touch her.

Without a word Talon slowly brought his hand to hers and gently rested his fingertips over her palm.

Iris shuddered from his touch.

"But I thought your magic wasn't working." Talon asked, keeping his voice low and not taking his gaze off her.

"We broke the curse," Iris admitted, hoping he didn't think that was a lie too.

"You did? How?" His face filled with light, and suddenly the old Talon had returned.

Iris hated to admit the reason again, but she did anyway, and she didn't even check to see if anyone might have been eavesdropping. "It was always about love. The love for my sisters…Fraywell." She hesitated there, but she had so much more to say. "You."

"Me?" Talon said and slipped his hand from her grasp. "You love me?"

Iris didn't answer his question before she blurted, "That's why I have to break this spell. I won't force you to stay. It's wrong." She grasped for his hand again, tears burning at the corners of her eyes. Releasing him was the last thing Talon needed from her, and nothing in the heavens above or on earth below was going to stop her from providing it.

But he pulled his hand back out of her reach. "You love me?"

"Give me your hand!" she pleaded.

"Answer my question." Talon crossed his arms over his massive chest while he towered over Iris.

Frustrated, Iris crossed her own arms to protect her emotions. "It's only the spell talking for you, Talon. It's trying to keep you here. You won't even make it a furlong out of Fraywell before it will force you to come back."

"I want you to say it," Talon demanded, his demeanor turned fierce. "Tell me if you love me."

"I love you," Iris admitted, the words flowing out of her. "I love everything about you. I love how you take care of me. I love how you take care of the cottage…the chickens. And no, I don't know their damn names…but I want you to take care of them. I love how you left me roses…how you kissed me and made me safe. I love how you found a little cow-shaped pitcher for the stolen cream. And I love how you are honest and care for everyone around you."

She had so many more things to say about Talon, but they all became nothing but blubbering into his chest. Iris didn't even remember getting there until he gently peeled her back.

The orc looked her deep into her eyes and said, "Then yes. You should break the curse."

Iris stood stunned. She didn't know what she should have expected, but it wasn't that. She wiped the tears from her face and worked to compose herself. "Yes. That's what I came to do."

After Talon presented his hand, Iris took it. She pulled her attention up to him and placed her other hand over the top of his and spoke.

*"Binding rise and binding fall
Ties release for once and all."*

Red magic trailed over their hands, and when Iris finished speaking it vanished.

When she was done, emptiness filled her chest. Her feelings had not changed, but his obviously would. Iris forced herself to look up at him and give a sad smile. "It's done." To make things entirely worse, the same stray piece of hair that would never behave had worked its way over her face.

A tear trailed down Talon's cheek, and as he looked at her, the corners of his lips quirked into a lopsided smile. He reached up and gently nudged aside the stray hair. "You are so beautiful, Iris Weyward."

Iris stood there stunned, having no idea what was going on. Why wasn't he leaving?

"I'm pretty sure there was no binding spell, Iris," Talon said and chuckled lightly. "It seems that didn't work from the beginning either."

"What do you mean?" Iris demanded. "Of course it worked. It's the only part that did."

He shook his head. "I didn't leave Fraywell because I

knew we hadn't said everything that needed to be said, not because I couldn't. I made it two leagues out of town right after I left the cottage before I decided to come back."

"Two leagues? That can't be right. You should barely have been able to make it out of Fraywell." Iris sighed in both confusion and desperation. "No, I broke the spell. You don't love me. You can leave if you want to."

"I feel exactly the same now as I felt before you released the spell." He grazed his large hand over her cheek. "The truth is…" He looked around for a moment and then back at Iris. "All my memories came back when I first saw Jamy. I wasn't a good person before we met. I've done things I'm not even sure you want to know about. The life I led is not one I want to go back to. I like it here. And I like the person I've become in Fraywell." He paused for a beat. "Somehow, I think I've been given a second chance to make amends for what I've done."

Iris certainly couldn't fault the orc for liking himself or tell him where he could or couldn't live. And now he'd said his piece. After turning her attention to the ground and taking a big gulp, she said, "Then I shouldn't stay in Fraywell. If you want me to go—"

"Go?" Talon said. "Why the snails would I want you to go anywhere else? *You're* the one who made all this happen. You changed me for the better… Whether you intended to or not, I don't think it was a mistake. Neither of us is perfect, but I'm meant to explore this new life with you."

Her gaze snapped back to his.

"Iris Weyward, I love you more than ever and plan to never leave your side if you'll have me."

"What?" Iris's tears began to flow again. She couldn't fathom what she had heard.

"Will you have me?" Talon asked while hope danced in his eyes and on his lips.

"Yes!" Iris whispered and nearly leaped into Talon's waiting arms.

He scooped her up and brought her lips to his. And for all Iris knew, the kiss lasted for a minute or a year. Either would have been too short.

Even so, her body loosened with relief as soon as she withdrew from the kiss. It was as if everything had been set right again in Iris's world.

Whatever *set right* actually meant. Iris's head spun as if she had been flipped upside down and back again. But it seemed that was exactly what she needed.

The events that had started with her waking from Quince nearly suffocating her (okay…an exaggeration), forgetting her daily affirmation—*Love the life you live…and destroy those who get in your way*—and tea leaves telling her she'd find love had ended in a way that actually had brought her everything she'd ever wanted.

And the *destroy those who get in your way* part meant even more to her as she gazed into Talon's smiling face.

Never again would she allow anything to get in the way of her happiness…particularly her own shortcomings.

And this meant every part of her life.

From that point forward, she'd do everything in her power to keep her vow and never let their differences come between her and her sisters. And not simply because doing so had conjured its own curse (and that had been annoying) but because she really needed them… They needed each other.

And Talon? Talon was staying with her in Fraywell. They would have a life together…and much more than him simply being her bodyguard. She couldn't wait.

Gray clouds had even rolled into the sky from the time she and her sisters had left her cottage… It was a perfect day.

Iris gazed at Talon's green features, and a grin played at the corners of her lips as she leaned in for another kiss.

That is, until the cheers began.

She gasped and looked around at the crowd that had gathered. And there were so many people she couldn't count. But she quickly picked out Poppy, Dahlia, Herman, and Lysander, who must have followed her even though they should have been back at the inn.

While her older sister stood with her arms crossed, her younger sister, with Oberon perched on her shoulder, looked ready to explode with happiness. Her hands were clasped together in front of her face, and Iris caught a glimpse of Poppy's wide smile.

"So," a strained voice came from below. "Does this mean we get to keep him?"

Iris and Talon gazed down at Quince, leaning half out of Iris's skirt pocket, his tongue lolling out as if he'd been trying to get a breath. His body was slightly squashed, his quills lying down along his back.

"Oh, I'm sorry. Are you okay?" Iris asked, drawing her familiar from her pocket and placing him on the ground.

"I'm fine," he answered.

Iris grinned. "Yes. We get to keep him. And don't get stepped on. I'd miss you if you got mashed," she reminded him.

"I appreciate the concern." Quince raised a paw then waddled toward Iris's sisters. "Now carry on, but I expect extra cookies later for the inconvenience."

Iris and Talon both gazed around at their audience as Puck loudly thrummed their lute and started in on a mediocre rendition of "Oh, Mistress Mine." Iris didn't even care when she brought her attention back to Talon, and the two of them broke into wide smiles.

Talon had changed more than just Iris…he'd also changed Fraywell. Losing him would be a tragedy none of them could afford.

With that in mind, Iris carried on.

Epilogue

A FEW WEEKS LATER

The last desperate sun rays of the day streamed onto the wooden floor, and everything was quiet…calm. Just the way Iris liked it.

The cottage smelled like sweet, caramelized butter and chocolate as she leaned back in the soft chair in front of the fireplace, where a small fire crackled and popped away. Relishing the aroma, she opened her palm and drew magic into it. The skin warmed and slowly turned from pink all the way to a luminous red. Heat rose over her palm and traveled between her fingers like swirling ribbons until she released the magic back to where it had come from, and it instantly disappeared under her command.

Iris sighed, feeling much more like herself these days. Even better than herself.

That is, until Quince snorted and snapped her from her revelry. He lay on the hearth, propped up against a small throw pillow he'd dragged out of the bedroom with his teeth. Iris had watched him struggle while doing it and never offered to help.

She was evil that way.

Her ridiculous familiar, as usual, snored like a dragon with a head cold. His front legs twitched, and he rubbed his little paws together, then smacked his mouth. "Nom, nom, nom," he moaned and then licked his lips. He was obviously having a dream about *something* tasty. But Iris couldn't really blame him. Since Talon had arrived, they'd eaten better than they had their entire lives.

Quince let out another snort, and his tongue flopped from his mouth and lolled to the side.

Iris scoffed and let out a quiet chuckle under her breath. But all in all she was glad to be back to normal.

Whatever that was.

She didn't really know, but so far she liked it.

Next to Quince lay the unfinished needlework Poppy had accidentally left when she and Dahlia had finally gone a couple of weeks before. The project lay in a basket on the left side of the hearth with the already threaded needle piercing the fabric alongside the words *I Am More Than Capable of Being Evil Today*.

Pursing her lips together, Iris thought about how Poppy

may not have forgotten it by accident at all. Could be it was her way of reminding Iris of herself.

But Iris didn't need the reminder. She already knew.

She was complicated. And that fact suited her just fine.

So, yes, she'd decided that if necessary, she'd always defend Fraywell with her magic, because she cared about the wellbeing of the people who lived there…as much as she hated to admit it. And Iris did like them. They deserved the protection.

She would also still absolutely destroy *anyone* who deserved it. There was no question of that fact, since she had to make a living somehow. So, of course, poisoned apples and such were still on her price list.

In the end, fair was foul and foul was fair.

Iris Weyward *was* admittedly very complicated.

Behind her in the kitchen, Talon clattered around with dishes and pans. "I'm considering painting the cottage," he said.

Iris twisted her neck toward the kitchen, but from the vantage point she didn't have a view of him. "Whatever for?"

It was true, the place still looked shabby from the outside, particularly with the newly cared-for plants and lawn…but Iris thought the decay still gave off a certain air.

And she didn't want to put out a welcome mat for just anyone.

Plus, Iris would *not* be hosting social gatherings anytime soon.

(Except Kate was coming for tea the next week, *and* they

had dinner planned with Lysander and Herman later that night. But those didn't count.)

The orc came into view, holding a plate in one large hand and two steaming mugs in the other. The scent of spicy orange tea filled Iris's senses.

She couldn't help but eye Talon up and down and wonder how she'd ever lived without him. He was dressed in a neat cotton shirt and a brown pair of pants, pressed just so at the seams. Despite the fact he was working hard in the kitchen, his hair was combed neatly and there wasn't a spot of flour on him. Like a top, her stomach did a little twirl at the sight of him, and she honestly hoped the feeling would never fade.

He not only looked good, but the orc took good care of her…in every way.

But that was her business…and not anyone else's.

"I think the new look would help your potions business," he said while sauntering over to Iris. "What about all black? Even the eaves."

Iris's interest piqued. Slightly.

He winked and placed the plate filled with four jumbo chocolate chip cookies and the two mugs of steaming tea next to a book titled *Evildoing for Beginners*.

He'd been intently studying the book every night before they went to bed. Talon, of course, had done more than his share of unethical deeds in his past life, but those days seemed to fade the more he focused on baking cookies and muffins.

Yet, since reading it, he had stolen a few herbs from Kate's garden in the middle of the night. But then he'd told her the morning after, and she hadn't even cared.

"Take as many as you like," Kate had told him. "Anytime."

But it was no matter. Iris liked that he was trying. It was really all she could ask.

"Increase sales? You really think so?" Iris asked and snagged a cookie from the plate. "Black? Hmm." The concept did have potential. She took a bite and the buttery sweet goodness, mixed with slightly bitter chocolate pieces melted in her mouth. She groaned and didn't know how his creations kept getting better.

"Plus," he said. "We want it to look nice if your father comes for a visit. My parents can come too."

Iris nearly choked on her cookie. They had discussed her father…but she really didn't know if she was ready for a visit from him and Talon's parents. Maybe she was. It would have been nice to find out how he was doing.

"Puck even volunteered to come over and help me paint," Talon said as he held up his cookie, eyeing it.

"*Puck?*" Iris knew Talon was distracting her from what he'd said about her father. However, she didn't really want to talk about Puck either.

"They're so grateful for your help with their singing. Said they doubled their income since you gave them a lesson." Talon contemplated Iris for a second, then popped the entire cookie in his mouth.

"I'd barely call it a lesson." Iris shook her head in

annoyance, but her magic still warmed in her palm. She *had* been half considering making them the potion they'd tried to pay for.

But she was only *half* considering it.

Iris chalked up the possibility to the potential relief that she wouldn't have to listen to any off-key renditions of "Sigh No More" when she made it into Fraywell. It was the only explanation Iris came up with for her potential generosity on such quick notice.

Still standing over her, Talon reached out and ran his finger across the edge of Iris's forehead and tucked her stray hairs behind her ear. "So. We're painting the cottage?"

She shuddered with pleasure at the orc's touch and couldn't help but (silently) admit he had quite a spell over her. "Fine. As long as there's no incessant barding around here. Might scare off clients." Iris took another bite of the cookie.

Talon chuckled. "Deal."

Before Iris said anything else, Quince's sleepy fidgeting intensified, and his beady eyes snapped open. He whipped his head around before his attention landed on Iris. "What's that?" he demanded as he licked his lips.

She held the cookie up as if she was examining it and said, "I don't know if hedgehogs can eat chocolate."

"Of course we can!" The familiar was on his hind legs and reaching out from the hearth as far as possible, making little grabby hands out in front of himself.

Iris chuckled, broke the cookie in half and handed Quince the uneaten part.

He took it with pleasure, fell back onto his rear and began munching the cookie. "You can never leave, Talon!" he said between bites, eyes rolling back into his head.

Iris stuck the rest of the cookie in her mouth and gazed up at Talon. "It's true. You're my prisoner."

With mirth, Talon held out his green hand to Iris in invitation.

A smile drifted across her own lips, and she gladly put her hand in the center of his and stood, her breath ragged.

His other hand snaked around her waist as Talon eased her to an open part of the floor. Iris gasped as he pulled her in close against his warm chest. His heart was strong and beat quickly against her touch.

"Promise?" He growled and led her into a dance while gazing deeply at her.

As they swayed, Iris wondered in the back of her mind if the binding spell she'd cast on Talon when she'd brought him back from the dead had actually worked, but in reverse. Maybe she was the one bound to him. What they had couldn't be real otherwise. Could it? Not to mention that whatever spell he held on her had helped her realize her dreams…to love the life she lived. "Only if I'm yours," she managed.

Talon reached up and swept his fingers across her jawline, and Iris relished the gentle touch. When he guided her into a spin the distance suddenly felt like too much until he brought her back into the home of his powerful arms.

"Always." And after that the orc drew Iris up into his arms and kissed her.

And this kiss was no small thing. It encompassed the romance, safety, and wholeness Iris never knew she was missing or even wanted. Talon had come to her in the strangest way possible, but the tea leaves had been right.

Love, in so many ways, had come into Iris's life, and it had *not* been the worst thing to have happened to her.

Breathless, she pulled away slightly and studied the orc's yearning amber eyes. "I love you."

Talon grinned and tightened his grasp around her waist. "I love you, Iris Weyward. You're the perfect amount of wicked for me."

And he kissed her again.

Keep reading for an excerpt from the first book in J. Penner's Adenashire series

1

A thyme-infused raspberry tart sailed off Arleta Starstone's rickety old wagon as if it had sprouted wings and taken flight of its own accord. The pastry smacked into the ground, the sweet, red fruit exploding through the thin shell and splattering its sticky juice onto the earth with a horrible little squelch.

Wasted.

"Oh, stars in heaven," the young woman muttered under her breath, her wavy hair sticking to the back of her sweaty neck, making the entire situation another level of worse.

Arleta pulled her wagon over to the side of Adenashire's rocky dirt road, her nose wrinkling at the ruined tart's fruity scent as it mixed with musty earth. She quickly adjusted her pastries so no more might escape.

As she was sighing, her gaze flicked up to the oak trees stretching above, where a group of ebony-feathered crows sat cawing and hopping from branch to branch. They hungrily eyed the awaiting breakfast, which it would be shortly since she had no time to clean the mess she'd made outside the main street.

She was late. *Again.* The timepiece in her pocket had told her so before she'd even left her cottage.

Arleta quickly glanced around, checking if anyone had noticed her mishap.

Other than the crows, it seemed no one had.

Wishing she had tied back her long chestnut hair better before leaving home, Arleta hiked up her tan linen skirt and brushed the loose strands from her face. Determined, she yanked on the metal handle of her overloaded wagon and soldiered on. Heart quickening at the exertion, she surveyed the rocky terrain ahead of her, mentally calculating the best route through the jumble of stones littering the way. There would be no more lost bake stock that morning.

All the while, the aroma of fresh bread and sweet pastries wafted from the back of the wagon; her stomach gurgled in protest, reminding her that she'd forgotten to eat before she'd left her cottage.

Again.

Verdreth and Ervash, the too-kind orc couple who lived

next door, would surely lay into her if they discovered she wasn't eating enough. They always tried to act like her fathers, but she was not a child anymore. She hadn't been for a long time.

Time. She just needed more time in the day.

But there was *never* enough time.

All the booths would be reserved if she didn't arrive at the market by half past, so she needed all the shortcuts she could take. Tonix Figlet, the stall renter, never held a spot for her. From the looks of him, the round, furry face and cute-as-a-button expression, one would think quokkans were a kind folk, but they had quite the sordid past in the Northern Lands—although who knew what was true and what wasn't. This one seemed to fulfill the rumors of their renown. Tonix, forever crabby, would have much rather rented the stalls to more *prestigious* merchants: elves, dwarves, even the rare ogre with goods to hock.

Magicless humans like Arleta were at the bottom of his list, along with anyone else with no magic.

No magic, no respect.

Even if she made it to the market on time, Tonix would surely relegate her to the back, where she'd need to sell her delights at a fraction of the price as those sellers who'd snapped up the premium spots.

"Despite everyone going on about how *good* the cardamom lemon bars are," she muttered under her breath.

As she rounded a corner into the village proper, Arleta's wagon wheels clattered against Adenashire's uneven cobblestones, the sound echoing through the narrow alleyway. The thick, pungent scent of refuse and decaying vegetables made her nose wrinkle. The smell was so strong that it completely blanketed the tempting aromas from her wagon.

She quickly approached the alley's entrance and the sounds of the opening market hit her ears. Tonix Figlet stood in the bustle in all his glory, his furry taupe paws firmly planted at his waist. His clothing, tailored wool pants and jacket over a freshly pressed cotton shirt, was simple but well-made, and of high quality, showing that he earned a good living as the market's owner. The marsupial's nut-brown eyes flicked over to her, and, for a moment, recognition sparked.

Then he plastered on a honeyed smile, turned on his heel, and walked away in the opposite direction, toward the linen sellers.

Arleta cursed more than the stars.

She gritted her teeth and pulled her wagon forward, determined to find a spot to sell her pastries no matter what the quokkan thought about her. Arleta knew there would be a decent amount of groveling on her part in the next few minutes, but going back to the cottage with this much inventory was not an option. Not that morning. Not since she'd spent most of her weekly budget to buy and make what was in the wagon. She needed to sell it that day, or everything would go stale.

"Mr. Figlet!" she called after him. The wagon's handle was slick with sweat, and her arms trembled with the effort of pulling the heavy load forward. Her voice rang out, slicing through the market noise, more than one seller looking her way.

"Mr. Figlet!" she shouted again.

The quokkan's worn leather boots scuffed against the rough cobblestone street as he came to an abrupt halt. Arleta would simply continue acting as a thorn in his side if he didn't speak to her, her tenacity no secret. He turned.

"Yes, Miss Starstone?" As soon as the words left his mouth, he pursed his marsupial lips and sucked his teeth. From his pocket he pulled out a golden watch, glanced at it, and held out the timepiece. "You know what time it is?"

Contempt was written all over his deceptively adorable features, but Arleta refused to let it get to her. Instead, she squared her shoulders, ready to do whatever it took to get a spot.

Beg. Plead. Offer Tonix Figlet free pastries for life.

She slid to a stop and the wagon behind her bucked, nearly dumping more raspberry tarts. While the quokkan waited for her to speak, tapping his foot, Arleta cleared her throat. She glanced over his shoulder and scanned the booths. Sure enough, the worst spot at the back was still available, and customers were only just starting to trickle in.

There was still time to set up.

"Yes, Mr. Figlet. I'm just a *little* late." With a small shrug of apology, Arleta made a pinching gesture with her fingers.

"Girl, you're *always* late. The vendor queue closes at eight sharp. It's now ten past. I'm sorry, Miss Starstone," he said, his voice drenched with false sympathy, tacking on a precious expression she felt was solely for the benefit of any onlookers.

Arleta winced. "Yes, I know." The quokkan was right, of course. She was always running behind, always struggling to keep up with life's demands, and she had given him all her excuses before.

She was the only person doing this work.

She had no magic to help her.

Time had gotten away from her when she was trying to perfect a new recipe.

The pastries needed to be sold somewhere, but Arleta couldn't afford a food cart or the license that accompanied it, or, stars forbid, save enough gold to actually buy a *bakery* in town. The market was her only option to sell her goods.

But Tonix Figlet didn't seem to care about any of those things, and especially not from Arleta. Now, if a local *elf* had fallen on hard times, he might have extended a small courtesy, although what Tonix *really* cared about was the reputation of his market. Everyone knew this.

And those without magic brought that reputation down.

"I'm afraid there are no spots left for today," the quokkan said and started to turn. "Perhaps you should try again next week."

Arleta was incredibly aware of this dance between her and Tonix, the one that kept her in her place.

"I have silver," Arleta said and quickly dug into her pocket to pull out the coins.

At the clinking of metal, Tonix twisted back, his demeanor changing in Arleta's favor, though just by a fraction.

Arleta took it as her in.

"You still have one booth open, and I can offer you...*six* coins for it." The booth was in the back *and* slightly blocked by a pole, so truly it was barely worth the usual four, but offering him more always seemed to soften the blow of renting to her.

A knot formed in Arleta's stomach as she thrust out the coins. The weight of them was heavy in her palm, a familiar, tangible reminder of the sacrifice she was making. Unless she sold out that day *and* generous customers filled her tip jar, paying the extra coins would mean choosing between not eating dinner for a few days and giving up some special ingredients for an upcoming test bake she was planning.

But right then, it didn't matter.

She *needed* that booth.

She had to stop living week to week.

Around her, the market continued to buzz with rising activity. Vendors preparing their wares mingled with friendly chatter and the occasional burst of laughter from a passing group of children. Fires were stoked, scenting the air with the roasting of all kinds of savory meats.

"Six coins," she proclaimed as if it were a fortune. Then she added, her tone dripping with honeyed sweetness, "You don't want the place to look *empty*, do you?"

Arleta was fully aware of how that last addition would knife Tonix a little. He had a reputation to uphold, after all, and even filling that space with a magicless vendor's goods would be better than the eyesore of an open booth.

As she waited for his reply, tension rose between her and the marsupial. Every word she said was a gamble, a delicate dance, and she had to get them just right if she wanted to secure her day's sales.

"Fine." The quokkan grabbed the coins from Arleta's hand. "Now get out of my sight."

"Thank you, Mr. Figlet," she said, not waiting for him to change his mind. With a grunt, Arleta took hold of her wagon's handle and raced to the empty booth, just missing the pole with the corner of her wagon.

To her left was a minotaur woman selling costume jewelry, clad in a flowing dress that shimmered in the sunlight. Her jewelry also glinted in the light, reflecting sparkling rainbow patterns onto the surrounding stalls. Arleta couldn't help but admire the intricate designs, each piece more beautiful than the last, though nothing she could ever afford.

On her right, the bouquet of rich, golden honey wafted toward her from the booth worked by a stocky, bearded halfling. The stall was adorned with jars filled with thick liquids of different shades, ranging from pale gold to rich amber. Each container glowed in the sunlight, casting a golden hue onto everything around it.

Neither vendor said hello, but just the thought of the honey lit the baking part—which in fact took up more than an average percentage—of Arleta's brain on fire.

Fluffy honey buns with silky whipped frosting.

Flaky puff pastry laden with honey and walnuts.

Rose water and honey cakes.

Her stomach rumbled, and she knew she would have to pick up a jar or two before the day's end.

If she made enough to afford it.

"Focus," she muttered to herself while she pulled out a fine lace tablecloth that had belonged to her mother and spread it out on the display table. Every time she used this particular cloth, it transported her back to a time when the family kitchen was filled with the redolence of her mother's freshly baked goods.

Back to when things were right in the world.

Arleta gulped the sudden swell of emotion down and spread the cloth out, taking care to smooth out every crease and fold, wanting it to look perfect.

Her mother had been an avid amateur baker. It was where Arleta had inherited the "pastry passion," as well as her noteworthy jawline.

Her father had run an apothecary business. When she was younger, his shop had always been a mystery to her. Back then there were just strange bottles and jars lining the shelves, but as she aged, she'd appreciated the herbs and plants, and eventually this knowledge had helped her create unique and flavorful treats. Plus, the tasty ingredients also had healing properties. She believed that when her customers ate them, the pastries healed them from the inside out. If not the body, then the soul.

It was Arleta's own "little dash of magic," the way the

ingredients came together and created something new and delicious. It was a kind of alchemy that she loved.

Even if she, or any human, *couldn't* use real magic, the only beings in the Northern Lands who the earth and stars guaranteed would not have it.

Over 50 percent of humans could be *affected* by magic, but they were not gifted its use, not by having it flowing in their blood or by having the ability to channel it from the outside.

Arleta arranged her offerings. The thyme raspberry tarts were her newest creation. The earthiness of the fresh herbs and the raspberries' sweetness was almost intoxicating, and she knew how the tart's delicate, flaky crust melted in the mouth. Next to the tarts were soft and chewy wild blueberry cookies. Verdreth and Ervash had sampled a taste of them last night—though, because they were orcs, sometimes a "taste" equaled more of her product than Arleta expected.

There were also several loaves of rosemary sourdough bread, cinnamon rolls, and petite lemon lavender cakes, each one a small work of art. Last, she arranged the wooden price signs that Ervash had carved for her. She'd told him it wasn't necessary, but he'd made them anyway. The orc was quite an artist, with a fine eye for detail.

When she had finally unloaded her stock, Arleta forced on a necessary grin. Tonix eyed her from across the way, and Arleta spread her arms out wide to show off her fully stocked and ready booth.

She might only be human, but at least her baked goods tasted magical.

TALON'S "DEMON'S FOOD" CHOCOLATE CUPCAKES

MAKES 24 CUPCAKES

INGREDIENTS

- 2¾ cups (330 grams) all-purpose flour
- ¼ cup (30 grams) cornstarch
- 1 cup (200 grams) white sugar
- ¾ cup (165 grams) packed light brown sugar
- ⅔ cup (65 grams) cocoa powder
- 1 tsp. baking soda
- ¾ tsp. salt
- 1 cup (about 160 grams) mini semisweet chocolate chips
- 1 cup water
- 1 cup buttermilk
- 1 cup vegetable oil
- 1 Tbsp. vanilla
- 3 large eggs
- 1 batch of Chocolate Buttercream (see page 297)
- About 2 Tbsp. shaved or grated chocolate (optional)

INSTRUCTIONS

Preheat oven to 350°F.

Prepare 2 12-cup cupcake pans with 24 cupcake liners, set aside.

In a large bowl mix flour, cornstarch, sugars, cocoa, baking soda, and salt.

Add chocolate chips and mix to combine, set aside.

In a separate large bowl mix water, buttermilk, vegetable oil, vanilla, and eggs until combined.

Add dry ingredients to wet mixture and stir until combined.

Fill prepared cupcake pans ¾ of the way full with the batter.

Bake for 21–23 minutes.

Remove from oven and cool completely before frosting with chocolate buttercream.

Optional: Decorate with shaved or grated chocolate.

CHOCOLATE BUTTERCREAM

MAKES 6-7 CUPS OF BUTTERCREAM

INGREDIENTS

- 2 cups (450 grams) softened unsalted butter
- 6 cups (780 grams) powdered sugar
- ⅔ to 1 cup* (65–100 grams) cocoa powder
- 4 tsp. vanilla extract
- Pinch of salt
- 2–4 Tbsp. milk, half and half, or whipping cream

*Amount will depend on how dark you like your chocolate frosting. I've done it both ways, and while each is delicious, I prefer less cocoa powder.

INSTRUCTIONS

Place softened butter into a stand mixer, and using the whisk attachment, whisk the butter on high speed until it becomes fluffier and lightens in color (3–4 minutes). Scrape down the sides as needed.

Add powdered sugar, cocoa powder, vanilla, and salt and beat on low. Add milk (or half and half or cream) 1 tablespoon at a time until the desired consistency is reached. Process should take about 3 minutes.

Use to frost or pipe onto cooled cupcakes.

Refrigerate the uneaten portion.

About the Author

Baking magic into every page, J. Penner crafts cozy fantasy from her sun-kissed San Diego home. With a cat on her lap and a pen in her hand, she invites you into worlds as warm and comforting as a cup of tea.

Website: jpennerauthor.com
Facebook: jpennerauthor
Instagram: @jpennerauthor
TikTok: @jpennerauthor